ASK ME TO STAY V
seafaring man seeking
village, and to subm
new vocation, but as
exposed by an unscr
the narrow minded
and want nothing to do with him, or his
wonder that is on offer before them is ignored in the blind acceptance of the story of his murky past, a story that grows more terrible with every malicious telling.

Cathryn, daughter of the County Squire, capricious, sometimes arrogant: but never less than beautiful. Janie, working at the village Inn with her father, she has a down to earth personality and a depth of understanding that is instinctive. These two women are so different in class and upbringing, but both of them young and appealing . . . and eager for love! And of two blue-water men, Richard and Jonathan, kindred spirits who form an immediate attachment, all four interwoven in an association of intrigue and passion: and ultimate betrayal.

Perranwithick is a tiny village, a confined community where the residents are reluctant to absorb anything . . . or anybody new. Can our flawed hero break down the barriers of small-minded prejudice and, even more pertinent, can he prevail over what appears to be un-surmountable odds?

Born Salford, Lancashire. Educated C of E primary school: and Salford College of Technology. Served three years in the Royal Navy. Rank Petty Officer, Electric Articifer. During which time developed a love of the sea that was carried on into private sailboats and after taking a sabbatical to sail full time for six months, my wife and I moved to Devon where I sold my previous yacht to buy a thirty four foot sloop which we moored at, and sailed from, Dittisham on the River Dart.

This love of the sea and sailing was a dominant influence in my early writing and fostered several stories, but of the early sailing ships. The romance of sail: The tall ships! My first was of an early East Indiaman outward bound for adventure and romance, and features a midshipman named Jason Queen. The second was a privateer on the Spanish Main: and a love story made in heaven! Both of these are standing in line for publication . . . However, my recently published novel, *Montaigne Barton*, is a romantic drama set in a Dartmoor village, and far removed from the sea, but the sailing theme is again dominant in this my latest novel, *ASK ME TO STAY WITH YOU*, where I feel there is also much for the reader to enjoy onshore, in the interwoven web of passion and intrigue between the four main characters.

All of my work is pure imagination and all characters are fictitious.

Other titles by Frank Smith

MONTAIGNE BARTON

Romantic Drama set in a Dartmoor village

THE COMING TO MANHOOD OF JASON QUEEN

PAVANE FOR A DEAD SEAMAN

JOKER

THE GORGE OF SABAEN

ASK ME TO STAY WITH YOU

Frank Smith

Higher Providence Publishers

This novel is entirely a work of fiction. The names, characters, localities and incidents portrayed in it are the work of the author's imagination. Any resemblance to actual persons, living or dead, is entirely coincidental.

First published in Great Britain 2003 by
Higher Providence Publishers.

ISBN 0-9541211-1-2

Printed and bound in Great Britain by
Short Run Press Ltd, Sowton Industrail Estate,
Exeter, Devon.

Higher Providence Publishers, Providence, Throwleigh, Devon.
E-mail: smit55.freeserve.co.uk

Cover picture: The Lizard Peninsula, West Cornwall.

Dedication

To my wife, Eunice, because this
is the one she likes best of all.

Author's Note

On examining an Ordnance Survey map the southern shoreline of Cornwall can be likened to the foot of a huge boot. The promontory of land called the Lizard that juts uncompromisingly into the Western Approaches to the English Channel is the heel of this boot and the bluff section that faces the gray wastes of the Atlantic, known as Cape Cornwall and Lands End, is the bunched-up toe end: the arch of the foot then being formed by the curving shoreline of Mounts Bay . . . Along this contrasting stretch of cliffs and monstrous crags can be found the coves and beaches made so infamous by the violent tales of dark nights and even darker deeds that are now so thrillingly part of Cornwall history and folklore.

The smuggler enjoyed a popularity that made him almost a seafaring Robin Hood, bringing warmth and enjoyment to all who could pay for, or earn, the price of a noggin. Thieves maybe!

But in local eyes, thieves only against the men of the Excise, a branch of the service of Her Majesty held in esteem by very few. Baiting the Excise men was a pastime indulged in widely and if the reward was only a cheap jug of "Cousin Jacky", need it matter if the sport was good?

It was only in the early part of the nineteenth century that the Excise men, combined with the strongly emerging Coastguard, or Preventative Service, began to squeeze the traditional smuggler from existence. When the risks became greater than the reward it seemed that the profit, and much of the sport, was gone . . . and we take up our story in the early nineteenth century in the reign of Queen Victoria!

Prelude

Just south of where Cape Finistere threads a tentative fist into the Atlantic Ocean is situated the estuary and entrance to the Ria de Tambre. The bay is beautiful: the shallows crystal clear and the Spanish sun baking the high ground and turning the sand along the water's edge into burnished gold. This is a Ria of fisher folk, indolent seekers after pleasure knowing no other way of life and taking their brightly painted boats to sea only when the weather suited. To the south lies the adobe village of Noya. To the north and adjacent to the Atlantic swell is the small fishing port of Muros.

Into this haven of fishing boats came sailing one day a distinctive looking ship. Rugged, yet with a pleasing curve to her sheer line and a tall, two-mast rig which gave promise of speed. Under a single headsail and moving very slowly she nosed her way among the packed fleet that was even then preparing to leave for a night's fishing. Three men on board: agile and with movements certain as they eased her in. Fending off, pulling on ropes. Careful not to cause damage or incur any, they warped the ship to a vacated berth alongside the breakwater and ship-handled her with a competence that earned appreciation from the observant fisherman. It was late afternoon: the tide just beginning its six-hour ebb.

The port of Muros saw few foreign ships. The Spanish seamen made no welcome, or hostility. Why make a fuss? Seafarers the world over have their own style of hospitality, knowing well that the need for a night's shelter may one day be their own. As long as the newcomer did not interfere with their own sailing! Anyway, this boat they had seen before. They knew she hadn't arrived in Muros to take fish, her business was more secret! They wanted nothing to do with her, or her crew!

She was painted dark green with white masts and varnished gaff and booms. Her decks were scrubbed clean. She looked trim. Her name was painted across the transom in flowing gold. She was called *Rose of Endau* but showed no register of a native port.

The tide ebbs and flows fast on the Atlantic seaboard. *Rose of Endau* settled on the mud with the harbour wall looming high and dank, its stone and dirt surface some three feet above her stern rails and with her masts carefully angled towards the roadway. Darkness fell. The estuary was silent. Well out to seaward flickered the white lights that were the stern cluster lanterns of the fishing fleet.

The *Rose* was alone.

1

Perranwithick

c. 1840

The sky was overcast with thunderhead rain clouds through which the sun rayed down to colour a pattern of alternate warmth and shadow across the meadow: and momentarily lingered on the lone horseman below. He had paused at a junction in the path along which he was moving, uncertain now of his way and regretting his decision to leave the highway to seek a shorter route across country. Though weary after hours of riding he gazed about with eyes alert under the brim of his hat.

'Which way now Mistral?' he asked. The ears of the dapple grey mare twitched and one hoof pawed impatiently at the dusty pathway. 'What do you care,' said the rider, 'we'll take the larboard hand and hope for the best?' His decision wasn't entirely due to guesswork, he had consulted a small, pocket compass even as he spoke. Working the head of his horse round they set off down a narrow track that meandered across the green slopes of the meadow unaware they were under surveillance and that their progress had been watched for several minutes by another horse and rider standing motionless higher up the slope of the hillside, camouflaged under an overhanging clump of trees. The change of direction brought an indignant frown and kicking her heels into the side of her mount she rode at a determined gallop towards the intruder. Mistral's ears flattened at the approach of the fast moving horse and, as her rider reined hastily in to face the intrusion, he realised he was being accosted by a young woman. She was dressed in formal black riding coat, highly polished boots of dark tan and, surprisingly, in tight whipcord breeches. Her mount was a huge Palomino stallion and from the tips of her boots to the lace at her throat she exuded class and affluence and also a threat, he had to pull Mistral aside as she thundered to a halt and so close it appeared almost a deliberate attempt to frighten. Then annoyance vanished before the incredible beauty of the young woman before him. She sat slender and erect in the saddle. Her cheeks were flushed rose pink and her hair tumbled in a windblown cascade of chestnut around her face and, as for a moment they looked at each other without speaking, her arrogant glare subsided before the calm, level eyes of the stranger. He was dressed as if for foul weather in a seafaring-type reefer jacket, cord trousers and knee length boots and, as he looked again at her he smiled, showing a flash of white teeth in a generous mouth, then he swept off his hat to reveal dark wavy hair that grew lush from low down in a peak over a broad forehead. He was undeniably good looking and as his smile widened she appeared suddenly unsure and at a loss for words.

'Whither in such a hurry, I pray?' He spoke in a resonant voice that penetrated even over the clamour of arrival.

'Do you realise that you are trespassing?' The calm bearing of this stranger confused, and brought a waspish tone to her voice as she snapped, 'This is private land and you have no right to be here at all!'

His smile faded at the imperious tone and he clutched his hat to his chest in mock alarm 'You alarm me, madam,' he said with a slight deference now evident, 'is it such a terrible thing to be a stranger and to have lost my way?' His eyes were deep grey and one eyebrow raised quizzically and he looked at her in an admiring way that forced her own glare to falter and a blush to diffuse her face. Uncertain now and feeling she was losing control she reined her stallion back a foot or two, finding great difficulty in maintaining composure.

'You surely must realise you are on private

land,' she said scornfully, 'this path is hardly a public highway?'

Bowing his head in acknowledgement he explained, 'The day advances and I was seeking a short cut so I might arrive at my destination before nightfall.'

'Just where is your destination?'

'The village of Perranwithick.' Upright in the saddle now with his fatigue forgotten in the presence of this tempestuous girl. A slow smile spread to the corners of his mouth as he spoke and his eyes focused on her as if taking in every facet and with such obvious appreciation that her own eyes reflected conceited pleasure but only for a moment and she then threw her head back in arrogant manner and snapped indignantly:

'You look at me too boldly, sir! I would have you know that I am the daughter of Sir Harry Sedgewick and inform you again that you are a trespasser on our land!' Eyes flashing danger signals now and cheeks aflame as she sought to intimidate this formidable stranger but her father's name seemed to have little impact and brought only a devastating smile and that damned expressive eyebrow lift as he doffed his hat to her.

'I make your acquaintance with extreme pleasure, Miss Sedgewick?' He placed emphasis and question on the name, as if trying to establish her status, before adding, 'May I introduce myself? Richard Mathieson, at your service and humbly apologising for my intrusion but if you will kindly point me in the direction of Perranwithick I will trouble you no further.' His voice was vibrant and hinted of good-humour and she was impressed, and in no hurry to dismiss him. But controlling wayward thoughts, she pointed an elegant gloved hand down the meadow.

'If you ride across the meadow' she instructed, 'you will find a gate that leads out on to the bridle path to Perranwithick. The way is sign-posted from there and when you get to the brow of the hill you will see the village, and remember in future, Mr Richard Mathieson, this is private land and my father's gamekeepers are under orders to deal very forcibly with intruders.' Her voice had softened and the threat carried little conviction, for he appeared unconcerned by her attempt to chastise and as he raised his hat to her then replaced it on his head with a cocky gesture he seemed highly intrigued and his eyes crinkled and held her own in complimentary gaze.

'My thanks to you, Miss Sedgewick,' he said, 'and if I look at you too boldly it's only because I have never before encountered so fair a maiden.' Preparing to move off, he added, 'May I hope we will meet again?' Softly spoken, the words sent a thrill of optimistic pleasure through her slim figure as she watched him ride away. A thrill that remained with her while she rode slowly back across the meadow towards the copse from where she had earlier observed the arrival of the stranger. His name resounded in her ears and she thought she would have to investigate further into this man named Richard Mathieson!

Reining to a halt at the brow of the hill. The bridle path along which he had been riding was deep in fallen leaves. Though still early in September already the approach of autumn could be sensed in the changing colours. Amidst a broad spread of green in the surrounding woods the recurrent flash of sunburnt gold gleamed conspicuous as a giant tree bowed with grace to the advancing season and allowed its foliage to change prematurely into glorious flame. The fields around had their own disorientated patterns of varying shades of green mingling with the sheen of deep yellow where a field of recently cut corn had been cleared and left with just a carpet of golden stalks as a reminder of the harvest, and over all, the wood-smoke from a nearby cottage chimney hung acrid on the evening air. As the village opened out below he hunched his shoulders against the increasing chill and murmured, 'Time we were bedded down for the night, old girl.'

Mistral's ears went back and her head nodded up and down as if in impatient agreement. They were both feeling the effects of the long day's ride and looking forward to a comfortable berth. Cantering down the main street of the village he halted Mistral outside a long and low building with a pan-tiled roof, whitewashed walls and a hanging sign on which was a faded painting of a ship under all plain sail, bearing the title '*The Blue Lugger*'. Tethering Mistral to a rail outside he bounded up the steps and through the entrance. The hallway smelled of polish. Copper utensils hung on the walls and a bowl of freshly cut flowers adorned the single low table of the attractive reception area. A young woman who had been polishing the copper work turned to greet him with a smile. Though quite small and perhaps a little on the plump side she had a pleasing fullness of figure that the apron she wore couldn't even begin to hide. As their eyes met and held for a moment he had a quick, moving impression of youth and laughter in the bloom on her cheeks and in the curve of a warm and generous mouth and he thought she was friendly and damned attractive and he also thought that if the two he had met so far were any indication, the womenfolk in this remote corner of the west country were exceeding fair.

She looked at him in polite enquiry and, at his request for a room for the night, moved behind a small, partitioned cubicle and without speaking offered a book for him to sign. Examining his signature she then asked, 'Would you be requiring supper, Mr Mathieson?'

'I surely would! I'd be grateful for anything but first would you allow me to stable my horse?'

The concern for his mount brought instant

approval. 'The stables are out back,' she said, 'bring your horse round and I'll show you where everything is.' Watching his lean figure move out through the front door she mused, 'Looks as if he hasn't had a decent meal for ages.' She had noticed the level grey eyes so tired in the taut thinness of his face and she looked again at his signature. The name seemed somehow familiar but putting aside curiosity she walked down the hallway in the direction of the stables.

With Mistral rubbed down and crunching oats from a wide trough he was shown to a tiny room overlooking the main street. There was already a pitcher of warm water and a blue-willow-patterned bowl on the dresser and he washed and shaved and changed into a clean shirt. His only clean shirt! White and with long flowing sleeves and a ruffle of Maltese lace at the throat. Brushing his hair back from his forehead he pulled in his belt another notch and went downstairs to find the taproom.

The man behind the bar was short on height but from the waist upwards had the build of a professional prizefighter, with heavy shoulders and long, powerful arms exposed by the rolled up sleeves of his woollen shirt. His hair was thinning back from a broad forehead and his eyes were deep brown, penetrating and observantly shrewd. Offering his hand in greeting he introduced himself. 'Glyn Ralston, proprietor of the *Blue Lugger,* my daughter Janie is preparing supper, would you mind having it in the bar room? The fire's burning well and you'll be more comfortable in here. Perhaps a glass of wine while you're waiting?'

'Prefer a jug of ale . . . a glass of wine would never quench a thirst such as mine.'

Ralston liked the style of this man and appreciation showed as he said, 'Sit by the fire, sir, I'll bring over a jug.'

Warming his back to the crackling log fire he drank deeply of his ale while taking in the surroundings. The room was low and surprisingly long with the polished woodwork of the bar reflecting the fire's glow. The bar front appeared to have been converted out of the stern of a ship, split and worn smooth over the years but solid as ever. The ceiling was yellowed with smoke from the open-hearth fire and a great beam of dark oak ran across the middle. The walls were decorated with ship's lamps and steering wheels and paintings of ships under great presses of canvas hung around the huge fireplace, and he relaxed in the conviviality and the ambience of a sailing community. Even at this relatively early hour the bar was busy and most of the tables occupied, with one being crowded with rough looking seafarer types who were conversing boisterously and downing ale as if to make up for time lost.

Janie Ralston brought food to his table and laid it out before him. Game pie: with a big dish of potatoes, a crusty loaf and a thick wedge of blue veined cheese. 'This ought to keep you going for a while,' she said with a smile.

'Janie, I can see you are a girl with an eye for a man's weakness.'

Her eyes shadowed. 'Think perhaps I see too much of the weakness of man at the Blue Lugger.' With which comment she moved quickly away and he looked quizzically after her then shrugged away the question and sat down to enjoy his supper. Working his way through the game pie, most of the potatoes and a goodly helping of bread and cheese he sat back with the remainder of his ale and drowsy in the warmth of the fire. He had noticed while finishing his meal that Glyn Ralston was no longer behind the bar and commented on this to Janie when she came to clear his table.

'Father had to go out on business but he won't be away long.'

The proprietor's absence hadn't gone unnoticed by the bunch of seamen at the long table and they were becoming progressively noisier and banging on the table with their tankards and calling for rum. Janie stood sheltered behind the bar unheeding their demands and Mathieson watched the scene with anxious eyes, wishing that her father would return to take charge. The noise from the table increased. They were five in number, rough and unkempt as if they had been at sea for weeks. He knew the type only too well.

Reasonable men normally and good seamen but with money in their pockets and some time ashore they could soon be reduced to a pack of animals, particularly as now, in a state fast approaching drunkenness. Pounding the table in unison they chanted, 'We want rum!' over and over again. They didn't appear bad-tempered, just ill mannered and boisterous but quite a few customers at the bar had begun to drift out the door and Mathieson had to wonder at the urgency which caused Ralston to leave his daughter to manage alone at such a busy hour. Suddenly she could bear the noise no longer and came out from behind the bar to face them at the table with her hands on her hips.

'You are getting no more to drink until you quieten down and behave yourselves!' She spoke to them as though they were recalcitrant children and Mathieson thought she was lovely and certainly had spirit because she stood only about five foot three and appeared positively diminutive before the bulky seafarers one of whom laughed out loud at the schoolteacher tone of voice and reached out and grabbed her and sat her down on his knee then, as she struggled to get free, he leered into her face:

'Give us a kiss then, darlin'.' He reeked of stale sweat and tobacco and ale and Janie was scared stiff by the sight and smell of him but the more she struggled the tighter his arms held her. His hands were rough on her and inflamed by her nearness he fondled with intent over the curves of her body but she jerked away from the man's clutch and her palm cracked with indignant force against the unshaven cheek of her oppressor. He started back with his hand to his face but the rest of the bunch was hilarious at this summary treatment and rolling about with laughter and one of his mates roared, 'Hard luck, Amos, more there than you can handle!' He lurched to his feet incensed by the laughter which he felt was directed at him personally and he reached for her again and raised his hand threateningly.

'You little bitch,' he snarled, 'I'll teach you to be more friendly!'

Janie didn't lack courage but she cringed away from the sheer size of the brute as he towered over her and her arms came across her face as if to ward off the descending blow. Whether he would have struck her was unlikely but he didn't get the chance, for the lean body of Mathieson eased between Janie and the startled seaman with Amos's hand held high and immovable. 'You are out of order,' he snapped in commanding voice. 'Pick on someone your own size!'

The intervention brought infuriated response from Amos. 'Let go of my arm before I smash you to a pulp!' This was more to his liking, for even in his alcoholic state he had only gone for the girl because of the taunts of his shipmates, but the situation had changed, now he had real provocation and a chance to show off and he growled, 'I'm going to beat you into little pieces, mister!' Mouthing the words with intent he deliberately ripped the lace from the front of Mathieson's shirt. A move greeted with roars of approval from his mates.

'Give it to him Amos, have the pretty shirt off his back!' This was proving the stuff of a good run ashore to sailing men and, secure in the support of his shipmates, Amos grabbed for another handful of lace but Mathieson thrust a hard hand over his face with the palm under the other's chin and heaved the bulky seaman away and the controlled strength spread-eagled Amos across the table and sent half-empty mugs of ale splashing into the laps of the unwary seamen. Now the place was in uproar as they rose in scrambling unison and with Amos back on his feet mouthing obscenities they came at Mathieson in a menacing shuffle. Retreating a pace he clenched his fists ready but suddenly realised he no longer stood alone for alongside him appeared a suntanned, husky-shouldered man who exuded a clean scent of salt water and Stockholm tar.

'Come on then, me hearties, let's see what you're made of?' The voice was soft and almost musical and with a definite lilt of amusement. His fists were held before him and moving in slow, anticipatory circles and Mathieson had the distinct impression that the newcomer was relishing the prospect of a stand up fight with these brutes.

‘Out!’ The disturbance suddenly quelled with the appearance on the scene of Glyn Ralston who jerked his thumb at the door in emphasis of the word. His shoulders were barrel hunched and his fists were clenched and menacing. He seemed to be held in awe by the burly seamen and they slunk out the door dragging the struggling Amos with them. Janie Ralston linked arms with the newcomer and her eyes riveted on his face and her whole being was lit up by his presence and he ruffled his fingers through her hair and stooped to kiss her on the cheek.

‘Hello, young Janie,’ he said cockily, ‘who’s your new friend?’

Ralston came towards them from the door where he had been keeping a watchful eye as the departing seamen weaved a precarious route down the street. ‘Sorry, maid, he said, ‘but I thought I’d be back before that lot became troublesome.’ Turning to Mathieson. ‘I must thank you, sir, it took real guts to stand up alone to a rough lot like them.’ Glaring round the tap-room he said with scorn, ‘More than the rest of my customers have between them.’ His wrath began to subside and he said in formal tone, ‘Mr Richard Mathieson, will you meet Jonathan Rudd, just back from deep sea trawling in the Channel.’

The hand of Rudd was warm and hard and with a firmness equally matched by Mathieson. Their hands clasped and held, grip tightening until it became almost a contest of strength with neither man relinquishing his hold. Mathieson looked at him and said with a smile, 'I'll let go, if you will?'

Rudd's eyes were an incredible clear blue and with deep sun wrinkles spreading from the corners, eyes that seemed to have been fashioned for the sole purpose of searching across vast oceans in quest for new lands and far-off horizons. His sun bleached hair was unkempt and long about his neck and matched by a bushy, drooping moustache and as he grinned and nodded in agreement the solitary gold ring in his ear reflected the glow of the fire and danced brightly against the background of his lush sideburns. 'You'll do! Richard Mathieson,' he said as he released his grip.

Janie was still hanging on to his arm and staring up at them puzzled at this exchange and not quite understanding just what went on in the minds of men. But she understood enough to realise that these two had just measured themselves and, without need for further qualification, had accepted each other as equals and the insight sent an unpremeditated glow of warmth surging through her. But the sight of his torn shirt brought her back from euphoria. 'Your lovely shirt is ruined!' she said in distraught voice.

''Tis but lace and cotton and nothing for you to be concerned about.'

Ralston's voice boomed from behind the bar. 'Let us drink to our new acquaintance,' he said as he filled glasses, 'and to the hope that he will be with us for some time.'

'I'll take just one glass of wine with you then I must be away to my room,' pausing for a moment, he then said, 'and I hope to be with you all for some considerable time.'

Janie's hand clapped over her mouth in sudden consternation. 'Now I remember,' she said almost in a whisper. 'Richard Mathieson! You are the new . . .'

'Rector of the Parish of St. Peter.' Finishing the words for her he drank his wine and bowed to them and turning on his heel moved away out of the taproom, leaving a silent hush behind him. Janie's eyes followed the departing figure with something approaching awe in their depths but the silence was broken by the wry chuckle of Jonathan Rudd.

'If this be a sample of the new preacher,' he announced with great appreciation, 'then I think church going might prove very interesting in the near future?'

'Amen to that!' said Glyn Ralston.

2

Breakfast the next morning, laid in the in the privacy of their own sitting room, a small and cosy retreat far removed from the public bar and taproom. It proved a quiet and rather formal meal served by a very subdued Janie and Mathieson found it difficult to conceal amusement at her deliberate solemnity. 'Why so serious,' he eventually asked, 'haven't seen a single smile this morning?'

'You might have told us who you were,' she answered with evident reproach, 'instead of allowing us to treat you as we would any normal traveller. I could have served your supper quietly in here and away from the noise and trouble in the bar.'

'I will hardly get to know the people of the village by hiding away. Have to begin my work somewhere and I don't believe folk will come running to me willy-nilly just because I am a minister.'

'The church going folk are not likely to appreciate a minister who frequents ale houses and gets himself involved in brawls like the one last night,' replied Janie candidly, 'or indeed that you should be here in the inn at all.'

'You think I might be an embarrassment were I to stay for a few more nights?'

'My father would certainly think so and it would be easier on yourself if you were to find . . .' hesitating, she then said with a wan smile, 'more respectable accommodation?'

'Do not decry your own very considerable hospitality,' he replied firmly, 'and while I must yield to your sound reasoning it may take a few days to organise my affairs.' His mode of speech caused Janie to regard him with conjecture in her eyes.

'You don't have the normal appearance or manner people expect from a minister,' she said with a curious inflection in her tone, 'and I have the feeling that you haven't long been ordained.'

He laughed out loud at this summary and his amusement was so infectious that Janie shed her former deference and smiled with him, warming to this stranger who had come with such impact into their small community. He stood across the room from her with his back to the fire and he looked fondly at her as he said, 'You are a shrewd young woman, Janie Ralston, and your feeling about my lack of experience isn't so far removed from the truth.' With these words his eyes met hers, so level and sincere, and Janie felt a strange magnetism and an indefinable quality which seemed to reach out and engulf her. Never had she felt so completely at ease when alone with a man and, as he stood there, so warm and friendly, he seemed to emanate a dignified yet almost humble manner that vibrated deep inside and which made her want to offer help in anyway she could.

'I know where you can find comfortable lodgings,' she stated, 'somewhere quite close to the church too, in the cottage of a wonderful old lady. It is very simple but Mrs Farquasan will look after you well . . . and she is a splendid cook.' Janie added this almost as an afterthought and he grinned at the jibe in her tone.

'Again, ma-am, you read me too well.' Looking at her in searching manner and her face coloured as he went on with, 'Speaking of cooking reminds me that supper last night was absolute perfection and I would have told you so if the evening had been perhaps a little less eventful.' Realising she was embarrassed he added, 'I'll accept your thoughtful suggestion and will call on Mrs Farquasan this very morning, but I hope this move won't be the cause of denying me the further pleasure of your company and guidance.'

Her cheeks coloured a deeper shade of pink and she didn't know how to answer this but her eyes held his without wavering. 'Don't worry about your lovely Mistral,' she said at last, 'I'll make sure she is well cared for.'

He thanked her for this comfort, and she followed him to the front door to direct him to the cottage of Mrs Farquasan, and lingered on to study the curious glances of the early morning passers by as he strode lithely up the main street.

Situated on high ground the little church of Perranwithick looked down over the high street and the surrounding straggle of buildings that eventually converged to form a picturesque village square. He paused at the lych gate for a reflective minute. While a most charming entrance to the church grounds it appeared uncared for and in a sorry state of repair with its twin gates hanging awry from hinges that had almost rusted through and he could see large gaps in the boarded under-canopy where overhanging branches of a huge elm tree pressed down on the worm eaten woodwork. Vine-like creepers clung in fibrous tenacity along the boards and mushroom growth added further to the scene of decay and he felt a surge of dismay at the air of despondency and neglect that encompassed the entrance.

'And this is only the gateway,' he murmured to himself as he opened one half and hurriedly closed it as it threatened to topple over. The main church building lay about thirty yards inside, rising from the granite steps to stand sheer on a surround of green sward. The church was small and constructed of local stone with corner quoins so massive that he pondered for a moment on the strength of the work force that had laid the stone centuries ago. Gazing with interest at the arch over the front doorway he judged the style of architecture to be about fifteenth century, an estimate confirmed when he walked around the side of the building to inspect two, low-level, Oriel windows which were masterpieces of the stonemason's craft and quite beautiful with multi-coloured glass set in lead. He wondered how they would appear from inside with a morning sun shining through, but overgrown as they were, he thought it unlikely that any light would shine through at all. The elevations were festooned with creeper that hung in lush confusion over the granite stonework and although some attempt had apparently been made to keep the front of the church reasonably clear the whole aspect was one of neglect and decay. Even so . . . he was suddenly moved by the atmosphere of peace and tranquility that reached out from this sacred place to embrace and bring comfort and a strong feeling that this lovely old church would not allow itself to be shamed by the lack of concern bestowed by the local community.

Instead of entering he yielded to the freshness of the morning and decided to explore further and after gaining the vantage of the high ground he stood for a while to enjoy his first view of the surrounding countryside with his gaze caught and enraptured by the glorious seascape now revealed. The church was perched on the very top of the cliffs and he could see down into Mounts Bay and clear across to Penzance over craggy cliff and great, overhanging bluffs of rock and he followed the sheer drop down to curving stretches of sand so pale and washed clean by the pounding surf. St. Michael's Mount was completely surrounded by water and the waves surged against the rocky base sending spray flying to be caught and carried by the fresh offshore breeze and the wind lifted his coat tails and blew chill up his back and he thought enough was enough and turned back to wander through the graveyard where most of the headstones were weathered smooth with the writings on them almost unreadable. Where he could make out the names they all appeared to be Trevellyanes or Tremaines or Tre-something or other and many of the headstones bore the legend 'Lost at Sea' and he began to realise that this was a village where the men folk were mainly seafarers and fishermen who plied their trade with the shadow of the Grim Reaper as constant companion.

His attention now focused on a gravestone much larger than most and wide enough to be a double grave, or a tomb, and the macabre thought sent a shiver down his already cold back. The headstone was tall and upstanding and below two dancing cherubs a plate of polished marble bearing no name, just the words *Gone from this World*. Surveying this with growing interest and conjecture he noticed that it was well tended with the grass verge cropped close and the soil inside the stone kerb showing dark as if newly disturbed. While contemplating this he had a sudden and uncomfortable feeling of himself being under scrutiny and, sensing a furtive movement in the brush and undergrowth to his right, he deliberately stooped to once more inspect the grave. Again came the stealthy movement and for a brief moment he could make out a shadowy figure that immediately disappeared as he turned for a clearer view. Shrugging away foreboding he walked quickly back to the front entrance and pushed open the double doors. They opened without ease of movement with their hinges squealing protest as if in some eerie ghost story. A short vestibule with a stone bench seat either side led to a smaller pair of doors that opened to the touch and allowed free passage to the main body of the church.

Small and compact with a high, barrel-vault domed ceiling and a stone flag floor entirely devoid of covering except for the rows of hard-backed chairs which stood forlorn and covered in dust. The walls hung with cobwebs and the cream wash that once had coloured them was flaking away in untidy patches. The windows offered little in the way of light except for one long window of stained glass set high in the end gable and splendidly arched in three sections through which streamed a resplendent blaze of colour down the centre aisle along which he was moving. His footsteps, staccato on the cold stone, hushed as he hesitated in wonder at this multi-coloured swathe illuminating his way to the altar that stood in proud dignity behind a rood screen of ornamental and delicately carved woodwork, then he sank to his knees in the dust and dirt and remained in silent thought for a long time. The absolute quiet and sanctity moved him to prayer and he raised his eyes to that wondrous light. His words came echoing back from around the walls as he said out loud:

'Help me to bring warmth and comfort into this Your House and to all who seek guidance herein!'

The next morning found him hard at work on the lych gate. His tools were basic. Bow saw for branch trimming. Smoothing plane. A panel saw and a claw hammer and a couple of wood-chisels all purchased only yesterday from the village store. His arrival in the village had apparently been widely spoken about and many a warm voice greeted him as he made his way up the high street, but none more so than the storekeeper, Stephen Tremaine, who was a tall, cadaverous man with hollow cheeks and thinning hair and a complexion sallow from always working indoors.

Shaking him vigorously by the hand he introduced his wife, Blanche.

''Tis high time we had an energetic minister,' said Mrs Tremaine. A dumpy woman with freckled face she stood with arms akimbo the better to survey him and the tools he had just bought. 'You've more work there that can be managed with one pair of hands, Reverend,' she said forcibly, 'and I reckon you could do with some help.'

'I can handle the more urgent repair work.'

Blanche Tremaine's stern look melted before his smile but ignoring his reply she continued with her train of thought, saying, 'You'll get little help from the men folk because they're mostly at sea or working the land from dawn to sunset.' Her mouth tightened as if determined, and she promised, 'I'll organise the women to do whatever we can.'

'Thank you kindly,' said Mathieson, then added tactfully, 'the church is in need of a thorough cleaning and I would be most grateful if I could leave the matter in your capable hands.' The manner in which he accepted and associated with her offer had Blanche beaming with pleasure.

'Think it needs decorating not just cleaning,' she stated in firm tone, 'but give me a day or two to get things arranged then we'll soon have the church looking shipshape once more.'

*   *   *

He was thinking about this as he straddled a sturdy branch and proceeded to saw through the sections that were pressing down on the lych gate roof and so engrossed that he didn't see her until she was directly below him. Janie was dressed as if ready for work, but under her somewhat austere overall a pale cream blouse with high collar was a becoming background to her slender neck and round-cheek face. With a fawn top-coat about her shoulders he thought she looked very pretty as he said, 'Hello Janie, you are a most welcome sight on such a fine morning.' With which greeting he swung down from the tree and descended the borrowed ladder and stood before her. The sun being warm and his work energetic he had stripped off his jacket. White shirt: open at the neck with sleeves rolled high above his elbows and muscles rippled in his forearm as he relieved her of the basket she was carrying. He was almost six foot tall and seemed to tower over her and Janie felt almost nervous at his compelling masculinity. She was bareheaded and her hair draped in windblown abandon about her face and she retreated a confused pace before his obvious approval.

'Mrs Farquasan had to go out shopping this morning,' she said as if in explanation, before adding demurely, 'said she had to stock up for her new guest so I offered to bring you something to eat at midday.'

'You knew where I would be?'

'The whole village knows! You are our sole topic of conversation.' Then with a shy smile. 'The womenfolk anyway.'

He was too interested in the contents of the basket to pay heed to this last remark, but then asked, 'Will you sit with me for a while?'

'If you wish, Reverend Mathieson, but not for long because my father is expecting me back very soon.'

Pleased at her acceptance he took her arm and led to a wooden bench situated on a pleasant stretch of overgrown lawn where the sun was warm. 'Why so formal,' he asked as he sat down beside her, 'my name is Richard, as you well know?' He drank from the mug of ale she had brought. 'I needed that,' wiping a speck of froth from his mouth he grinned as he added, 'it's frightening to know my weaknesses are so very apparent.'

Her shyness gave way to pleasure at his appreciation. 'It's a warm morning,' she said, 'and not wishing to do anything that might be misconstrued I almost brought a glass of milk.'

'There's little harm in a pint of ale on such a sunny morning,' said Mathieson through a mouthful of bread and cheese. Downing the last of his ale he replaced the jug in her basket with a flourish and said, 'My thanks, Janie.'

'It is a pleasure to serve such an appetite,' she murmured, and the rather sly tone brought a smiling:

'Must have something to do with the fresh air around here.' He found the company of this attractive girl most pleasing and sought to delay her departure. 'May I steal a few more minutes of your time,' he queried, 'perhaps you'll stroll a few yards with me before returning to the *Blue Lugger*?'

Janie hesitated, she ought to be getting back but the hour was still early and her father could manage easily enough . . . It really was most tranquil here with Richard.

'Just a short while,' he said, sensing compliance, 'and I need an excuse not to climb back into that tough old elm.'

Reaching out to take her hand and together they strolled across the green sward around the church side with the midday sun warm on their faces and the clean fragrance of pine trees about them and the silence broken only by the dull clop of a horse trotting in the roadway. Pausing before a small granite headstone that bore the title "Margaret Jane Ralston" she said sadly, 'My mother.'

He had wondered about this but had thought it prudent not to enquire.

'I'm sorry, Janie,' he said.

The solicitude in his voice brought a wan smile then, shrugging away melancholy, she said in explanation. 'Mother died over five years ago but I still miss her so very much, so does my father, probably more than me, so I took over with the work she used to do at the Inn and help him in every way I can, and being busy was the best medicine for us both. My brother, Simon, was the worst affected . . . he took her demise so much to heart, so Jonathan straightaway took him on: didn't allow him time to feel sad and he soon got over losing her.' Then, in fond tone. 'He is so very young and loves being part of the *Rose*.' Mathieson thought she was very young herself and was more than impressed with this strangely mature girl with those penetrating eyes of darkest brown. Moving on, they resumed their stroll, the grass was long and she could feel the cool damp through her shoes then the sudden pressure of his fingers above her elbow halted her sauntering tread. Came a rustle in the grass at her feet and she stepped back in haste as a sinewy shape slithered away.

'It's only a grass snake,' said Mathieson, then, noticing her alarm he added with a smile, 'and probably more frightened than you are.'

'Why didn't you step on it?' she said with a distasteful shudder. 'I hate snakes!'

'Such snakes are harmless enough,' looking at her as he said this, 'and there is a place on earth for all His creatures, even such a tiny snake.' Still holding on to her arm as if he enjoyed touching her his statement brought a probing glance from Janie.

'You are an unusual man, Reverend,' she said, 'do you realise this is the first time I have heard you speak words that sound like religion?'

'I hope to practise religion rather than speak it.' The words were spoken softly but with great feeling and she sensed that he was unsure, as though trying hard to find his way in what was obviously a new vocation. His quiet humility overwhelmed her and she had the strangest feeling: of wanting to reach out and comfort him. Her eyes on his were searching and she looked at him for a long moment as if seeing right through him.

'I watched you run down that ladder,' she said at last, 'and I have lived among seamen long enough to recognise the style, and the manner of speech.' Looking him full in the face, she concluded, 'You have spent much of your life at sea!'

Shaking his head in no small amusement he looked wryly at her. 'I begin to think there is something of a witch in you, Janie Ralston,' he said, 'some mysterious gift that enables you to see through me with such ease and accuracy and I shall have to remember that you are a formidable young woman, one with whom I must measure every word lest I be found wanting.'

She glanced up with something approaching dismay in her eyes. 'How strange?' she murmured, 'for Jonathan said the same thing almost word for word except that he called it frightening.'

'Jonathan Rudd! I've been thinking about him this morning. Now there is a buccaneer if ever I saw one.' Looking down at her as she tensed he added quickly, 'Steady now, I meant it only as compliment.' Her reaction had confirmed his earlier impression and he continued in probing voice, 'You think very highly of Rudd I fancy?'

'Is it so obvious?'

'Not until this very moment, but I can see how any woman would find him exciting.' Then, cupping her chin with gentle fingers he lifted her face and forced her to look at him. 'Beware, Janie,' he said with great deliberation, 'for this is a giant of a man and there are few such men in this world.' His voice sounded full of regret and somehow haunted as he went quietly on with, 'But like the great winged albatross which roams the vastness of the Southern Ocean his soul will not easily be confined to any one horizon, and to try and clip such restless wings is to invite disillusion and heartbreak.'

'I don't want to clip his wings!' she cried with a break in her voice. 'I know he likes me but never says so and always so casual and uncaring and because he and my father are such good friends and because my brother sails as mate on the *Rose of Endau* he treats me as though I'm his sister!' Her tirade faded into a sob, then she blurted, 'And it's all so unfair! With this final outburst she rushed away in extreme discomfort. He called after her to no avail and he shrugged his shoulders knowing he had intruded enough for one morning, then his eyes came to rest on the empty lunch basket and a slow smile started and he said out loud:

'I'll use the basket as a valid excuse to call at the Blue Lugger this evening.'

3

Two heavy oak gates, open and pegged back against granite pillars and a weathered name post stood at one side with the title Sandford Barton in faded black lettering.

He reined in to take a few moments in contemplation. This invitation had been more in the nature of a summons to attend and he felt most apprehensive knowing how vital the moral and financial support of the wealthy Sedgewick's could be to a new clergyman striving to establish himself in what had so far proved a very poor and run down parish. Though he did not relish the thought he had to accept that he had come here cap-in-hand. On trial almost! Needing tact and subservience . . . a quality that didn't come easy. Then his mind cleared and optimism took over. It wasn't all gloom because he might see her again this very morning.

Mistral cantered up the gravel driveway

skirting a natural pond on which paddled a squadron of mallard ducks in line astern, then on towards a block of stable buildings where two young men grooming horses paused in their work at the approach of the big grey. He sprang down from the saddle and one of the grooms came to take the reins and regard him with interest and deference.

'Good morning to you, Reverend,' he said in friendly manner, 'leave your mare with me, Sir Harry and Lady Sedgewick are expecting you at the Barton.'

The main house lay about fifty yards from the stables up a widening track that opened into a wide crescent fronting the main doorway. The elevations were faced with dark brown stone so rich in colour that in places it appeared almost red. Built in the style of a medieval fortress it appeared more mansion than dwelling house with the front walls culminating in a heavily ornamented parapet wall, castellated into battlements. The windows were narrow but high and arched with the glass in small squares set into strips of lead and as he approached the dark-oak and somewhat forbidding front door he saw a hanging bell cord. Pulling on this he winced at the cacophony of disturbed bells from within, followed almost immediately by a rush of feet then the door opened to reveal the young woman he had encountered on his way to Perranwithick. Her eyes were dancing mischievously and he felt his breath catch at her incredible beauty. She wore a flowing skirt that reached her ankles and a pale blue blouse with puffed and transparent sleeves, and tantalizingly open at the neck. He wore no hat and bowed his head to her. 'Miss Sedgewick.'

'The Reverend Mathieson, I believe?' she said in a slightly mocking tone and as she spoke he saw the figure of a man behind her. Dressed in butler's regalia he at that moment had a very disapproving look on his face, and she admonished, 'Don't fuss Hawkins, the Reverend and I have met before, when he was riding without permission across the brook meadow.'

Mathieson refrained from comment, sensing that her arrogant manner at their first encounter could be the reason behind her rather uncomfortable levity. He wanted to say something to put her at ease but didn't get the chance as she said, 'Mother and father are in the library waiting for you before we take morning tea.' Bidding him to enter with a coyly spoken, 'If you will kindly follow me, sir?' Proceeding through a spacious hall and his eyes lingered on the curve of her slender waist and hips as she moved with swaying grace before him. Her perfume hovered so enticingly and he thought she was lovely and, at that moment, felt more man than minister. Then they entered a long and comfortable room. Persian carpet. Hide-covered easy chairs, bookshelves lining the walls and the room smelled of leather and polish: and exuded affluence! There were three others in the room and Mathieson hesitated, feeling well out of his depth as they turned to face him. Then his arm was gripped and he could feel the tingle of her fingers above his elbow. 'Come along preacher-man,' she said, 'don't be shy!' Steering him in she brought him close to the large settle. 'Mama, may I present the Reverend Mathieson.'

'Lady Sedgewick.' He took the proffered hand and smiled down at her.

'I am very pleased to make your acquaintance, Reverend.' Her cool tone conveyed disapproval of her daughter's lack of respect and she rose from her sitting position to stand and look at him. Tall and slender: dressed in a gown of burgundy velvet. Her hair was darkest brown slightly tinged with grey and framed a high-cheeked, oval and attractive face. Her eyes were hazel flecked and warm yet slightly interrogative and her hand lingered on as if in welcome . . . Then he broke the silence to state:

'Good of you to ask me to call so soon.'

'We could hardly wait to meet the new minister,' she said, adding with a smile, 'and you certainly made an impression on Cathryn!' This remark brought pleasure and he glanced quickly at her but her eyes were demurely downcast.

'Bring him over, Cassy!' The voice resounded across the room and he turned towards the two men by the fireplace, then advanced towards the speaker.

Sir Harry Sedgwick stood over six feet tall but was so bulky he appeared almost squat, accentuated by strong thighs bulging inside tight fitting breeches. He wore no coat, just a wine coloured waistcoat that strained ominously around his stomach. He had a strong face with a square chin, and a shock of wiry hair the colour of spun silver accentuated his determined good looks. This impression had to be taken in retrospect as his hand was grasped and pumped up and down.

'Not much like your predecessor,' said Sir Harry, 'but we bid you welcome to Perranwithick and hope for your long and rewarding stay among us. Sarah!' he said loudly, 'are we ever to have any damned tea?' His outburst was premature for just then a maid appeared bearing a massive silver tray which she set before her mistress. A thought occurred to Sir Harry and he suggested, 'Perhaps the Reverend would prefer something more stimulating?' Crossing to the sideboard which hosted a set of decanters and glasses he poured a measure of golden liquor.

'Thank you sir, but tea will be most welcome.'

'How about you Captain?' Sir Harry looked enquiringly at the other man who declined with a negative gesture.

'Shake hands with our new preacher then! Richard Mathieson, meet Captain Wilder Faraday of Her Majesty's Excise Service.' Taking a gulp of brandy he then announced, 'The Captain has been recently appointed from London to rid Cornwall of its pestilential smugglers.'

The two shook hands. They had time for no more than a polite greeting before Lady Sedgewick served tea while the pretty parlour maid followed with plates of tiny savouries. Mathieson's interest had been aroused by Sir Harry's last remark and he now had the chance to observe Wilder Faraday from over the rim of his teacup. The Captain looked a hard man. Of medium height but with powerful arms and shoulders and a thick trunk of a body and while not in uniform he was fashionably dressed in navy blue jacket and waistcoat and white, stove pipe trousers with a broad band of silk complimenting a taut waistline. His shirt had embroidered lace up the front, and with a swarthy complexion and jet black hair smoothed back from a narrow forehead he was quite striking but in brutish fashion and his face was dominated by a wide and sensual mouth. Mathieson thought him impressive, in a repellent sort of way. 'Surely Captain,' he said politely, 'there is little enough smuggling in this remote corner of the West Country to warrant the attention of so high a rank?'

'You appear to lack local knowledge, Reverend, the Cornish coastline is notorious and smuggling is part of the folklore about here.' Faraday smiled in sinister manner as he then said,

'Smuggling goes on wherever there are seafarers, for seamen always seem to believe they have some divine right to break the laws of the land. But I am not here on business. Like yourself . . . I am just learning my way about the countryside and taking the opportunity of calling on upon those who have great influence and who are concerned with maintaining law and order.'

Mathieson winced inwardly at the ingratiating tone, and while realising he was being less than charitable couldn't help but wonder how the Captain felt about the vast and open expanse of Cornwall when compared to the congested Port of London. The derogatory comment about seafarers had also aroused resentment, so he probed, 'Was it promotion that brought you to Cornwall?'

Faraday came out of his relaxed stance to look calculatingly at Mathieson and his eyes were wary. 'I had considerable success in London' he said coldly, 'substantially more than enough to place me in an area where I can assume sole command.'

'Sole command is important to you?'

'I like to run things my own way.' Faraday was smiling, but in a snide manner indicating he did not appreciate having to explain. His eyes remained cold and very watchful as he said, 'Because I believe that wherever there are deep sea sailing men I will find rogues and thieves who deliberately run contraband, and make no mistake, Reverend, there also will I be: ready and waiting to catch and hang the offenders!'

'Come now, gentlemen!' broke in Lady Sarah. She had no liking for this conversation or for the conflict that had arisen between her two guests and she said firmly, 'No more of this wearisome talk, I beg you.' Now addressing Mathieson she enquired, 'Tell me, Reverend, when are you hoping to start regular service again?'

Grateful for her intervention he replied, 'Thank you for asking, but I need to carry out a few jobs of renovation about the church and it will be quite a while before I am ready for services.'

'I know the church has been allowed to fall almost derelict and feel somewhat ashamed that we haven't tried to help a little more with maintenance.' Pausing for thought, she queried, 'Are you acquainted with the retiring minister?'

'Only by name,' said Mathieson, before going on to state. 'I have called twice at his place of residence but received no answer to my knock on either occasion although I could sense that the house was occupied.'

'Reverend Foxer always seemed in poor health and unable to cope with the parish work and because of his lack of incentive, attendances dwindled to pitiful level and about two years ago he finally gave up. He's been little more than a recluse for a long time . . . his wife also, poor dear, although she had to act as an unpaid servant for many years.'

Mathieson had always wondered about the alacrity with which he had been granted this incumbency. Now he knew why? Probably no one else would take it on! Morose thoughts quickly dispersed as Sir Harry broke in with a brusque, 'Nonsense, Sarah, women like Mrs Foxer enjoy being downtrodden, it's the only way they find justification and contentment.' He poured another glass of brandy before continuing with, 'Now then, Reverend, how can we help, perhaps the use of a couple of my men for a day or so?'

'You're most kind Sir Harry, but I have some skill with word-working tools, enough at least to carry out the more urgent repairs.' Pausing . . . he then suggested hesitantly, 'I'll need all the help I can muster to repaint the interior.'

'Offer stands when you are ready. This village has been without its church for too long. Doesn't do the folk any good, you know? They need spiritual guidance, or else they get into bad habits.' He accompanied this statement with another gulp from his glass, the despairing glance of Lady Sarah not going unnoticed by Mathieson, but Sir Harry had more personal matters to pursue and, addressing him directly, said, 'Like the looks of that dapple-grey of yours. How about selling? I'll find you a mount plenty good enough to hack around on.' His voice was dominant in the confines of the library and Cathryn stirred with sudden interest. This was typical Sir Harry, for his passion for horses was common knowledge, but she knew also that he couldn't be thwarted in an overwhelming desire to own the finest stock in the area. Glancing across at Mathieson she noted the worn cord jacket with leather patches at the elbows and the sturdy legs encased in tight trousers and knee length boots, themselves a little down at heel but showing a high polish beneath the scuff marks, and his face was dignified above a badge-of-office dog-collar. He wasn't outstandingly handsome, she concluded hastily, but certainly of interest. She found the quiet authority of this man intriguing and as their eyes met she caught a suggestion of a conspiratorial wink. Then, concentrating his gaze firmly on Sir Harry, he said:

'You compliment me, sir, but my mare is not for sale.'

'Name your own price!' Twirling his empty glass as if confident that his money offer would be accepted.

'Mistral is not for sale,' repeated Mathieson with his voice conspicuous in the hush that had fallen, and Wilder Faraday leaned back against the oak beam that was the lintel of the open hearth fireplace, the better to enjoy the tension . . . and the conflict. He had noticed the deepening hue on Sir Harry's face and waited with malicious anticipation for the axe to fall on Mathieson who, in Faraday's opinion, had far too much pertinent comment for a humble man of the cloth.

'There's a price for everything Reverend.

You drive a hard bargain but I want that mare!' Sir Harry's money usually commanded due respect and he said forcibly, 'I'll double whatever you paid for her! Come on, man, and don't play the fool with me, I know you can use the money!' Confronting him in aggressive pose but Mathieson stood his ground and Cathryn could sense something immovable in his stance.

'Mistral is not for sale,' he said again, 'and I beg you, sir, not to pursue the matter to a point that becomes unpleasant.'

Inflamed by frustration and the brandy he had consumed Sir Harry thrust forward. 'Sell me the mare,' he thundered, 'and I'll paint your church from top to bottom as it has never been painted before.'

Mathieson's mind reeled at the thought of his little church in newly found splendour. But he had come to seek help: not to grovel! He shook his head and said ruefully, 'You bargain unfairly Sir Harry, but I will not sell Mistral to you or to anyone else,' smiling his gentle smile now, he added, 'as for the church: it will be done one day, I promise you.' The atmosphere was far from cordial and he hesitated for a moment unsure of how to handle the situation but certain that the meeting had been a complete disaster. He had offered confrontation instead of meek subservience and had lost his cause before it had even started and, looking at Lady Sarah he said, 'I have rewarded your hospitality in very poor fashion, my Lady, and so I thank you and take my leave with great regret.' He nodded a brief farewell to Faraday but saw only the back of Sir Harry who had turned pointedly away and stood staring out the window.

'Show the Reverend to the front door, Cathryn,' murmured Lady Sarah. Her face reflected concern as Mathieson immediately turned and followed her daughter into the hall.

Mistral had been groomed and was tethered ready at the front entrance and he paused before mounting. 'I'm sorry to have upset Sir Harry,' he then said.

'You are the least tactful person I have ever met,' she replied scornfully. 'Couldn't you have evaded him a little? Promised to think about it or something similar, because your uncompromising refusal left poor Papa with no dignity and he isn't used to being denied, especially in front of his family, and Captain Faraday also.'

'Among other things,' he said, 'I came to ask if he would kindly read the lesson at my opening service.'

'You have a strange way of gathering support. He'll get over it but don't expect much help from him for a while.' Smiling, she looked at him and her eyes sparkled with mischief as she said, 'Mama approves of you though, and together we'll work him round.'

'Does that mean you also approve?'

'Do not pursue your good fortune overmuch,

preacher-man,' she replied with a slight goading edge in her tone, 'you've done quite enough damage to the Sedgewick family for one day.' She heard a quick chuckle as he mounted and then, with a lift of his hand and a clatter of hooves, he sped off down the driveway.

Back in the library Lady Sarah regarded her husband with reproof in her eyes. 'Really Harry,' she said, 'you weren't very charitable? Neither was it necessary to get all worked up over a simple matter of horse-trading.'

'The man's an upstart!' snapped Sir Harry in a voice waspish with annoyance and humiliation. 'He'll not reign long in Perranwithick!'

Immersed in thoughts of his own Wilder Faraday mused, 'Mathieson? Sounds familiar! There was a First Mate of the same name on one of the Far Eastern clippers operating out of the pool of London and I wonder if there is any connection.' Looking at Sir Harry for confirmation as he suggested, 'I could write to a colleague in the shipping company and find out if any mystery surrounds your new minister.'

'No business of ours,' replied Sir Harry. Still irritable and more than a little embarrassed he added spitefully, 'But it could be interesting to learn more about Mathieson.' Shrugging away Lady Sarah's disapproving look with a scowl, he concluded, 'He's too damn sure of himself for my liking!'

4

High tide at Newlyn, where the *Rose* lay secured against the dockside with her decks almost level with the cobble-stoned roadway and her fishing nets piled up ashore. A heavily built man moved among the salt encrusted coils in bare feet that were almost hidden in the thick folds of netting. 'They seem in pretty good shape, skipper!'

Straightening from a kneeling position where he was engaged in fitting a new section of teak planking in the deck alongside the doghouse, Rudd said, 'If you think they are still usable, Jake, spread them out and leave them to dry for the rest of the day, then give Simon a hand to fix the broken rail on the foredeck.' Kneeling again to his work he looked up when another voice interrupted his labour. Brushing aside the momentary irritation he greeted the intruder with a welcoming smile. Her hair was long and the morning breeze blew dark strands across her rose-tinted face. She had a wide sensuous mouth and her eyes were as dark as her hair and his glance went instinctively to her bosom as she leaned forward over the stone bollard in a posture that allowed the low-cut dress reveal the first, full swelling of her breasts and the deep cleavage between. 'Kathleen, me-pretty,' he greeted, 'you're a sight to behold on such a fair morning.' Her reached out a hand to her but she backed away, feigning reluctance.

'Not so fast Captain, you said you were coming to see me last evening.' Her mouth drooped at one corner as she said petulantly, 'I waited in for you.'

'I know, my love, but I was working on this damned deck until after dark and by then I was much too tired to come ashore. Only had enough energy left to climb into my bunk and fall asleep and dream sweet dreams of you. Oh. Kathleen, such dreams!' Leaping on to the quay he slipped his arm round her. 'Don't be angry,' he murmured in her ear, 'you know I would have come had it been humanly possible.'

She glared at him but her petulance was fast disappearing under his infectious humour and as he brushed the hair from her cheeks her mouth softened into an involuntary smile and she gave him a look that held a blend of fondness and resignation. 'Just don't know why I bother with you,' she said, 'you're a rogue and a romancer and no decent girl should be allowed within sight of you.'

'Kathleen, Kathleen, how you wrong me, you know I seek no other but you.' Moving one hand in caressing motion along her arm he said in cajoling tone, 'May I tell you I have a present, brought all the way from foreign lands just for you.'

'A present: what is it?' There was excitement in her voice then her eyes narrowed and she asked with meaning, 'Where is it?'

'Where do you think?' said Rudd with snide innocence. 'Where else but down in my cabin just waiting for you to come and claim it.'

'You swear that you have present for me?'

'My love, I deceive you not, it but needs your presence down below and all doubts will be vanished from your lovely brow.' He knew her too well and straightway lifted her in strong arms and swung her down to the deck and then led her to the main hatchway. They paused at the entrance and she looked at him with her eyes dancing then ran with a peal of laughter down the wooden steps with Rudd sliding eagerly behind her with his hands on the rail and his feet not touching the steps.

Simon glanced at Jake, who just shrugged his shoulders before resuming work on the damaged guardrail. A full hour passed before the saloon doors again opened and Kathleen emerged with Rudd. He handed her across the deck onto the dockside, all the while showing great courtesy. As she gained the sweep of the roadway she turned to enquire, 'Tonight Jonathan?'

'Of course!'

'You sure?'

'As long as we finish work and get the ship ready for the early morning tide.'

'Oh!' Stamping her feet in frustrating and he watched with amusement as she stalked away with her shoulders back and her head held high and her long skirt twirling about her ankles. He jumped back aboard as Simon came back from the after deck towards him.

'You're a terrible liar Jonathan,' he said with a boyish grin.

'Only in affairs of the heart and in pursuit of willing young women such as the lusty Kathleen.'

'And where tonight, or will we be to tired after our hard day getting the ship ready for sea?' Of medium height, Simon was a lean young man dressed in a check shirt and matelot-type trousers with bell bottoms. His hair was sun-bleached blond and he had a rugged, weather-tanned face with a snub nose and his eyes were brown and just now bright with humour.

'Now then young Simon,' said Rudd with an unconcerned grin, 'you forget who's captain here, and you know the laughing eyed Susan at the Landfall tavern is expecting me again. Fancy that her bed will be warmer than a cold bunk below.'

Jake had been watching Kathleen's departure. Suddenly alert, he scurried aft. 'Coach coming!

Looks as if we are in for a visit from the Excise men.'

Rudd's relaxed manner gave way to uncertainty and he stared along the quayside as a smart open coach and pair rumbled to a halt. A man in Excise uniform jumped down from beside the driver and moved speedily to open the door and Wilder Faraday stepped down and looked around with a lace handkerchief held to his nose as though he found the strong stench of fish and seaweed far too unsavoury for his delicate nostrils. Formidable in full uniform his glance seemed to take in the whole of the untidy dockside scene. Then his eyes fastened on the flushed and hurrying Kathleen and lingered on the brightly dressed bundle she cradled in her arms before focusing on the *Rose* and her crew. He sauntered with apparent lack of haste along the harbour wall towards Rudd, who had met the Captain only once before, on which occasion he had formed an instinctive dislike which went far beyond the customary disdain of seamen for men of the Excise. Looming over Rudd from the vantage of the dock wall Faraday strode on deck without invitation.

'Do come aboard, Captain.' Rudd spoke with heavy sarcasm as Faraday's boots ground dirt and dockside grit into his newly stoned deck planking. The Captain was immaculate in a tailored uniform coat of dark blue with snug fitting trousers running into polished boots, and a silk cravat adorned his throat. His eyes were diamond sharp and his penetrating survey took in the ship from stem to stern to where Simon and Jake stood poised warily amidships, then back to the new board in the deck planking.

'Had some trouble I hear?' he said insolently.

'Nothing unusual,' countered Rudd, 'trouble and deep sea fishermen are constant companions.'

Regarding him cynically Faraday stooped to pick up the splintered piece of plank Rudd had cut out of the deck. Turning the plank over he ran a finger along a gouged hole in the wood. 'Strange wound,' he suggested, 'and looks like the mark a stray musket ball might leave.' His voice took on a biting edge and he focused calculating eyes on Rudd. 'How would a simple fisherman come by such a hole in his decking?'

'We had a small shark caught up in our trawl and had to gaff it,' answered Rudd without hesitation. 'I can tell you we don't get too close to a shark's teeth no matter what the size.'

Greeting the reply with contempt Faraday probingly queried, 'I hear that Spanish brandy is proving very popular and I imagine it could be a trade that pays much better than fishing.'

'If you think you can find any brandy,' said Rudd with an angry gesture, 'you're welcome to inspect below?'

'Don't play the innocent with me, if I suspected you had contraband aboard you would have been rummaged inside out by now!' Throwing the board down Faraday gave Rudd a calculating glance. 'The woman who just left,' he asked slyly, 'friend of yours?'

'Kathleen? Yes, she's a very good friend.'

'I wondered what such a whore was doing on the dock at this time of day?' His tone was deliberately offensive and Rudd's fist came up in hasty retort but Simon sprang between them to place a restraining hand on his arm.

'Easy Jonathan, remember we have to sail on the morning tide.'

An ominous sound came from the quay as an Excise man cocked and aimed his musket but Rudd wouldn't be restrained and he thrust forward and brandished his fist at Faraday. 'I'll smash your beak of a nose if you don't get off my ship!' Anger brought great menace into his stance but Faraday was unmoved. In fact he felt satisfied and pleased with his interrogation and thought that if Rudd had a weakness it was obviously an over-fondness for women.

'Remember I am here on official business,' he said disdainfully, 'and any further violence will have you languishing in prison for so long a period of time that you won't sail on a morning tide ever again.' His eyes focused keenly on Rudd as he added, 'I just wonder how your woman friend came by the little bundle she carried.' Allowing a moment for this to sink in . . . he then said with snide meaning. 'Correct me if I'm wrong, but wasn't the doll dressed in Spanish national costume?' Leaping lithely ashore he turned for a final thrust. 'Don't treat me as your usual naïve Excise man, Rudd, for when I catch you smuggling, and I certainly will if you continue, I'll take great pleasure in hanging you from the nearest gibbet!' With these words he signalled to his watchful escort then wheeled away and marched back to the coach and pair with Rudd staring after him in anger and no small consternation.

'I'm going to enjoy crossing swords with you, Faraday,' he growled out loud, 'just watch out for me on some dark night!' Looking into the worried face of Simon he said, 'Don't look so forlorn, lad, he'll need to rise early if he wants a sight of the *Rose* ghosting in.' As a rattle of coach heralded the departure of the Excise he glanced after them and said with a grin, 'Perhaps we'll catch fish this time, just to perplex our not-so-naïve Captain!'

5

Mathieson counted himself lucky to be lodging in the home of Mrs Farquasan. The widow fussed over him as she would her own son and took great pleasure in his company. His bedroom overlooked green meadowland and in the evenings he would sit and read, or sometimes write, in the warmth and comfort of a cosy sitting room when only the click of her knitting needles would intrude upon his thoughts.

They had just finished supper and he looked up with a contented smile as she began to clear away. Indignantly declining his offer to help she instructed him to relax for a while. A plump little woman with clear blue eyes in a smiling, rosy cheek face that always appeared well scrubbed she soon reappeared from the kitchen and taking her usual seat on the sofa arranged herself with her knitting and started conversation with. 'You've been very thoughtful this evening, Reverend.'

Welcoming this opening he glanced at her to enquire, 'Is there someone about the church grounds I should know about?'

'Why do you ask?'

'Because today again I had the feeling that someone was watching me.'

She hesitated, but her knitting needles worked smoothly on before she cautiously replied, 'Reverend Foxer used to employ a man to work on the grounds a few hours a week . . . a funny sort, who would sneak away if anyone came near'.

'Did he pay the man a wage?'

'Doubt it, but he allowed him to stay in a little hut under the trees. He lives there still so they say, just like a hermit. I've only had a glimpse of him, but he is crippled in some way and with a badly deformed back.' Shuddering at the thought, she then said, 'Wouldn't go near that churchyard at night, not for anything!'

He noticed at once the very real fear on her face but his interest had been aroused 'Something else I find intriguing?' Her needles stopped their intricate work as she became engrossed in the dialogue and she looked up with foreboding as he went on to explain, 'There is a double grave with two marble cherubs on the headstone and of which I can find no mention in the church records.'

The comment brought a glance of discomfort and, in a voice that hinted she knew more than she was willing to disclose, she said, 'The early records were destroyed in a fire some fifty years ago.'

'Seems more than a little mysterious?'

'Not when you realise how hard a time churches in this part of the country have endured over the ages, it's a wonder any of them are left standing . . . losing a few scraps of paper can't be so drastic?' Her voice hushed as she stated, 'Folk here say that the graveyard is haunted and that evil spirits roam free in the dead of night.'

'But has anyone actually seen the evil spirits or is it just a part of local superstition?'

'Nobody goes through the lych gate at night.'

'Do you think these ghost stories have anything to do with the strange man you mentioned?'

Her involvement caused her to drop a stitch so she laid down her knitting and looked at him. 'I think he's harmless enough,' she said, 'and I'm fairly sure he's more afraid of people than they are of him.'

'Have you any idea where he came from?'

'Rumour has it that a long time ago his father played the organ at some big Cathedral up country but that he took to drink.' Her voice took on a gossipy note as she went on to explain, 'They say he went funny in the head and died early because of the drink. He was supposed to play the organ here in the church but I don't know of anyone who heard him but this happened a long time ago and so far as I know, the hermit has been living in his little shack ever since.' Pausing for reflection, she then said, 'People wondered why the last minister put up with him, the man is so strange and does no work about the church at all, I think Reverend Foxer was afraid of him too!'

It was turning out to be an interesting, if somewhat bizarre, story. Deciding he would have to look into this strange affair: there might be some information in the church records, he then queried, 'Didn't know there had ever been an organ in the church?'

'Just a poor broken down affair and eventually one of the sides split and fell off.' Mrs Farquasan took great satisfaction in sharing her fund of local knowledge with the new minister and went on with a suitably sad smile. 'The organ was never played and in the end they carried it out and left it to rot in the barn. Imagine the woodworms have eaten it away by now.'

'I'll have a look tomorrow, an organ would be so wonderful and what a difference it would make to the hymn singing.'

'You first need the organ, then someone to play it, and finally a congregation to sing. Reverend, you have a long road ahead!'

'What a picture of despondency you do paint, ma-am!'

The following morning he completed work on the lych gate by hammering home the last oak peg, planed a shaving from the closing edges where they threatened to close too tightly and swung them a few times. The gates moved smoothly on greased hinges and closed with a satisfying click and he stood back for a moment and surveyed his work. While in idle contemplation he recalled the conversation about the organ that had been carried away in pieces, and after brushing away the wood shavings he strolled without haste around the church and into a stone-built barn that stood some yards from the rear of the main building. Here again the picture was one of neglect and decay. Window frames rotting and in danger of falling out. The door was non-existent and the floor a mess of dirty straw and bird droppings and numerous tiny bats hung as though dead from the roofing timbers and he gave a wry smile and thought it no wonder the churchyard was shunned at night if these little creatures flew there. But the craftsman Thatcher of long ago had done his work well and the roof was intact and firm. The inside of the barn might be cold and draughty but it was as dry as the dust on the floor. He ducked his head involuntarily as a flock of sparrows flew out in panic at his intrusion into solitude, then venturing inside he saw the organ immediately. It was the only thing of substance in the barn. Against the wall in broken down disarray it leaned over on its side and he inspected it with resignation. The keys had faded to a dirty yellow and there were many gaps in the keyboard. Both the front and remaining upright were riddled with woodworm and crumbled to dust under his exploring fingers. Even as he touched it, the organ sank a little further into the ground as if ashamed to be looked upon and he dusted his hands together and gazed sadly at the derelict instrument.

'What music had once been made by you old friend?' he murmured. The sound of furtive movement from outside banished the train of melancholy. He stood very still apparently lost in thought, and a long, breathless minute passed. Then out of the corner of his eye he saw a head and shoulders rise above the stonework of the window and his startled gaze met the searing flash of scary-dark eyes then the head dived away out of sight and he heard a hurried movement of withdrawal and he sped out the door and round the side of the barn.

Rustling in the undergrowth away to his right, he caught the glimpse of a shadowy figure disappearing into the dense thicket. An ungainly shape but even as he focused the bushes closed to give thorny refuge to the fleeing figure and leaving him with an impression of a dragging, awkward leg pulled along from a misshapen hip and back. Nerves tingling with apprehension he followed in the wake of this frightening apparition. Not in undue haste because the damp grass showed a clear trail and he had no intention of turning pursuit into a chase. Carefully opening up the prickly undergrowth he eased through the first clutching of the brush and out under the spreading branches of the woodland behind. The tracks wound unsteadily under the trees parallel to the church grounds then out on to a small meadow and at the edge of the wood he saw a wooden hut, no larger than a garden shed, and he paused for a moment under the shelter of a huge elm tree before approaching. There appeared no window at all but he could make out the outline of a narrow doorway. Moving warily up to the wooden shack he took a quick glance around then knocked on the door. No response, so he knocked again. 'Is anyone there?' Again no answer and he pushed tentatively at the door, which swung open to reveal a dim interior. The doorway seemed the only means of illumination and he took a careful step inside. Wood-shingle roof. Boarded walls through which showed an occasional circle of light from a gaping knothole. A wooden bench served for a table and a single packing case as a chair. In one corner a low settle made from rough boards was obviously a bed and there was no other furniture except for a neat shelving arrangement on the end wall that housed a series of leather bound books. The gold embossed lettering aroused interest so he reached out and opened one. It proved to be a book of music and as he rippled the pages he could see that someone had made notes on the music scoring at different positions and while the ink had faded the lettering was in a fine copperplate hand, and still legible.

Replacing the book with care he looked around with growing speculation. The room was pitifully small, but clean and tidy. The bare floorboards, though warped and twisted, had been scrubbed so clean they were a pale, creamy yellow in colour. A circular stone chimney rose from the centre and there was a warming glow from a slow-burning log in the hearth and on a nearby metal tripod stood a smoke blackened cooking pot. The whole atmosphere reflected a simple but lonely air of self-sufficiency and Mathieson knew he had no right to be here. That he was intruding into privacy! So he stepped outside and closed the door behind him. A rapid glance confirmed that he was alone and he walked away brooding upon the strange man who chose to live in this isolation.

The next few mornings before starting work he first of all would grope through the bushes and leave some small item of food at the door of the shack. He could sense that his every movement was being observed yet never again did he open the door of that humble shed nor in any way reveal his awareness of being under scrutiny.

On the fourth morning, as he stooped to lay a loaf of newly baked bread at the doorway, he sensed the nearness of another human being and as he straightened and turned it was no surprise to see a strange shape emerge from behind an adjacent clump of bushes. He made no move and the man stared somehow defiantly up into his face and a surge of compassion swept over Mathieson as he surveyed the onlooker. The man's body was twisted and hideously crooked down his left side with the leg spread out at a grotesque angle and his back was hunched at one shoulder. A tense moment followed with neither giving way.

'Why are you here preacher,' the man said angrily, 'what do you want with me?' His voice was harsh and forcing, as if his mouth had not formed words aloud for a long time.

'Do I have to want anything?' Mathieson's motives were plain curiosity and interest but he tried to make his words sound casual, while excited by the contact he had no wish to force the other into flight.

'Everyone wants something, except me, and I want only to be left alone!' The words were bitter and his hands clenched and Mathieson's eyes were drawn to the nerveless talons that were the fingers of his left hand. The man saw the look of concern and took a shuffling step forward and held out his misshapen arm before him with his fingers drooping in twisted confusion. 'Drink your fill, preacher!' he snarled through a contorted mouth. 'Look at me with pity if you dare! Hideous though I am! Deformed! Mutilated! I need not your pity!' With these tormented words he stooped and lifted the loaf of bread from the doorway. 'Or your charity!' Throwing the loaf at Mathieson's feet he cried with angry crescendo in his voice, 'Can you not leave me alone?' Rearing to full height he seemed about to run away but Mathieson caught the outstretched arm and ran gentle fingers over the twisted hand. The man's face registered immediate shock. His eyes were dark caverns of pain but held a soft and glowing luminosity that served to soften the harsh look on his face and Mathieson felt a momentary flicker in the hand he was still holding, an almost desperate fleeting move to reach out to him. Then the hand pulled free to fall down to the crippled side. 'Can you bear to touch me?' he asked in wondering tone. Some of the anger seemed to have disappeared and he said, more quietly, 'People always turn away in fear when they look on me, my father was the only person who ever touched me.'

'Your father was Mathew White the organist.' He had gained this knowledge from the church records but, glaring like a trapped animal, the man shouted:

'Why do you want to know about my father?'

'I don't! I want to know about you.'

'All you really want is for me to leave here? It frightens the gentle people of your village to have me around.' Though his voice was sneer of contempt and heavy with bitterness, Mathieson found educated eloquence apparent in the mode of delivery, and as he strove for words of comfort he had a moment to notice the shabby clothes that hung loose on the thin frame and the coverings of animal hide on his feet and he thought that this man had not lived among other people for a long time and he thought he didn't care for other people and that he was pretty damned self sufficient. A quick summary, that brought caution.

'You are wrong, Mr White,' he said, 'for you can stay here as long as you desire and you have my word that I will never disturb you again. But even if your door should remain closed to me, I want you to know that the door of the church will always be open to you.' Looking at him as he said this, he saw a tremor shake him and the eyes that had been downcast suddenly flared and focused angrily.

'Were the sacred doors open when my clay was cast into this mould of degradation?' A sob shook him and trembled his words. 'Is this mutilated shape of mine some part of the great universal scheme of things to be, and can you tell me this, preacher? Where was your God when I was being formed? Or how much agony of body and mind has to be endowed into one insignificant human being like me?' The way he looked as he said this and the way he spoke seemed to indicate God and the world had made of him an outcast and that if the world had outcast him he didn't want to be a part of the world and that he didn't care and that it was the way he wanted it to be, and Mathieson shook his head in considerable anguish. How inadequate he felt as he said:

'You ask questions to which I do not have the answers.' He spoke with sadness and with humility but his gaze burned into the man before him. 'But this I do know,' he then said firmly, 'that if there is a place for every one of us in this great scheme as you have named it, then it will never be found by hiding away from the eyes of the world but only by accepting what small virtues we have been granted and using them with dignity and pride.' Stooping to retrieve the loaf of bread. 'Mrs Farquasan baked this especially for you this morning, how sad she will be when I take it back. Dirty and dishonoured.'

A terrible, choking sob shuddered through the twisted frame. His hands reached out and tore the loaf from Mathieson. Then, clasping it to his breast and with eyes blurred with unshed tears he dragged blindly off through the bushes. The sound of stumbling withdrawal died into silence and Mathieson walked away with those haunted eyes scorching in his soul.

He didn't see any sign of the strange recluse all that day or on the day after. But on the second morning when he was hard at work in the churchyard there came movement from the undergrowth and the figure of Thomas White limped through. He was clad in a working overall and threadbare, woollen waistcoat. His shoes were scuffed and oversize and he wore no socks and, coming up to Mathieson, he stood like a frightened bird poised for instant flight. 'I can do that for you,' he said, 'if you'll allow me?'

Straightening with a deliberate, tired sigh. 'There is such a lot to do,' said Mathieson, 'and I'd be most grateful for any help.' Ecstasy surging and flooding at this contact but he forced himself to suggest calmly, 'Perhaps we can work together on this path, side by side?'

A glimmer of relief and acceptance appeared and brought amazing gentleness to the barren face. 'Suits me,' he said with a sidelong glance, 'but no obligation and no interference with my way of life.'

'Whatever you wish, Mr White.' Mathieson smiled for the first time since they had met and the little man felt the warmth reach out to embrace him.

'Will you not call me Thomas?' he very timidly asked.

Placing a firm hand on White's shoulder he looked at him and, as their eyes met, he said, 'Thomas. I bid you welcome.'

They began work along the overgrown path that wound a meandering way into the church-yard but after a little while he noticed White beginning to falter so he feigned tiredness. 'Let us sit for a while,' he said, 'and perhaps you'll share some food with me?'

White nodded thankfully and they sat on a grassy bank in the midday sunshine and quite close to the double grave that so interested Mathieson. He stole a speculative glance but the little man seemed oblivious so he looked again at the dark line of freshly disturbed earth about the stone and casually remarked, 'My landlady claims the graveyard is haunted at night.'

''Tis probably me who haunts the place?'

'I think not! Mrs Farquasan said she imagined you were harmless enough,' seeing White grimace he added, 'she tells me that on the darkest night the gravestones are said to come alive and float around the churchyard.' Watching for reaction as he went on. 'You live nearer the church than anyone, do you feel that strange things happen here?'

'I've never seen any ghosts.' The voice held a blend of amusement and qualification that brought a probing:

'You have seen something though?'

'I'm always locked away in my little house at night and I neither wish to see ghosts or talk to them.'

He thought White knew more than he was prepared to say but not wishing to press any further he rose to examine the gravestone and again to ponder on the absence of grass or weed growth inside the marble kerb.

'Odd to find a grave without a name yet so well-tended?' He stepped on to the marble slab and tried his weight, springing on heel and toe but there was no movement, the slab solid and unresisting. White watching every move, and Mathieson grinned and said, 'There is mystery here to be revealed one day, but I can be patient. Now then Thomas . . . on with our work!'

6

‘By the deep, seven!’ called Jake Ward from the bow. The *Rose* ghosting over the water with just one large foresail set while the light breeze hardly kept the sail full and did nothing at all to dispel the tendrils of mist that enveloped them in cold and clammy embrace.

‘What’s on the bottom, Jake?’ The coastline couldn’t be seen but Rudd knew they were almost home.

Hauling in his line, Jake scowled at the tallow served base of the lead weight to declare, ‘Mud and weed!’

‘Look for mud and shingle at five fathoms.’ Rudd’s hair was soaking wet and he brushed a trickle of water from his sideburns.

‘Blast this fog!’ said Simon Ralston from the helm where he was intent on the compass binnacle, glowing a dull red in the gloom.

‘Not to worry lad! Always remember that even

if we cannot see, then by the same token we ourselves must be invisible and this fog is a good friend, providing we don't run the *Rose* on a rock before we get the cognac landed.'

'Six fathoms and weed!'

'I'll take the wheel. Stand by the anchor chain, shore shelves steeply here and we'll need to let go quickly.' With this Rudd took the helm. It needed but an hour to daylight and he had no intention of being caught so close inshore. Already the sky above was turning into a shade of pale grey and he cursed the fog that had delayed their night passage across the Channel. Should have judged our time of arrival more accurately he reproached inwardly. After all, they had only been to Roscoff on the Brittany coast. Less than half the distance they sailed to Spain. The morning was still and eerie with the only sound the gentle slap of wave running against the hull. As the cry of 'five fathoms and shingle' reached him, Rudd's straining eyes caught a glimpse of a land shadow and almost, it seemed, on the end of the bowsprit.

'Let go, Simon! Stop the chain on twenty fathoms then watch it until you are sure we have good hold. The tide runs fierce here and we have no margin for safety if she drags.' Rudd then commanded Jake to, 'Launch the longboat!'

The ship's tender hung ready with the davits swung out over the side and Jake clambered down as she settled in the water. Simon remained on the bow to ensure the ship had her anchor down snug, while Rudd handed down casks. Over thirty in number they could not all be accommodated in the little boat. Rudd boarded and the two men took an oar each and from a standing position rowed the few yards to shore. Running her stern on to the beach. Jake leaping out with his bare feet splaying wet holes in the sand. They soon offloaded the casks and Rudd rowed back to the ship where Simon, satisfied that the anchor was holding, was ready amidships and now proceeded to hand down the remaining casks then jumped down to grasp an oar and they were quickly on shore where Jake waded out to haul the boat above the water line.

At this stage of the tide there was but a few yards of beach exposed and the bare, rocky cliff rose sheer above them and Simon ran along the sand and started to scale the base of the cliff using the lumpy mounds of rock at the foot to begin, then, miraculously it seemed, finding foot and hand holds along a ledge so narrow as to be undetectable from below. He climbed about twenty feet before disappearing behind a growth of stunted bushes growing out from the open rock face. Then a rope ladder came hurtling down. While he scaled the cliff the others had carried all casks to the base. Rudd climbed the ladder to join Simon on the ledge and now a dark cave was revealed and seemingly endless and leading deep into the hillside. Without delay they fed a stout double rope down and together par-buckled the heavy casks up and into the cave, stowing them side-by-side in the dark tunnel. An urgent operation that bespoke of much practice with not a word spoken or a moment wasted. Ropes and ladders hauled and stowed Simon scrambled down. Rudd then carefully re-arranged the stunted growth to hide the cave from prying eyes before hastily following. Boat launched they were soon back aboard ship.

With the longboat secured inboard, Simon straightaway hauled in the slack until the anchor chain was straight up and down. Jake set the foresail and the ship's head paid off to seaward. The anchor broke from its hold on the seabed and came rattling up to stop with a dull thud against the hawsehole trailing a slimy length of weed. The shoreline disappeared in the mist as all plain sail was set and the *Rose* gathered way and, heeling to the wind, was soon running free into deep water. Dawn was breaking. The morning mist hung about them in wreaths of wet vapour and they seemed to be in some strange no-mans land unable to see more than few yards around the ship and yet above them the sky was paling-clear and beautiful.

'We cut that run a little too fine,' said Rudd, 'if we get delayed in such fashion again I'll stay out in the Channel for another twenty-four hours. Shouldn't really have taken such a chance,' scowling at the thought as he added, 'especially with Faraday on the prowl.'

'It's not only the Excise we have to think about,' said Simon, 'the new preacher could give us trouble when he realises we're using his churchyard to unload brandy. Don't think he'll be as accommodating as old Foxer, that one would do almost anything for a free jug of brandy.'

'Then we must find some diversion to keep Mathieson out of the way,' said Rudd with a smile, 'I rather think your Janie could be the answer there. Perhaps we could find a way for her to look after the Reverend for an hour or so.'

'I don't want Janie involved. Better for her own sake if she has nothing to do with this.' Simon looked troubled and went on to say in warning tone, 'You know she'd do anything for you, Jonathan, and I wouldn't want to see you taking advantage.'

'I don't take advantage of young girls, in any way!' Rudd's eyes sparked fire but his anger faded as quickly as it had flared and he added with a grin, 'Just thought it might be to their mutual profit if we were to arrange for them to be entertained elsewhere. I'll talk it over with your father, Glyn may have some ideas as to how we may occupy the very Reverend Mathieson.' Serious now as he mused, 'We've had a good run with the brandy but it's becoming too chancy, too many obstacles, and it's time we lay low for a while. At least until Faraday is removed from the scene: one way or another?' cocking a sardonic eyebrow as he added, 'I'll give that one a run for his money! The *Rose* can outrun any ship he can put into the water and I'd just love to get that evil sod out at sea and run him ragged, aye, and his ambitions with him. Break out the brandy, Jake,' he called in laughing voice, 'let's drink to the Captain's downfall.'

Jake needed no further prompting and quickly returned on deck with mugs of cognac. 'To the *Rose*,' cried Rudd, raising his mug, 'and a speedy riddance to Wilder Faraday!' Toast drunk with due ceremony, Rudd said to his appreciative crew. 'Better get back into the Channel and fill our holds with fish. Then we'll set sail for Newlyn and the delights of the lovely, dark-eyed Susan . . . or Kathleen perchance?' Adding as an after-thought, 'What a pity a man can't be in two places at the same time, such sport we would have.' He spun the wheel turning the ship almost abeam to the south westerly wind. She heeled rail down and the sails hardened and the bow wave began to foam white as she dug her nose into the first of the long, Atlantic swell. His stout legs, encased in thigh boots, straddled the deck. His long hair streamed in the wind and the morning sun shone bright on the gold earring. Rudd about his business, doing what he knew best. 'Come on, me-beauty,' he shouted, 'we've a hold to fill before we can put into Newlyn!' His carefree manner had them responding with enthusiasm and while Jake got ready the hand lines Simon scurried below to prepare breakfast.

The *Rose* beat her way down Channel all day and her crew were kept busy pulling in mackerel by the hundred and her fish hold filled to the brim before Rudd turned his ship for Newlyn.

The following morning's flood tide found them creeping into harbour. The last shred of sail taken off, the ship bumped her rubbing strake against the wall and soon lay tethered fore and aft to the huge bollards built into the quayside. A dull and blustery morning and the keen wind slapped the rigging against the mast in vibrant resonance as a fat, soft looking man came aboard to stand amidships and look at the teeming fish. 'Just in time to get your haul to market,' he said, 'but we'll have to get a move on.'

'Not so fast, Rudd,' commanded Wilder Faraday from the dockside, 'I want my men here before your cargo is off-loaded.'

'If I miss the auction the catch will be worthless!'

'How very unfortunate.'

'You know damn well I only have fish aboard!' Glaring heatedly at him, Rudd's eyes narrowed as he snapped, 'I don't think you have the authority to harass a fishing vessel in this fashion and I'll make formal complaint against you to your superiors!'

'I have no superiors in this area,' said Faraday with a sneer, 'and as for authority, I need only a suspicion that you are smuggling and my powers are without limit?' His face was pinched and hawk-like and his eyes were diamond sharp and evil as he scorned, 'Find it hard to believe you've spent more than five days at sea for a miserable load of mackerel?'

Forcing himself to calm, Rudd said, 'Unlike yourself, Captain, I have no control over such matters and if the fish choose not to come aboard there is little I can do to persuade them, we just keep on trying until our holds are full. Might take weeks even, but once at sea we don't return until we have a catch worthy of bringing in.'

By now a line of dock-labourers stood waiting to begin offloading and with the belated arrival of a squad of four armed Excise men, Faraday had no option but allow work to start. The men skillfully packed the fish into boxes and loaded them on to a long handcart poised ready on the quayside. Watching every move, often halting the work while he surveyed some triviality, Faraday appeared to deliberately hold up the transfer of fish to shore and Rudd grew ever more menacing as the morning wore on. The fish auction would be over by now and his mackerel virtually without value after payment of his costs. With a sad shrug the overseer finished his tally. The last box was loaded on the cart.

'Sorry, Jonathan,' he said, 'I'll do my best but you know how it is?'

'No fault of yours, Sam, just do what you can and pay off the men.' Turning to Faraday with no indication of the anger seething deep inside. 'Are you satisfied now or have you some further indignity in store for me?'

Pulling up his coat collar against the wind, Faraday said with an evil smile, 'I knew you wouldn't be such a fool as to bring contraband into Newlyn under my very nose.' Standing on the deck amidships close to the unloading operation he pressed a handkerchief to his nose. 'It passes all understanding how you can live with the stench!' His cold eyes turned again on Rudd and there was intense dislike in his look as he stated, 'This has just been to warn that I'm watching you very closely because you haven't been fishing for a full five days or you would have shown more concern about the loss of your catch. Make no mistake, Rudd, I'm going to apprehend you and others like you, and soon, so that I can return to more civilized society in London.'

'So brilliant an officer, I wonder how the Port of London could let you go, or how they can hope to manage in your absence?' Sarcastic, jibing words, and watching Faraday closely he saw the sudden irritation that lined his forehead and flamed to anger in his eyes. Then, intuition brought whiplash into his voice as he snapped. 'Or did they kick you out, my high and mighty Captain, did they choose to boot your arse as far from their sight as they possibly could?' Laughing into his face and convinced that his taunt had struck home and hurting him in the place where he was most vulnerable, squarely in the man's self-righteous front of pride and dignity. 'Face it, Faraday,' he goaded, 'they wouldn't take you back with a bucket of gold: much less the head of a poor Cornish fisherman.' Rudd's voice took on an elated note as he savaged his enemy with a biting, 'You're through, Captain, almost finished, and this is as far as you are going to rise in the service of Her Majesty!'

He half-turned away but Faraday gripped his shoulders with hands of steel and jerked his face to within a few inches of his own. A speck of spittle appeared on his lower lip and his voice was intense and threatening as he growled, 'Think what you will, Rudd, I care not for your foul opinions and promise that you'll regret the day I came to Cornwall but this will be a very short lived regret: before the hangman's noose chokes the life from you!' Overcome with rage, and hatred, he relinquished his hold and pushed Rudd away with brute force. Brushing angrily aside the helping hand of one of his men he jumped ashore and snapped commands that had the men moving off at the double.

'He aims to get you, Jonathan,' said Simon worriedly, 'by any means he can.'

'He'll first have to get his backside out of that plush office chair . . . hasn't hung me yet and he can piss off and think again if he expects me to cut and run!'

'He could be relying on you thinking along those lines and gives the impression that he's deliberately goading you into making some gesture of contempt so that he can get his hands on you.'

'Then we'll have to be very careful and very smart, young Simon!'

7

The courtyard at Sandford Barton hosted a score of smart carriage and pairs. Lanterns shone around the entranceway and every ground floor window shed welcoming brightness and as he reined to a halt he wished again that he could have found some logical excuse to decline this invitation to the ball at the Barton. Remembering the frustration of Sir Harry on the occasion of his previous visit he had been surprised to have his attendance requested at all and envisioned the hand of Lady Sarah behind the invitation and, with a surge of anticipation, perhaps the influence of the headstrong Cathryn?

Looking around for somewhere to tether Mistral but a groom appeared at his side. He knew him well by this time and said, 'Thank you John, but please keep her handy because I'm not expecting to stay long.'

'She'll be ready when you are, Reverend.'

A formally dressed manservant took his invitation card and was about to announce him when Mathieson caught his eye in a plea for silence. 'Not too loud, I pray,' he murmured, 'especially as I am so late arriving.' Sidling into the banqueting hall. Spacious: with a polished wood floor and the walls paneled in dark oak. Devoid of pictures but set in each panel was a rampant coat-of-arms. Wall lamps and numerous candelabra lit the room with intimate glow, and at the far end a raised platform hosted a string orchestra playing with distinct lack of enthusiasm with the music barely audible above the din of constant chatter from those thronging the room. All were in evening dress with the glorious colour of the ladies gowns in striking contrast to the black tie and dinner jackets of the men, and he winced inwardly at the thought of his own, dour appearance. Catching sight of Sir Harry and Lady Sarah among a small group by the buffet table he moved to greet his hosts. Wearing an ankle length party dress of royal blue that fitted her slim figure to perfection, Lady Sarah greeted him with a smiling, 'How nice to see you again.'

'Thank you for your kind invitation and I beg you to excuse my late arrival.'

'I'm sure the cause was worthy.'

'You are most charitable and understanding, Lady Sarah.'

Sir Harry greeted him with cold indifference then introduced the others in the group. The only two he was familiar with were the doctor from Penzance and his wife with whom he conversed pleasantly for a few minutes.

The orchestra struck up a gay waltz. The glorious melodies that had swept Europe off its dancing feet were only recently arrived among Cornish society, the music was at once lively and provocative and the dance floor immediately filled with couples. Lady Sarah looked at him and her foot tapped to the rhythm. 'I do so enjoy the waltz.'

The covert invitation in her voice brought immediate concern and a hesitant. 'Have I your permission to approach Sir Harry?'

'My husband never dances, which leaves me with few opportunities,' adding in soft tone, 'I don't think my reputation would suffer if I took a turn around the floor with our own minister.'

He had little experience of women, society women none at all, and suspected that Sedgewick women had determined minds of their own. Uncertain, and thinking he was inviting trouble but had no option but to make a gallant arm.

'May I have the honour, my Lady?'

She acknowledged with a flashing smile and he led her out on to the dance floor and so attentive he missed the irritation that crossed Sir Harry's face. After a few turns she stated, 'You dance well.'

'And you, ma-am, are a very accomplished

teller of fairy stories.' But he was enjoying the dance and the mobile lightness of Lady Sarah in his arms.

Smiling appreciatively at his reply she asked, 'When are you hoping to open up the church for service?'

'The Sunday after next . . . must begin my work although I am far from ready.'

'You'll be fortunate if the village folk support you immediately.' Speaking in serious tone as she explained, 'They are slow to absorb anything or anybody new and it will take time to gain their confidence.'

'Yet I have met with only friendliness and a desire to help: but I don't mind starting small. I need to build on solid foundations and will eventually gain their acceptance.' His voice hardened as he added, 'I must!'

'Is the need theirs, or yours?'

'With perseverance it could prove mutual.'

'Wish you luck, Reverend, and offer any help I can.'

'By attending church on my first service?'

'I'd really love to, but my husband isn't exactly enchanted with you right now and I couldn't attend without him, for what would the village think?' She spoke with genuine regret and as if she would have liked to say more and she looked at him with warm eyes and as their glances met and held, Mathieson thought she was lovely and realised again the source of her daughter's beauty. But the qualification in her voice caused him to change tack, and say:

'I was surprised to receive your invitation, especially after our first encounter. Do I see your guiding hand in this?'

'Only lent a little support to the suggestion, the idea really came from Cathryn. We had long talked about a coming out party for her and it was rather obvious how she re-awakened the proposal after your visit. We both felt that Sir Harry couldn't be quite so demanding of you a second time.' She spoke with feeling as she added, 'There are only two areas where he can be so unreasonable – his horses – and our only child, an overriding passion for both allows him no room for logical behaviour and it was sheer bad luck that your Mistral is so handsome a mount and caught his eye. Such a pity, for we had that very morning been contemplating the extent of our financial support.' They were engrossed in the dialogue and in a growing appreciation for each other and many a curious feminine eye scrutinised the elegant Lady Sarah held close in the arms of the new, and very good looking minister. Pressing his arm she whispered, 'The music has finished you know, perhaps we had better rejoin the others.'

Looking around with a start, they were alone on the dance floor, and offering his arm with a boyish grin he escorted her back to the buffet table, this time catching the full blast of frowning irritation from Sir Harry. But a flutter of silk at his side drove away trepidation and a breathless voice asked, 'A glass of punch, preacher-man, or would you prefer brandy?' Dressed in a gown of dusky-pink silk cut low off the shoulder she looked captivating. Her hair was piled high on her head showing her oval and high-cheeked face to full advantage and a double link of pearls shone, like an imperious choker chain of lustre around her slender neck and he looked at her admiringly for a long moment.

'You take my breath away,' he eventually said, 'but a glass of punch would be very acceptable.'

Taking a long stemmed glass she ladled a generous measure and one for herself. 'How long have you been here,' she asked in demanding tone, 'you weren't announced?'

'Arrived late and sneaked in.'

'Watched you dancing with Mama, you seemed to be enjoying yourselves.'

'Lady Sarah is charming and yes, I enjoyed dancing with her.'

'Watch out for Papa,' she warned, 'he's so very possessive.'

Glancing over to where Sir Harry stood with some of his guests, and with his face flushed and far from pleased. 'Already had the evil eye treatment,' said Mathieson, 'seems I have a way of annoying him without even trying. Does the possessiveness also include his daughter?'

'I take that remark as an invitation to dance.'

Consulting her dance card with mock solemnity she said, 'I have one dance left, and it just happens to be this one!'

She led him on to the floor as the music began again and he noticed a tall, sallow faced young man stop short in his approach towards them and had to smile at the crestfallen look appearing on his face. Shrugging, she returned Mathieson's quizzical look with a roguish toss of her head. 'I have to be hospitable and share dances between all our guests. Besides,' she went on, 'if I adhered strictly to my dance card I wouldn't be able to dance with you at all.'

'So it seems this is the only one you and I will share.'

Her smile dazzled and she made no answer but he was making heavy weather of the minuet and looked down in consternation as he missed a step and trod on her toe. Her intimate nearness shattered concentration and he felt a sudden heat that had nothing to do with the temperature in the ballroom. 'My apologies,' he said, 'not much good am I?'

'No!' Shaking her head in agreement, then a look of mischief appeared. 'It's terribly hot in here, let's take a chance and creep away while they're all busy dancing. I want to show you something very special.'

They were circling at the bottom end of the room and without further comment she took his arm and propelled him through an open, double doorway, into a glass fronted conservatory where plants and flowers hung in profusion with fragrance earthy and appealing. The outside door stood open and led on to a side terrace where daylight had almost merged with the pale velvet of dusk, and light from the windows spread shadows across the terrace and cast a glow over and beyond a low boundary wall on to a shingled area in the centre of which rose the stonework of a well. Intrigued, he moved across the terrace to stand beside it. The perimeter wall was just below waist height and had been skillfully shaped into a small circle from out of which rose a beautiful, sweeping stone arch. This in turn supported the spindle and turning handle and from the spindle wound a thin rope that dropped sheer into the depths below and after his inspection he approvingly announced, 'A wishing well!'

She looked at him and the look was one of pleasure and sharing and of pleasure doubled by the sharing and she said happily. 'This is my favourite place on the whole estate. I sit here in the summer when the day is warm and sometimes when I just feel the need to be alone.' Running her hand lovingly over the wood spindle, she said, 'When I was a little child it was neglected and derelict but when Papa realise how much I loved the well he had it renovated and rebuilt.'

'Your father loves you very much, I think. Why does he call you Cassy?'

The question took her by surprise, then she

explained, 'Because my initials are C.A.S!. Cathryn Ann Sedgewick. So I am Cass for short, or Cassy.' Perching on the stone side of the well, shivering a little in the cooler air, and he instantly whipped off his jacket and spread it around her shoulders. She yielded to his concern by pulling the jacket about her with one hand while the other reached out to touch his shirtsleeve and as she glanced up at him she found herself responding instinctively to his courtesy, and to his rugged good looks. His shoulders were broad in his white shirt and a leather belt outlined the lean column of his stomach. She noticed that his legs were spread apart and well balanced as if used to being that way. His face was in shadow as he returned her survey. 'Sit here beside me, Richard,' she said softly, 'where I can see you better.'

He felt a flush of pleasure as she called him by name. Her hand was still on his arm and as he sat with her she noted with concern the worn cuffs and the frayed and threadbare sleeves and her eyes flicked away as if she wished she hadn't seen what she had seen then came back to his face as he said with a wry smile, 'Knew I shouldn't have taken off my jacket.'

'Are you so very poor?' she whispered. She felt the breath catch in her throat and a wave of tender emotion engulfed as she said this and he looked at her as if he felt the same emotion, then said in deliberate, solemn voice:

'As one of the mice that live in the church.' She

knew he was laughing at her, then his hand sought hers and held it tight. 'Do not concern yourself, lovely Cathryn, he said, 'poverty is part of my calling for whom among you among you would place faith in a minister who is rich and waxing fat? I have to reach the people from a level they can understand and associate with,' pausing, he said, 'and if to reach this communion I must be reduced to rags . . . then so be it!'

Cathryn thought with sudden compassion how easy it would be to reach out to this man, and the thought filled her with a disquiet that was almost frightening and she drew away and her eyes were cloistered under long eyelashes and he read her thoughts and rose to his feet. 'Does the thought of poverty frighten you so much?' he asked in searching tone.

'How would I know,' she replied frankly, 'think it might?' She looked at him and there was conjecture in her eyes and in her voice as she said, 'I just don't understand you, Richard Mathieson. You claim to be poor yet spurn so decisively my father's offer to pay well for your horse.'

'But don't you see? Mistral doesn't care if her master is poor and has to wear an old shirt to a fancy dress ball?' He spoke in jesting tone, then she heard his voice soften. 'I know only this!' he said. 'She loves me and endows me with everything such a wonderful creature can offer a man and she gives me of herself without hesitation and without conditions: and I'll not betray such a trust for a handful of coin!'

A quick moistening started behind her eyes and a tear began to trickle down her cheek and he caught it on a gentle finger. 'Cathryn, is such a lovely pearl shed for me? Then here is treasure beyond any price!' He held his finger over the well and let the tear fall into the depths and his hand raised high over the well. 'If a man can wish on such a priceless gift?' his voice seemed to hold her in a trance and she gazed starry-eyed as he slowed his rhetoric, before concluding, 'then I wish this tear to remain in the warm embrace of this lovely well: to shine bright on the darkest night and forever to reflect how a beautiful girl bequeathed a precious part of herself to a humble preacher.' His words seemed to hover on the still night air. Her eyes were wet with tears as she raised her face and reached for his hand to clasp it close into the softness of her breast and hold it there and he felt his breath catch in the moment of wonderful communion that engulfed them both. Then she looked across at the lighted windows. The music was muted and far away. 'Oh, Richard,' she whispered, 'I don't want to go back in there, can I stay with you for a little while longer?' She spoke as a child and he looked at her and thought she was all he had ever dreamed about.

'You are asking me to incur the wrath of your father: again!'

'I can handle Papa, but I don't think you are afraid of him, or anyone else for that matter.'

'But you are so wrong, Cathryn, for I am mortally afraid of lovely young women like you, who weave wonderful magic upon a night such as this and who without knowing can reduce a man to a mass of quivering jelly forgetting every desire except the one, overwhelming need to possess such beauty.' Hesitating. Unsure! As if he had said more than he was entitled to say, before going on very thoughtfully, 'And it ill becomes someone of my chosen calling to in any way place so captivating a young woman in a position that might cause embarrassment.' His words caused a look of disappointment to cloud her face, so he sat down again. 'I've made some kind of attempt at propriety,' he said with a smile, 'but must admit that I also have no wish to return to the ball.'

They looked fondly at each other, like two conspirators, then Cathryn said, 'I haven't wept without apparent reason for a long time.' She snuggled deeper into the warmth of his jacket and her arms were soft and inviting in the lantern glow. 'Tell me about yourself, Richard,' she then said, 'I want to know all about you.'

'What's to tell?' He didn't want to talk about it but she was looking at him in a demanding way and with obvious interest, so he had no choice but to accommodate her and he said in clipped, economic voice, 'I am from seafaring stock, my folks are natives of Bristol where they still live.

My father was a sea captain and secured me a post as apprentice officer on a clipper ship when I was just seventeen.' Shrugging as he explained, 'Took me nine years to work my way up to the quarterdeck, then to First Mate, next step was to be my own command, but fate intervened and I resigned my position . . .' Ending his narrative abruptly, he had said more than he had intended and she looked at him as if she wanted more, but nothing was forthcoming and she wondered why he was so reticent about his past?

'They say in the village that you have been a seafarer,' she said curiously.

'You've been talking with Janie Ralston.'

'Only in passing,' she said with some attempt at dignity, 'but it seems an odd change of lifestyle for men are reputed never to be able to settle down ashore after years at sea.'

'Sometimes such decisions are made for us: if indeed they haven't been made when the Book of Life was first written. As for a change of life pattern,' reluctantly involved in the dialogue he looked deep into her face before continuing with, 'there are few men who can sail the vast oceans without coming to believe in the presence of an all-embracing Being, some great overall influence on the formation of sea and sky and wind and sunshine.' The words were delivered with compelling belief and she scarcely dare breath lest she break down the rapture as he went on with his personal narrative.

'To be on watch in the middle of the night with my hands on the wheel: and the great clipper rushing on through the dark seas. Such music does a fine ship make! The constant throb of the trade wind in the rigging and the roar of the bow wave as she ploughs her way over the endless fetch of the Southern Ocean. Or to lean over the rail while she ghosts into the calm water of a south Sea Island lagoon with the insistent growl of breakers away to windward and the afternoon sun blistering the paintwork and bubbling up the pitch in the deck planking. Such moments in life that have to be taken and enjoyed and then let go for no man can forever sustain the surge of youth and energy that drives us on to discover just what lies over that sunlit facade that is our own, personal horizon. Oh, my lovely Cathryn,' he said in reverent voice, 'I truly have seen the glory of the Lord in all His wonders to perform.' His face raised to the heavens and through his words she had a vision of him, barefoot on the deck of a tall ship and sure-handed on the wheel as he conned the sailing vessel through the night. She was emotionally moved as never before and, as a sudden whisper of wind rippled through his hair to waft a dark curl over his forehead, she instinctively reached to smooth it back from his brow. Their faces were very close and she threw her arms round his neck and kissed him passionately on the mouth.

Immediate: urgent response, then he was

up and pulling her on to her feet.

'Now you see what I mean about reducing me to a mass of jelly, and you've already learnt far too much about my former way of life.' Smiling as he said this, but so sadly it seemed. Then feigning severity he said, 'It's high time I let you rejoin the party and also, your dance card has few empty spaces and your prospective partners must be distraught at your absence.'

She could feel the bruise of his mouth against her own and was about to remonstrate as if she wanted more then shrugged out of his jacket and gave it to him but her hand lingered as she said, 'I would much rather spend the rest of the evening alone with you, for you bring colour into my life, even tears.' The thought bringing her back from euphoria she added quickly, 'I must look a terrible sight!'

'Never have I beheld so fair a maid.' Shaking his head and adding with a smile, 'Come now, my vain one, it's back to the ball for you: and to face the disapproving music of your father for me.'

But the doorway of the conservatory already heralded the irate presence and voice of Sir Harry.

'Cassy! Where the devil have you been hiding? This party is in your honour and at your instigation and it's damn discourteous to run off this way and leave your guests!'

'The fault is mine, sir.' He felt the pressure of her fingers on his arm as he faced her father and gained confidence from her support and he said contritely, 'and must beg your pardon for keeping her out here so long.'

'You don't have to tell me, Mathieson, I know with whom lies the fault!' An evenings indulgence with liquor had further inflamed resentment, but Cathryn stood her ground and faced him without flinching.

'There is no fault, Papa,' she said, 'we have just been sitting by the well in wonderful conversation.'

'Conversation? Looks more like he's had you in tears. Better see to your face, girl, before your rejoin our guests.'

Hesitant . . . for she knew only too well his lack of control when laying down the law according to Sir Harry . . . she looked at Mathieson for guidance but he just smiled at her. 'Don't worry, Cathryn,' he said, 'I'll come to say goodnight before I leave.'

She moved reluctantly away and Sir Harry took up position between Mathieson and the entrance. 'Just don't know what to make of you,' he snapped, 'first you charm my wife into going against me then I find you alone with Cassy and her in tears. Hardly the discreet behaviour I expect from a man of the cloth?' Glaring at Mathieson before grinding on. 'I had no wish to invite you to my house but allowed myself to be persuaded by the two of them, but you appear determined to cause trouble and to prolong this bad feeling between us.' Anger brought spite to his words as he stormed on with, 'Seems I was right about you the first time, but get one thing clear: you will not be allowed to upset the harmony of my household!' The flush on his face grew deeper and Mathieson was silent and had no answer to the tirade as Sir Harry raged, 'I want you to leave before you inflict further humiliation on my family, and forbid you to call at the Barton or try to see Cassy without my permission.' The forcible way he said this made it clear that such permission was unlikely, but if Sir Harry expected apology or words of conciliation he was about to be disappointed. His unreasoning accusations just caused Mathieson to look at him sadly before requesting:

'May I be permitted to take my leave of Lady Sarah?'

Sir Harry reared up about to refuse, then natural hospitality, combined with the dire thought of a possible stricture from his wife, caused him to step aside and growl, 'Make it brief!'

8

Darkness was closing on the little township . . . the warmth of evening handing over to a clinging-damp autumn mist . . . causing beads of moisture to form on the paintwork and trickle in slow rivulets down the inside of the portholes. Dressed in their number one's the crew were making ready for a run ashore and Rudd slid the hatch tight, turned the key in the padlock. 'First time I've locked up the *Rose* when berthed in Newlyn,' he said with a disgruntled snort, 'but with Faraday on the prowl?'

'Should I stay aboard?' asked Simon.

'Time to worry about the Excise is when we have something of interest aboard and Faraday will need blue water under his keel for that to happen. So let's forget about him and go seek the fleshpots!'

Jake's impatient stance on the quayside

brought a grin from Simon as he stated. 'He's thirsty: again!'

'Finest drinking man I've ever seen,' acknowledged Rudd, 'but never a drop does he drink when at sea, at least,' he qualified, 'not without invitation.'

'Probably needs to make up for time wasted, hope we don't have to carry him back?'

'Haven't carried him yet,' said Rudd indulgently, 'but he's been pretty close on several occasions.'

Forty years of age, Jake Ward was a big man, heavy, but without any surplus flesh. He had spent all his life since the early teens in ships and on the sea and any schooling that had been forced on his reluctant mind was long forgotten in a haze of salt water. He could neither read nor write except for his own name and because of this many unscrupulous captains under whom he had sailed had constantly cheated and ill-used him and until he joined Rudd aboard the *Rose*, had just drifted aimlessly between any ship owner who would feed him and supply the price of a run ashore.

From the beginning Rudd treated him fairly. Allowed him to live permanently aboard ship. Paid a regular wage and an extra bonus when earnings were good. Encouraged him to salt away part of his wages. An uphill task! For money and Jake Ward were short-lived companions and whenever he had coin to jingle in his pocket the only beneficiary was the nearest alehouse. In return, Jake gave a loyalty that was nothing short of devotion, following every move with a dedication that often bothered Rudd, who wasn't convinced that responsibility for another man's future lay on his own shoulders. But, he had great regard for this gentle giant, whom he knew would lay down his life for him without question if the need were to arise

Sauntering with jaunty seafarers gait along the quay. Light from the windows of the fishermen's cottages shone over the still waters of Newlyn dock and spread shadows among the tethered ships. Simon glancing back to make sure his foredeck riding light was burning well. A riding light was unnecessary in harbour but they would probably need some illumination on an inebriated return. Coming to a halt at the bottom of a narrow alley that rose steeply from the main street, Rudd announced, 'Be busy for an hour or so but I'll join you later at the Landfall.'

'What gift have you to offer Kathleen this time?' asked Simon innocently.

'Just calling out of the kindness of my heart, and you know how I hate to disappoint a young woman when she expects my company.' The glow from a nearby cottage window cast a glow on his earring as it spun with his quick laughter.

'Does this kind heart of yours also feel kindly towards Susan at the Landfall, fancy she's expecting you also?'

'Later, Simon, you wouldn't wish me to spend all my time charming just one of these lovely creatures. Such a capacity for romance must not be confined to one alone.' Adding without modesty, 'Tis a hard path I tread having to share myself with so many, and if the fair Susan should mention me in passing, you know how busy I am on board studying charts for tomorrow's departure.'

'Let's go, Jake,' said Simon, 'our so-gallant captain has other things on his mind.'

Don't be envious,' laughed Jake, 'you're too young to concern yourself with such fancies.'

'Look out for the lad, Jake,' instructed Rudd as they parted company. 'Rough company at the Landfall when the fishing fleet's in harbour.'

'Aye, skipper.'

The Landfall Tavern boasted only one public taproom. Long, and low ceiling with a massive, timbered bar running the length of one wall. Fumes from the open-hearth fire and countless years of tobacco smoke had coloured the paint-work drab and the bare wood floor appeared well worn although just now it was liberally spread with sawdust. A central column of dark oak supported the misshapen beam that held the weight of the floors above and this beam was adorned with gleaming horse brass and copper utensils which reflected the glow of the log fire and lent a warm and friendly ambience to the austere taproom. The centrepiece and most outstanding feature of this display was a long drinking horn exquisitely fashioned in copper with rings of brass reinforcing the softer metal. Over the years this horn had sustained many a knock and there were innumerable dents in the copper, and it hung from a brass chain directly over the middle of the bar top.

The evening was well advanced and the tavern teemed with men, seafarers all, with the mood one of increasing revelry. In the far corner a grey-bearded old sailor played a small accordion surrounded by a group who sang with gusto: when they knew the chorus. Simon and Jake sat at a table in the centre of the room listening idly to the music and drinking from pint mugs. Behind the bar despatching foaming pints to her eager customers worked the barmaid Susan helped by two men of indeterminate age and the insatiable thirst of the sailing men kept them at full stretch.

Susan had a sharp tongue and a quick sarcasm that she delivered with the ease of long accustom. She wore a pale blue sleeveless blouse open at the neck and throat and which threatened to burst asunder against the thrust of her full breasts. Her hair was long and hung well down her back in black, cascading confusion and her arms were soft and shapely. The customers treated her with respect and returned her sarcasm with a repartee that was often suggestive, but it was woe-betide any misguided stranger who sought to make improper advances. Just at that moment her eyes took on a serious aspect at the entry of a group of men who had just pushed through the doors and swaggered up to the bar. Ordering ale, they threw money down as if they had plenty and stood with their backs to the bar surveying the company.

They were the crew of *Barracuda*, the largest fishing boat out of Newlyn, a cocky and ill-mannered bunch to whom the rest of the fishermen gave a wide berth. The skipper and ringleader of this unsavoury crew was a heavy, balding barrel of a man with a pockmarked face coloured livid by years of over indulgence. He was dressed flamboyantly in a red silk shirt with long flowing sleeves and his cord trousers were held precariously below his vast girth with a gold-buckle leather belt. He was named Curtiss but no one had ever heard his Christian name and he was known only as Curt. His rivalry with Rudd was legendary and these two old adversaries wasted no chance to score against the other and as his searching gaze came to rest on the table at which Jake and Simon were sitting a look of devilment crossed his ugly face. Simon tried to ignore him but a feeling of apprehension started deep inside but Jake just carried on with his drinking, as if he wasn't there. Sneering at this lack of response Curt reached for the drinking horn 'Challenge any man in the house to drink a yard of ale faster than me!' Harsh words, reflecting great confidence, and the hubbub suddenly hushed, for all knew his capacity for making trouble and nobody responded. The silence seemed to inflame Curt and he glared around. 'Isn't there a single one of you who can drink like a man?'

Jake looked up at this, but Simon placed a warning toe against his foot. A lack of interest, that brought a contemptuous, 'How about the *Rose of Endau*?' No acknowledgement so he turned away, sneering, 'Gutless: just like their skipper!'

Jake's chair went back with a screech.

'Fill the horn, Curt, let's see if you can drink as well as you talk!'

'The man has a tongue, after all.' Handing over the horn Curt said with an evil grin. 'You first! Loser pays for the ale.'

A buzz of anticipation went around the room as interest became riveted to the contest between the two big men and a space hastily cleared in the centre of the floor where Jake and Curt stood face to face. Jake straightaway lifted the horn to his mouth and two tankards were poured until the horn brimmed over. The crowd chanted in unison as Jake opened his throat to swallow. 'One – two – three – four – five -six.' They were really enjoying this and the count roared with increasing volume and even Simon began to lose apprehension and gaped in awe at the speed Jake emptied the horn.

Now it was Curt's turn. Again the tankards were poured. 'One – two – three – four – five – six!' Excitement in the shout. The two were evenly matched and the count was identical. Without allowing Curt time to get his breath Jake said, 'Again!'

Susan's eyes flashed as she saw a flicker of alarm cross Curt's face. Drawing another four pints and kicking off her shoes she climbed on the bar top to make it easier to fill the horn. 'Show him how 'tis done, Jake me-handsome!' she laughingly called.

Again the count roared. 'Six for Jake – six for Curt.' The two were breathing hard but still they faced each other with neither giving way. 'You ain't crowing so loud now, Curt!' said Jake, grinning into his face The crowd shouting approval and chanting in concert.

'Again! Again!' Susan's bare feet slapped a quick fandango on the polished wood of the bar top as the tankards were re-filled. Jake raised the drinking horn to his mouth. 'One – two – three – four – five – six!' The man with the accordion joining the throng and squeezing his instrument gaily in time with the rising crescendo. Jake lowered the horn with a gasp. Not a drop escaped his lips but he stood as though his legs had turned to jelly for a moment then handed the horn to Curt without a word. All in the room tensing with expectation while the horn was filled. Then the chant began. 'One – two – three –

four – five – s . . . !' The count had still to reach conclusion before Curt gagged and pulled the horn from his open mouth and a retching sound came from his throat and the last trickle from the drinking horn ran over his chin and down his neck on to his fancy shirt and Simon couldn't control a shout of triumph.

'You beat him! We won! We won!' Dancing round Jake in his excitement. Jake's eyes were glazing over but he grinned widely at Simon's exuberance, then Curt grabbed Simon by the collar.

'I got it down quicker than him that time,' he growled heatedly, 'the count didn't go to six.' The room fell silent. Simon's look of joy was wiped off his face and his eyes narrowed.

'You lost!' he said bluntly. Gesturing at Curt's dribbling mouth. 'It's all down your mouth and shirt. Pay your dues like a man and stop whining!'

The contempt in his voice inflamed Curt to shouting point. 'I'll not be put down by the *Rose of Endau*!' With this he jerked Simon forward, snarling, 'Let's see how you perform with a yard of ale.'

'You won't make me!' Simon ripped away his hand. His voice had gone deathly quiet and the circle about them suddenly widened as the onlookers shuffled away from confrontation, engrossed but wanting no part in this. Though just a stripling of a youth and lean to the point of thinness, Simon's upper body had the beginnings of the bulk of his prizefighter father, and his shoulders were just now hunched powerfully under his cotton shirt.

There were seven in the crew of *Barracuda.* Rough, crude looking men, and they now formed a menacing barrier against the alarmed onlookers, who had no liking for this but few in the room sought a sore head for interfering. Shaking his head in an attempt to clear the haze that threatened to engulf, Jake shambled forward with angry intent, but his arms were seized from behind as two of Curt's crew held him in tight grip. Jake was immobile but the burly men were finding difficulty in restraining him

Simon backed away as Curt advanced brandishing the drinking horn. At a glance from Curt another two of his men grabbed Simon. One pinioned his arms behind while the other took the horn and, forcing his mouth open, thrust it between his lips.

'Fill 'em!' Curt pounded the bar with a brace of empty tankards. The man behind the bar took one look at the bloated face and scurried hastily to do his bidding. The two men forced Simon to his knees and Curt towered over him. 'Now my little fighting cock, drink!' They yanked Simon's head back by the hair. Curt steadily filled the horn and Simon choked as the liquid ran down his throat and the man holding him down clapped his mouth closed as liquid began to trickle from his lips. His eyes were staring wide in a suddenly pale face and his throat convulsed in spasms as he strived to swallow the incessant flow of dark ale. Curt kept the horn raised and started to pour a third tankard. He seemed without any feeling except one of glee and Simon choked in nausea with his eyes staring in hopeless anguish at the unrelenting hand. The crowd began to fidget and murmur protest. Susan was flaming mad and took an angry step forward to help the youth but was immediately blocked by the rest of Curt's crewmen.

The hand over Simon's mouth pressed harder and harder and squeezing his nose so he couldn't breath and he tried in vain to open his mouth and as he gasped for air he choked horribly as the ale flooded his lungs. The foul ale began to slowly drown him but Curt just laughed evilly at the boy's torment and kept pouring and so engrossed in dire intent that he failed to notice the path opening through the crowd to reveal the entry of Jonathan Rudd who took in the scene with one searing look and instantly shouldered Curt aside then drove his boot into the back and kidneys of the man holding Simon, and down he went with shriek of agony. Simon slumped sideways and the horn shed its content onto the sawdust. In the same smooth surge Rudd's leap took him to Jake who, finding the grip on him hastily released, turned to his captors and his hands closed with relish on their necks. Picking up Simon's retching body, Rudd placed him on a stool, then with a look of consuming anger he confronted the poised and waiting Curt. 'Still picking on boys?' he said with menace. 'What are you like with men!' The dire threat in his voice had Curt retreating, but only momentarily then he straightaway threw the heavy pewter tankard but Rudd swayed to one side and the tankard sailed past and into the people massed behind, showering them with ale. Following behind the tankard Curt swung a fierce right hand that flailed only emptiness and the impetus of his wild strike sent him surging out of control past the nimble Rudd who leaped high and kicked him on the point of neck and shoulders and pushing him hard on his staggering way and down onto the sawdust floor, and Susan's dark eyes gazed approvingly into Rudd's face.

'Very neat, captain,' she said.

'A Spanish Count taught me that trick when I was down in Corruna, it can be very irritating.'

Curt was more than irritated. Wild with humiliation he launched to his feet and roared into attack but Rudd met him with a flowing leap and drove his foot hard into his chest and the force of the kick sent Curt hurtling back and crashing to the floor on the same spot from which he had just risen, and Rudd resumed a nonchalant stance with his elbows on the bar top. A smile of satisfaction was on his face and he cocked an eyebrow at Susan as she linked her arm in his.

'Spanish Count again?' she queried.

He kissed her full, inviting mouth and shook his head cockily.

'French matelot in Roscoff! Look out, here he comes again!'

Curt had learned the folly of rushing at Rudd and now came at him again, but slowly and in shambling menace with his face contorted and mouthing obscenities and Susan took her hand hastily away. 'What trick this time, Johnny boy?'

'No more tricks.' Determined now. 'This time it's pure Jonathan Rudd!' Levering away from the bar with his fists held up in front of his crouching body and moving slowly up and down as if inviting his opponent to strike first. The two circled in wary stance then Rudd closed up and breathing easily and his eyes narrow and unwavering, so Curt swung a clubbing fist that went whistling harmlessly by. A growl came from Curt's mouth and he struck again fierce but wild as Rudd leaned aside. Curt shuffled forward, snarling, 'Stand up and fight like a man!' He reached to grab Rudd in a bear hug but again his tormentor neatly eluded his grasp but this time Rudd came in and his arm rose to block a looping right hand and as the heavy bulk jarred forward with the momentum of his swing, his iron hard fist exploded into Curt's stomach driving the breath from him and leaving his mouth gasping wide open. Rudd picked his spot dispassionately and smashed a hard one-two into the mouth and face sagging before him then as Curt reeled away Rudd hit him with a clubbing right hand smack on his unshaven chin and Curt's head flew back and he went hurtling down to slide along the sawdust until his head crunched hard against the centre post.

Placing a disdainful boot under the unconscious man, Rudd rolled him over on to his back. Looking into the battered face he took a half-full jug from a nearby table and trickled the liquid over the balding head. Curt began to splutter so Rudd emptied the jug over him, saying coldly, 'He'll live!' Susan called warningly and he immediately dropped to his knees and one of Curt's crew went flying over his crouching body with the heavy stool that had been wielded as a club sailing from his hands. The man groaned once: then was still and prostrate. The two remaining crewmen were advancing in support of their skipper, but cautiously and Rudd heard Jake swearing out loud as he banged together the heads of the two he was holding and alternatively shaking them like a pair of rag dolls.

'Need me, skipper?' he asked.

'Not this time, Jake.' Simon on his feet, and with these words he took position alongside Rudd. While still pale only the dampness of his shirtfront portrayed his recent ordeal and Rudd's eyebrow lifted at the peculiar, flat tone of his voice.

'Which one do you want?' said Rudd.

'Him!' gesturing at the man who had been holding him down.

'He's all yours!' Rudd stepped forward and reached out and took hold of the second man's nose with hard fingers as he retreated in sudden haste. The man gasped in pain and tried to tear away the vice-like grip that made his nose scream in agony and brought tears to his eyes but Rudd forced him down on his knees. 'Just squat there and watch,' he commanded, 'and just be thankful he didn't choose you.'

The solitary figure of a boy in one-to-one confrontation brought a sneer to the face of the crewman. He closed confidently, but without hesitation Simon hurled at him. The beating was quick: and brutal! Once, twice, three times his fist blasted into the fleshy stomach. He started to sag but Simon coldly held him by the neck of his shirt and belted a vicious right into his face then, stepping back a short pace, hit him with both hands clenched like a club, smack on the side of his jaw, and the man spun and dropped without a sound.

'Reckon your father taught you well, lad.' Throwing some coins at the bearded tapster, Rudd said. 'That'll pay for the wasted ale!' Looking with contempt at the onlookers he gestured at the men prostrate on the floor. 'Throw this unsavoury lot into the alley!' Suddenly willing hands dragged the battered crew of *Barracuda* outside and dumped them with relish at the rear of the

Tavern and Susan looked at Rudd with dismay in her eyes as he gathered Simon and Jake and prepared for departure.

'Do you have to leave so early?' Leaning over the bar in open invitation she said suggestively. 'The night's still young and you know I have been waiting all evening for you.'

'I've lost my liking for the customers of the Landfall,' Rudd replied, 'and must see my crew safely back aboard.' He brought her face down with gentle fingers and her petulant pout turned into a smile of anticipation as he whispered in her ear, 'Leave your door unlocked: I'll be back!'

9

Echoing from the sheer cliff side, a bird's shrill cry broke into meditation and he paused his sauntering tread to observe the seagull in graceful flight. The clean whiteness of the bird outlined stark against the backdrop of lush greenery where it seemed to be following with lazy precision, the bottom edge of the overhanging foliage, the edge that would just dip into the sea at high tide and where the dense matt of green formed a horizontal line as if in protest at the twice daily douche of salt water. The morning was bright and clear, silence broken only by the wash of surf on sand and gravel and from overhead the musical whine from the wings of two Canada geese as they flew with purpose high over the hillside on their way to find some quiet, inland sanctuary

Of late, he often walked this route where sea and sand and green hillside all conspired to form a sheltered, sweeping crescent and where there was little to distract his thoughts. He was concentrating, rehearsing the sermon he must prepare for his opening service. So vital! He had to make it interesting, worthwhile, so they would come again! Normally he was alone with his thoughts, but not this morning, for the peace was disturbed by the sound of a horse ridden fast along the shallows and, raising his hand to shield his eyes from the sun, he recognised the Palomino stallion of Cathryn Sedgewick. At the same time the horse altered course and raced towards him at full speed then reined to a skidding halt with nostrils flaring and steam rising from its haunches. She swung lithely down, her eyes sparkling like diamonds and her chestnut hair in windswept disarray. Her cheeks were flushed rose pink and he looked at her in admiration.

'Whither in such a hurry, I pray?' he said with pleasure rampant. The words were those used on the occasion of their first encounter and the repetition was deliberate.

'Hoped I might run into you.' She said this as if she knew he would be there and that her appearance on the beach was no coincidence. No secrets around this community he thought but was too delighted to see her to ponder the thought.

'That you most surely did,' he said.

'Stood your ground well enough.'

'Only because I was too terrified to move, you ride that horse like a man!'

'Father taught me.' Then, imperiously. 'I have no time for side-saddle, ladylike nonsense.' Scraping a furrow in the sand with her foot she asked, 'Do you think I also look like a man?'

'Vanity, vanity!'

She raised her face and her eyes were the colour of deep hazel framed with long curling eyelashes and the urge to touch her and to hold her was almost irresistible but instead he took the reins of the restless horse.

'He needs walking.'

She fell into step with him and they sauntered along the sand at the water's edge: and so close he had difficulty maintaining composure. 'Haven't seen you since the night of the party,' she said and reproach was so petulant in her voice that he hesitated, before answering:

'I wanted to, so very much, but you know how the sparks fly between Sir Harry and me.'

'Does he have to know?'

He let the reins fall and the stallion dropped behind then wandered off towards the greenery. Brow furrowing, he queried, 'Are you suggesting we meet in secret?'

'You just said you wanted to see me,' she said defiantly.

'More than you know: but not in a way that might appear furtive. When I call on you it will be by the front door . . . out in the open for all to see.' His hands sought hers and gripped on tight. 'Oh, Cathryn, I will not play the role of a back door vagrant, sneaking in to see you like a thief in the night!' His voice had taken on a biting edge and she could sense the fierce pride that burned within but always suppressed in the need to affect a bearing of simple humility. Having to consider feelings other than her own was a new and uncomfortable experience and she didn't like the experience!

'Papa would never allow you to call,' she said tartly, 'I don't imagine his ambitions for me would tolerate such an arrangement.'

'Do you think I'm unaware of this? Every eligible bachelor in the county must be at your feet. Men of title and with everything affluently possible to offer, including the continuance of the kind of luxury to which you are accustomed and which, if you are to be honest, you enjoy so much.' Slowing his rhetoric he said in wry tone, 'Now tell me, Cathryn, what have I to offer by comparison?'

'Comparison!' Dismissing the word with contempt. 'I don't balance my feelings against cost. You ask me what you have to offer as though it were some kind of contest with the highest bidder taking the prize? Do you have to offer anything?' She seemed strangely pensive as she went on, 'This alone could prove more than I deserve, but one thing I am very sure of is the way I feel when you are near me. Whatever else? I know you are a man among men and I have constant and overwhelming need to see more of you.'

Rushing on with words flooding as if long confined. 'I need the gentleness of your smile. The touch of your hand in mine! To feel your confidence surround and enfold me, and to recapture the magic we created on that wonderful evening by the wishing well. Richard, Richard! Surely this false and mocking difference in our life style isn't so formidable that it can't be bridged if desire is strong enough?' She looked at him and her eyes were those of a woman in love as she pleaded, 'Is it so wrong to take happiness where we can?'

The morning sun shone bright on her upturned face and the fitful breeze threaded her hair in colourful abandon. Her cheeks were flushed and her mouth curled in slight anger as she spoke the last words, and he had never seen anything so beautiful and could no longer keep desire in check. His hands were on her shoulders and her face lifted instantly to his and he couldn't do anything about it but kiss her. On the forehead as if in supplication and as if asking permission then his arms enfolded and her body snuggled against him as if just waiting for his move and her warmth and softness devastated and he buried his face in the cascading fragrance of her hair. Stomach muscles in a tight knot, driving all breath from him, his mouth found her cheek, then her neck, before fastening on her lips with a hunger no longer to be denied and they clung to each other with desire rampant. His kiss was more and more demanding and bruising the ripe mouth that was open to receive him and he felt her body surging in response and he broke away with a gasp of torment and he led her to a slab of rock worn smooth by the pounding surf and he spread his coat and pulled her down beside him. She came easily and he looked down the curve of her neck to where her breasts surged so invitingly under her blouse front and he held her tight and all the while warm sunshine flooded them in glorious heat and added further fire to their embrace.

A seabird dived low over the water pursuing an endless quest for food and its harsh cry echoed round the bay in mocking discord to hang suspended in the vast bowl of sea and sky and intrude into passion and her eyes opened to see him looking at her body. 'Still think I look like a man?' she said in secret whisper. He could feel her fingers creeping round his waist and for a mad second desire engulfed, with a need to possess so overpowering it threatened to tear away all vestige of control. He knew a desperate yearning to yield to the demands of his body. To immerse himself in the exquisite wonder of this lovely woman and he lifted her face, his fingers tremulous as he traced the curve of her mouth with his fingertips. Her lips fluttered response and her eyes were wide and unafraid and his senses reeled in the exuded scent of this young woman, willing and eager for love, and all the while his hands trembled with a wild longing to caress her body and he had to clench his fingers and fighting might and main to break from a spell that was rendering him bereft of control and dragging him down into an abyss of abandon: so threatening and yet so completely inviting!

'Help me, Cathryn,' he gasped, 'in God's name help me! I cannot fight this alone!'

She stirred: impatiently. He knew she was waiting. Anticipating! He sought release from tumult. Knowing he had to do this on his own. His hand tore free and fastened on a spur of granite with fingers white under the strain and bearing mute testimony to indecision. Words rasped from him. 'Let me sit and watch the sea for a moment, my love, and try to restore sanity to this wanton frame,' agony brought fervent appeal to his voice as he gasped, 'and pray for guidance!' These words brought movement and with petulance very obvious she jerked upright and his withdrawal brought a flush of anger to her face.

'What's the matter with you,' she snapped, 'do you find me so undesirable?'

'So desirable that I almost took you, here on the sand, by force if need be!'

'You know well that you would have needed no force.'

It was truly spoken and he didn't know what to do or what to say but he was breathing more easily now and his eyes were tender as he gazed into a face flushed with emotion and he found voice at last to say, 'It was a moment of wondrous feeling, Cathryn.' Sensing an ominous change in her manner and choosing his next words with care. 'I need you so much that I lose all control when you are near and have to force myself to remember what I am and the work I have to do.'

'What are you seeking then, a more private place, I thought you wanted me out in the open for all to see?'

A spiteful echo of the demanding Sir Harry had appeared in her voice and brought a frown. 'You deliberately misconstrue my words,' he said, 'if we are to have any future together there has to be more for us than a coupling of animal passion: here on the beach.'

'Suppose it proves the only way, will you deny us this happiness for always?'

Gripping her shoulders he pulled her upright and his hands moved in hopeless caress down her arms. 'But today has brought happiness,' he said quietly, 'and despair also, for never have I known such emotion as we just shared, but this is all I can allow myself to take at this time.' Calmer now, he spoke with a quiet authority that cast a chill of disappointment over Cathryn, whose every nerve cried out for fulfillment and she wanted him so much and didn't know what she had to do to make him realise and sought refuge in arrogance.

'You evidently did not hear when I said we should take happiness where we can,' she said in angry retort. 'Never forget that there are others who find me desirable and who do not share your noble inhibitions.'

Frustration had hardened her voice and brought increasing dismay and he said in admonishing tone, 'Were I to take advantage of you in such a way I would stand condemned as a weak and loathsome hypocrite and I cannot permit this passion to overwhelm us so easily.' The words sounded hollow and he knew they were and he knew she was questioning his manhood and had to convince her otherwise. 'There is another way,' he said determinedly. 'Let me call on you at Sandford Barton. Your father will eventually bow his head to us when he is forced to accept the love we have for each other. If only we stand firm we could face the whole of Cornwall without flinching.' He spoke with urgency and with desperation in his voice. He had to reach her! Make her understand, but sensed only growing antagonism. She was very young and very proud and couldn't face rejection without showing deep resentment. She needed to inflict equal pain and said with deliberate scorn:

'Perhaps the minister is stronger than the man?'

He gave a rueful shake of his head before replying, 'Sometimes, but certainly not this morning. Would you think me more of a man if I were to possess your body without thought: or honour. Could I . . . without forever destroying our chance of a wonderful life together?

'Don't think I am ready to face life as the lady of a poverty stricken minister!' Very much a Sedgewick who could not easily deny herself of anything she might desire Cathryn wouldn't be appeased and her words were spoken in spite and with bitterness and she realised that her thrust had gone deep as his head drooped and he looked suddenly vulnerable as if she had stripped away his veneer of calm dedication and she knew instant regret and also the sobering thought that he was in more torment even than herself. Her own emotions began to subside, to be replaced by a feeling of hopelessness and of being completely lost in circumstance beyond her control. She could have bitten off her tongue but instead hid from sight behind a proudly spoken. 'If you approached my father in such a way he would send me immediately away from the Barton and from Cornwall, so far away that we could never see each other again.'

'No matter how far away . . . a love such as this could reach out to touch across any distance . . . need only for you to command and I will confront Sir Harry. Indeed,' a suspect thought intruded and he paused for a moment before continuing, 'were I sure this was what you wanted you would have no need to command because I would surely know, and make sure that no one in this world had power to keep us apart.' Cupping her face in his hands he looked at her but saw only the frown of uncertainly furrowing her brow. 'Does the thought frighten you so much, Cathryn?' he asked. 'Can you not see how golden life would be with all opposition and indecision smoothed away if only you and I can be bold enough, and certain in ourselves.'

'I'm not afraid, but you must realise that I am not sure I can so readily adjust to your dedicated way of living. Not just now, anyway, I need time to think, but on my own because I don't reason too clearly when you are close to me.' Her voice trembled on the words and she managed a wan smile as she said in contrite tone, 'If only I could let everything go and submerge myself in your confidence.'

Silent for a few moments, he then said, 'It has been written that the measure of love can be calculated by the degree of how much we are prepared to sacrifice for its fulfillment.' His words were sad and somehow self-derogatory and she couldn't bear the look of loneliness that clouded is face. She threw her arms round him and held him close and looked into his face.

'Forgive me, Richard, I know you are offering all you possess in this world, but I can't decide just yet. Can you give me a little more time?' She was distraught and it showed and he wanted to hold her, to comfort, make love to her, but he had just come back from that inviting abyss.

'Oh, Cathryn,' he said, 'I have no right to

expect you to turn your back on all you know and love, take all the time you need.' The mood between them had changed. Passion still smouldered, but without consummation the fires were slowly extinguishing. They were both unsatisfied yet drained of emotion. 'Will you come to see me again,' he asked, 'I walk here on the beach most fine mornings?'

'Knew that already, but I'm the one who should be asking.' Then, in sotto voice. 'Can't promise to behave.' She spoke almost as a child then turned from him in considerable haste and ran to mount the palomino. Digging in her heels she sent her mount accelerating into the water's edge leaving him torn asunder in a conflict of emotions. His withdrawal had brought only embarrassment and a sense of terrible hurt, yet even more damming was the knowledge that he had denied her the one thing she so imperiously had demanded. Himself! What should he have done? Taken her? Questions knifing into him as he stared after her: then horse and rider sped behind a bluff of rock and were gone from sight.

10

Polite knock on the vestry door and at his request to enter the door pushed open to reveal the jaunty figure of Jonathan Rudd. He was dressed in a navy-blue Guernsey jumper and tan-coloured sailcloth trousers and looked very lean and healthy-fit and, greeting him warmly, Mathieson said, 'I was just thinking about you.' He saw a bewildered look flash across Rudd's face then the strange expression vanished to be replaced with his normal cocky grin.

'Sounds ominous!'

'You might think so when I tell you why.'

'Now I'm really worried,' said Rudd in mock alarm.

'I need someone to read the lesson at my opening service and hoped I could prevail on you.'

'You must be at a low ebb, Reverend, why don't all your solid citizens stand up and be counted?'

'They won't stand still long enough,' smilingly replied Mathieson. 'Anyway, I want to bring colour into church service and you are by far the most colourful person I know. Except Captain Faraday,' he added, 'now there is a man who could be interesting.'

'If you can call a poisonous snake interesting . . . forget it . . . the man's evil! A monster wearing the uniform of authority!' His tone reflected intense dislike and Mathieson looked at him for a long moment.

'Hope you are not falling foul of him?' he then said as if in warning, 'he could be a very powerful enemy and make life awkward for a seafarer such as you.'

'Forget about Faraday, he doesn't cause me any anxiety, although 'tis not for lack of trying.' Beckoning to the door he said excitedly, 'Something special to show you!'

Intrigued, he followed Rudd's seafarer's gait outside into the roadway where waited Simon and Jake by the long cart from Newlyn dock, this time drawn by a sturdy work horse and surrounded by a strong smell of fish but Mathieson's astounded gaze fastened immediately on the church organ and sections of piping that lay among the heap of straw. He couldn't believe it! And Rudd took personal reward from the incredulous look on his face.

'Found it in a disused chapel in Marazion,' he said with obvious delight. 'Janie knew of its whereabouts and the village folk made a collection to raise the money to buy it, and though it was your landlady's idea to begin with, when the villagers got to know they all wanted to help. Whatever,' he concluded, 'here it is and I hope it still works?'

Speechless, Mathieson ran his hand slowly over a section of organ pipe, now realising there was another man in the background who he recognised as Jan Coggeshall, the village blacksmith. Face coloured red from close proximity to the furnace, huge shoulders and bulging forearms and with his taut waist strapped with a broad leather belt. A resourceful craftsman, Jan had the enviable reputation of being able to fix almost anything. Touching his cap in greeting. 'I took it down, Reverend,' he said, 'and I'll soon have it back together.'

'It's good to see a man who enjoys a challenge,' said Mathieson smiling at the blacksmith and at his lack of modesty.

'You and me both, Reverend,' said Jan meaningfully, hefting a bag of tools he added, 'let's get it inside before it rains.'

Manhandling the heavy organ up the steps into the church along the centre aisle and into the sacred area behind the rood screen. True to his word, Jan soon had the pieces assembled and when it was placed to his satisfaction Mathieson stood for a while in rapt contemplation looking at his organ then, turning to thank the men for their labours, found to his surprise that Rudd was the only one there.

'They've gone down to the *Blue Lugger*,' Rudd explained. 'Janie's preparing a meal and Jake fancied a glass of cider before eating but you were too engrossed to notice them go. She asked me to invite you as well, if you've the time?'

Declining with a shake of his head, Mathieson said absent-mindedly, 'Thank her for me but I'm too excited about the organ to think about food.' Adding sincerely, 'You have done me a great service, Jonathan, and hope that one day I can do something for you in return.'

'You could come out fishing tomorrow,' instantly replied Rudd, 'we need an extra hand for trawling and a sea breeze will put a little colour back in your face.'

Hesitating. Feeling a quick, instinctive desire to be afloat again, a feeling he had thought long suppressed. Then he asked, 'How long do you expect to be away?'

'All day and perhaps through the night, we'll be back in port early enough to catch the auction.'

'Haven't done much fishing.'

'You're going to take the helm, I'll do the fishing.'

His exuberance was contagious and Mathieson responded in like manner. 'Find me somewhere to stable Mistral and I'll be in Newlyn at daybreak.'

'Pray for a fine day, Reverend.' Delighted to

have his offer accepted, Rudd then said, 'Janie will be disappointed if I don't bring you back for a meal.'

'She'll have enough on her hands without me. Give her my thanks: and my regrets.' Mathieson was already on his way back to the organ, so Rudd shrugged resignedly and ran out and off down the street after the trundling cart.

Duster in hand: flicking straw from the ivory coloured keys. He was elated, not just by the organ, but because the people of the village had joined in support. Accepting him! He sensed movement from behind, but continued clearing remnants of dirt and straw from his newly acquired treasure. Then a face peered through the rood screen.

'Come in, Thomas, and take a look at our new organ.' He knew that White missed no happening around the church and was intrigued by his unusual appearance inside. Standing back he surveyed the instrument, with gratification in the knowledge that he now had the means to fill his church with music.

White came close, with his shuffling walk slower even than normal, and he appeared most uncomfortable at the close proximity of the altar. As if oblivious, sitting on the long stool that came with the ensemble, Mathieson ran exploratory fingers over the keyboard. They depressed with a dull thud so he bent down to search for some way of pumping life into the dead console. There came quick, eager movement and White slid alongside pulling impatiently at his trailing leg. His good foot worked the pedal board up and down a few times and Mathieson was amazed at the look of childlike excitement on his face.

'Really needs someone pumping,' explained Thomas. 'Try now, Reverend.'

Mathieson pressed a key and laughed out loud at the tuneless wheeze that greeted his effort. Easing off the stool, he said, 'You try it!'

Hesitating, looking around in guarded manner, White spread his hand wide and played a chord, then another, the organ came to musical life under his gentle touch, and Mathieson, remembering the rows of leather bound books that adorned the wall of the little shack, placed both hands on the crippled shoulders and turned him round to face him. 'Thomas,' he exclaimed, 'I believe you can play the organ.'

'This instrument hasn't been played for a long time and needs careful tuning.'

'Do you know how?'

'My father taught me, but such a long time ago I hardly remember where to begin.'

'Did he also teach you how to play?' Sensing this must be a painful subject, he spoke in coercive tone and very carefully.

'He tried!' White's hands were clenched on the keyboard with the knuckle bones protruding through the taut skin. 'For a long time he tried, but how can a cripple hope to make music like my father could?' The desperation in his voice and in his eyes dulled his face and pulled down the corners of his mouth, then he said, 'I think his despair of me finally broke his spirit, so much that he started to drink heavily, and the love for the organ and the music he made began to leave him.' The deformed shoulders slumped but only for a brief moment and then straightened and he gave Mathieson a fierce look. 'When Mathew White played the great cathedral organ,' he said proudly, 'people would gather in the road outside to stop and listen. Queen's of the Realm even, and illustrious Men of State would come from far away to worship: just because he was playing there!'

'You loved him very much.'

'He was all I had, you see. I do not remember my mother… she died when I was a baby. My father educated me, sheltered me from the prying eyes of the world outside. But for me he would have been rich and famous and his music would have lived on for all time.' A sob shook the frail body and Mathieson felt a surge of compassion, realising now that in addition to great deformity, Thomas carried the weight of his father's downfall on his shoulders. He also thought that Mathew White had carried shelter too far and to a point that did not allow Thomas any hope of facing the world outside. Sitting alongside he placed his arm round him and said, ever so gently:

'The music of Mathew White could come alive again through you. It can be possible that here in this humble chapel we two together could bring his music back to the ears of the world.' Willing the little man to look at him he said insistently, 'Is not the memory of your father worthy of such an effort?'

'You know not what you ask.'

White's voice was a whisper of despair, but Mathieson persisted. 'I'm asking you to play the organ for me: here in the church at Perranwithick.'

'Who do you think would come and listen to someone as miserable and deformed as me?' The harshness of the words that tore from his mouth wracked Mathieson, then the voice broke with a heart rendering tremor. 'They might come out of curiosity to feast their eyes on the freak who plays the organ!' Voice rising in sudden anger but it was the anger of despair and the anger of shame and the anger of desperation. 'No, Reverend Mathieson!' he blurted, 'you want more of me than I have to give and I ask you again to leave me alone and in peace! You always seek to arouse desires that have long faded into oblivion, and above all else, why do you keep expecting me to expose myself to the pitying and frightened eyes of your people?'

He could find no answer and just bowed his head in silence and White looked at him for a long moment with the reproach fading from his eyes. Then he reached out and touched him. 'Don't be sad for me,' he entreated, 'when alone, at least I am my own man. I do not see the misery of my body anymore and long ago accepted that this is the way it has to be. Please try to understand that only when I am forced to see myself through the eyes of other people do I face again the agony of my own being, and I cannot any longer bear the revulsion of those who look upon me.' Anger rising once more as he said harshly, 'Pity is an emotion I can well do without!'

'This barrier you erect could be torn down if only you would help me.'

'I will not subject myself to humiliation and further agony of mind. The outside world and me are happier in isolation!'

11

Early morning at Newlyn: keeping out of the way while Rudd and his crew expertly squeezed the ship from the crowded harbour. Warping her round, then setting a small jib to allow her to gather way. She came out from under the sheltering lee. The wind came free. The mainsail hoisted and filled with a loud thump and she heeled rail down. He noted that Rudd steered close inshore and wasn't surprised when he heard the order to lower the mainsail, and the ship proceeded under flying jib and mizzen. Grinning at the scrutiny, Rudd jested, 'Standing in too close for your liking?'

'Fancy you know these waters better than I ever will,' glancing round before adding, 'you run a tight ship, Jonathan.' Wondering again why he had been invited. Couldn't see himself as anything but a passenger on this trip. Shrugging the thought aside he relaxed and began to enjoy the clean tang of salt air and the feel of a sloping deck beneath him. It was a long time since his legs had braced wide against the surge and roll of a tall ship. He was dressed in a white, roll-neck sweater, reefer jacket, dark blue sail-cloth trousers and soft-leather deck boots, and Rudd surveyed him with approval and thought he looked more comfortable in seafaring rig than in his robe of office.

'We're just picking up a few lobsters before we start fishing in earnest,' explained Rudd. Spinning the wheel even as he spoke and the ship poised alongside a bobbing can coloured bright red and bearing the name ROSE in bold lettering. The ship's tender trailed astern and Jake clambered down to gather in the red can with a boat hook, then hauled in a length of line and finally a dome shaped basket. .

'Nothing skipper,' he called, 'but the bait's gone!

'Renew the bait and reset the pot,' ordered Rudd. 'Can't imagine how the lobster got the bait out but good luck to it.' With the crew back inboard they sailed a short distance to another red can.

The hauling in process repeated, Jake announced. 'Same as before . . . neither bait or lobster!'

Raising a sardonic eyebrow, Rudd murmured, 'Curious.' After a further three abortive attempts he had the longboat secured inboard and queried, 'What do reckon, Jake?'

'*Barracuda* sailed before dawn.'

'Thought we might have trouble with Curt,' mused Rudd, 'but never imagined he'd be reduced to stealing a few lobsters. Seems he and his crew are looking for another hiding.' Then he shrugged and said, 'Take the wheel, Richard, while we set all sail and get out into deep water. Tide's falling and I have no fancy to put us ashore on a mud bank for the rest of the day.'

Moving behind the wheel Mathieson glanced up at the masthead pennant and steered to bring the ship's head into wind. She lay quiet with the foresail flapping while the crew winched up the heavy wooden gaff to which the head of the mainsail was laced and the massive spread of canvas rose slowly up the mast. The crew worked well but in a casual manner that suddenly fired him into command. 'Simon!' he roared, 'get that flying jib hauled further out! Quickly man before she fills! Jump to it, Jake . . . ease away on the main sheet! More! More! Now make fast!' The commands rang out and so incisive and the crew obeyed without hesitation and the *Rose* picked up her skirts and creamed over the sheltered waters. 'We need more sail, Jonathan, your mizzen staysail's rigged so get it up there!'

'Aye, aye, sir!'

Straddling the wheel and relishing the kick of the rudder as she heeled rail down and cut through the short waves with increasing speed. Knowing again the thrill of commanding a tall ship as the *Rose* sped away from the confines of Mounts Bay into deeper water and the sweep of coastline began to open out behind.

'We're going out fishing you know, not crossing the Pacific.' Rudd alongside him, leaving his sweating crew amidships, as if awaiting further command. Mathieson's eyes were intent on the open water ahead and came back from the distance only with reluctance. Then he grinned a little shamefacedly and made as if to relinquish the wheel. Declining the invitation with a gesture, Rudd said, 'Haven't seen the *Rose* respond like that for a long time.'

'Sorry about the hustle, old habits die hard, I guess. Hope Simon and Jake don't take offence?'

'Looks as if they enjoyed it.' Rudd gave him speculative glance before adding, 'Janie said you have been a blue water man.'

'So that's why you asked me to come? To find out for yourself?'

'Yes! To both questions.' Looking at him Rudd said with a shake of his head, 'What a waste, you and me would have made a great team.'

'Doing what, hardly think you need a partner for fishing?'

'There are more lucrative ways to use a ship like the *Rose*'

'Probably be better for my peace of mind not to learn of them.' Carrying this thought further Mathieson said, 'Captain Faraday is convinced that smuggling is commonplace down here in

Newlyn and seems determined to catch the offenders red-handed.'

'He'll have to get his backside out of that plush office chair, never catch any of these mysterious smugglers from so easy a seat.' Contempt in his tone and dislike of Faraday showing in the grim look that accompanied this statement and Mathieson thought he was complacent to a degree that invited confrontation: and disaster.

'Don't underestimate him,' he cautioned. 'Faraday is anxious to make his mark here so that he can all the more quickly be transferred back to London and the kind of society life to which he thinks he is entitled. He's a dangerous man who would go to any lengths to make a name in Her Majesty's service.'

Shrugging, as if he didn't want to talk about Faraday and, pursuing his former trend of thought, Rudd said, 'Don't look so concerned, Richard, I wasn't going to ask you to smuggle a few miserable casks of brandy. I was talking about real adventure . . . of sailing to remote islands and perhaps finding treasure beyond dreams. With a ship like the *Rose* we could sail to anywhere in the whole world.' His eyes were afire and the boyish enthusiasm brought a smile to Mathieson's face and a reflective tone appeared as he looked at him.

'Dreams!' he said, 'such as I once had, and I have seen places such as you talk of. I've also known men who found these treasures. Pearls particularly! Black and shining: with a lustre that would burn into the very soul. Pearls for which you might search for ever and not find.' In a tone that hinted of personal experience he concluded, 'But I have yet to see riches bring true happiness.'

'Every man has his own idea of happiness,' retorted Jonathan Rudd, 'can you think mine would be realised by a lifetime of seeking fish in the cold water of the English Channel?' His voice carried conviction as he went forcibly on. 'Surely it's far better that a man should follow his dreams and desires even if they crumble to ashes rather than live out a frustrated life in contemplation of what might have been: had he but dared?'

'This is a question that each of us has to answer for himself and it's but a few short years since I felt the same,' said Mathieson with great feeling. 'I know only too well the terrible force that can drive a man to sail the great oceans and I'm not the one to advise otherwise.' Gesturing around, he stated, 'You're half way there because you already have the vehicle, your own magic carpet . . . one that waits on every tide at Newlyn. Take the *Rose* if you must and together seek this destiny, but this is not for me any more because I tried and failed: miserably,' a look of pain filled his eyes and he hesitated before continuing with, 'not only failed, for the cost of my failure was born by someone else.' His voice faltered and he gripped the steering wheel tight and he slumped into it as if for support in a mode of distress that had Rudd looking on in consternation.

'I'm sorry, Richard,' he said contritely, 'you make me feel an intruder.'

'Just a momentary lapse, won't happen again.' Must exercise restraint, he thought dolefully. Making too many errors of judgment lately. Coming out with Rudd was another! Under control again he enquired with a smile, 'Does your invitation also include breakfast?'

As though he had been awaiting the summons, Simon emerged on deck with steaming mugs of soup and chunks of fresh bread.

'I sense the hand of the lovely Janie,' said Mathieson.

'She mentioned something about you always being hungry.'

'That young woman has a capacity for pleasing that is wonderful to behold.'

'Intend to marry her one day,' boldly announced Rudd'

'Have you asked her? Does she know of your designs upon her?'

'I've not asked, but she knows!'

'Don't delay over long or someone else might get in first.'

Looking him over, Rudd said mischievously, 'Hardly think there is any danger from you because from what I have been hearing you are finding much pleasure in the company of the impetuous Cathryn Ann Sedgewick.' Grinning widely at Mathieson's startled glance he added, 'There are no secrets in our small community.'

'Didn't realise my movements were worthy of such interest.'

'Beware, Richard, the countryside is strewn with the broken hearts of men who laid siege to the door of Sandford Barton in the vain hope of carrying off the prize of our bewitching Cassie.' The words were light-hearted yet with strange inflection and he moved uncomfortably away to look over the side rail and look down into the frothing bow wave. His voice came back on the wind. 'Stay on the helm while I take some sail off,' shaking his head in no small amusement as he added, 'wouldn't catch many fish at this speed.'

Drifting along the Western Approaches, the crew now dressed for fishing in waterproof aprons and thigh boots. The cold waters were alive with fish and the holds began to fill and it was still early in the day when Rudd declared enough and turned the ship for Newlyn.

'Sail ahead, skipper!'

Rudd looked up at the call. There were quite a few sails ahead but he knew to which Jake referred and his eyes hardened on the unmistakeable schooner outline of the *Barracuda*. 'Right then, Mr Mate,' he cried, 'now's your chance to get sail up in earnest! We'll give Curt and the *Barracuda* a fright before they reach harbour.'

Hurriedly discarding their heavy fishing clothing, Rudd and Ward re-hoisted the huge mizzen staysail while Simon wriggled forward along the bowsprit to set a large inner jib behind the two already flying. Then last of all they broke out the topmast triangle that sets in the angle formed by the topmast and the mainsail gaff and the *Rose* fairly flew through the water under all the sail she could carry.

Sudden commotion aboard *Barracuda* as Curt realised that Rudd was closing with dire intent and from a ship sailing casually back to port the *Barracuda* became transformed into a ship knowingly being pursued. Chase on! Simon and Jake poised by halyard and sheets, in a position and stance that indicated they had done this before, and Rudd surveyed with malicious amusement the tall masts of *Barracuda* heeling further and further over under the press of canvas she was being forced to carry. 'Overtake to windward,' he ordered, 'she's no match for the *Rose* and we should just beat her to the fairway.'

Wrestling the wheel over and struggling to hold her on course. 'Give a hand here, Jonathan!' called Mathieson, 'becoming too much of a handful for one pair of hands!'

Rudd lent his weight to the wheel but his gaze stayed unwaveringly on the ship ahead. 'She's coming back to us, fast,' he shouted, 'bet Curt's having a heart attack!' There was elation in his voice, and also determination, and Mathieson thought that he didn't take kindly to the loss of his lobsters and was out for recompense, but the ships were closing at a rate of knots and all the time the entrance came nearer with the buoy marking the channel now in clear view but the two ships raced on with the bowsprit of the *Rose* coming up on the stern of *Barracuda* with menacing intent.

A gust heeled the *Rose* over, dipping her lee rail into the surging bow wave. Mathieson's sure hand steadied the wheel until she came up with water rushing along the lee decking and streaming in torrents out the scuppers. The wheel needed hands of steel and he straddled the deck with legs braced wide and controlled it with strength and confidence: and exhilaration! Never for a second taking his eyes off *Barracuda* in case the ships rolled together, for at this speed any touch would bring disaster and all the while the dark green hull of the *Rose* seemed to be trying to mount the black *Barracuda* like a rampant stallion and so close that he could clearly see the foaming wave that roared away from her bow and came racing down her side to surge in force over her bulwarks and her lee scuppers were awash, dragging in the water and slowing her.

The *Rose* came up on *Barracuda* and as her bowsprit drew alongside the pursued vessel Rudd raced down into the waist of his ship to exchange obscenities.

'Get away from me you bloody fool,' raged Curt, 'you'll sink us both!

'Then get out of my way!' The fairway buoy looming ahead, Rudd scurried aft. The *Rose* had moved just ahead now but there appeared no more than a few feet separating the racing ships and a collision began to look inevitable should there come the slightest increase in wind, but without care or caution Rudd screamed, 'Leave the buoy to starboard! Push the bastard in the mud!' His wild recklessness and the intense excitement of the chase brought exuberant response and Mathieson gave a maniac shout as he spun the wheel. Turning just enough to miss the towering structure of the fairway buoy and *Barracuda* had no choice but to helm out of the channel, or hit the buoy!

'I'll swing for you, Rudd!' Pummeling the air with his fists in emphasis but now the canvas of the *Rose* effectively shielded the wind and the sails of *Barracuda* drooped in the lee and she slowed dramatically as she lost her wind and wallowed astern, a slowing that enabled her helmsman to steer away from the mud shoals and back into the safe water of the fairway and they rounded the buoy in the wake of the *Rose*. Curt's face was a picture of murderous rage but with all sail to take off before entering the rapidly approaching entrance he had little time for thoughts of what he would to do to Rudd and joined his crew in the rush to drop all sail and smothering them hastily on deck entered Newlyn dock at far too fast a rate of knots and fetched up alongside the stone jetty with a sickening crunch and with their fumbling disorder greeted with hoots of derision from Rudd and his crew who were lined up on the dockside enjoying the spectacle. Curt jumped ashore and grabbed him by the shirt collar.

Tearing free, Rudd suggested calmly, 'I'll have my lobsters back now.'

'What bleedin' lobsters?'

'You lifted my pots early this morning!'

Eyes narrowing in sudden comprehension Curt thrust forward. 'Listen, Rudd,' he snarled, 'I'll smash your face in anytime but I don't need to steal lobsters from a fellow fisherman . . . even one whose guts I hate as much as I do yours!'

'Then why run your ship from us?'

'What the hell else did you expect with you bearing down on me that way? I've never refused a challenge in my life and if you wanted a race for the entrance I was bleedin' well going to give you one!' Raging, spitting mad, he shouted, 'You're a bleedin' idiot! I could have lost both my masts with all that canvas up!'

'Not if you kept your gear in good condition.' Gesturing at the shambles on the deck of *Barracuda*, Rudd said scornfully, 'You run a sloppy ship, Curt.'

'How I run my ship is my business!' Curt's shoulders hunched and his fists clenched like

Devon shovels and Rudd responded in the same manner as he stated:

'I'm taking six lobsters.'

'Put one foot on board and they'll have to carry you off!' His crew had formed a menacing barrier behind and Curt growled, 'We're seven against your three.'

'Four!' Mathieson shoulder to shoulder with Rudd.

'Who the hell are you?'

'My helmsman,' said Rudd proudly.

'Helmsman!' Glaring at Mathieson. 'Bleedin' lunatic more like it!'

'Are you going to hand back my lobsters,' insisted Rudd, 'or do we have to come and take them?'

'Tell you one last time! I didn't lift your bleedin' lobsters!'

'Let's take 'em, skipper.' Jake spoke as if he was looking forward to an all out scrap, but Mathieson placed a retraining hand on Rudd's arm.

'Easy now, Jonathan, I believe him . . . don't think he'd belittle himself to steal a few lobsters from you.'

Rudd stayed his forward move. 'If not the "Barracuda",' he frowningly queried, 'then who else?'

'How the hell am I supposed to know?' snorted Curt, 'it was still dark when we sailed and we went straight out to sea.'

Under Mathieson's calming influence much of the heat had gone from the encounter and the opposing crewmen relaxed their belligerent stance. 'Forget it then, Curt,' said Rudd, 'I'll bow to the sound judgment of the Reverend and give you the benefit of the doubt.' Adding ominously, 'This time!'

'If you ever pull another stunt like the one today I'll skin you and nail the hide on your own masthead!'

'Look forward to it,' said Rudd.

As the crews dispersed Mathieson looked at him and Rudd looked back and there was friendship between them, and something more! A sense of accomplishment together: and an appreciation of mutual ability. They were kindred spirits, and with a broad grin, Mathieson said, 'Thanks for a most fulfilling day, Jonathan. But please! Don't ask me to come out fishing again. Can't stand the excitement!

Wilder Faraday sat at his desk contemplating the sheet of notepaper in his hand. The Excise office overlooked the roadway and the harbour. A square-shaped building it had been painted white many years ago but the colour had faded to a dubious grey and the further ravage of wind and salt air gave the frontage an air of neglect and general lack of maintenance. Faraday's office however, was warm and comfortable. Furnished with a large desk and leather armchair and with a long sofa under one window. On a sideboard of polished mahogany lay a fine silver tray on which stood a pair of decanters and six matching glasses of sparkling crystal. A rich tapestry covered the floor and the office held an ambience of well being in diverse conflict with the austere appearance of the exterior of the building.

His lip curled in a sardonic grimace as he re-read the letter and he swiveled his chair to gaze out the window. Then, taking a long cigar from his vest pocket he lit up with exaggerated care and with the fragrant smoke hovering he leaned back and sat brooding with his eyes hooded and half-closed, but his satisfying train of thought was interrupted by the sight of two ships arriving almost simultaneously in harbour. *Barracuda* docking behind *Rose of Endau* and hardly had time to tie up before both crews spilled out on the dockside and he surveyed the scene with considerable interest.

'There are many ways of dealing with smugglers like Rudd,' he murmured to himself, 'perhaps the filthy louts will kill themselves off and save me the bother.' His eyes opened wide as he saw the figure of Mathieson leap ashore to join the melee, and with speculation rampant he mused, 'Now there is real interest, Rudd and the Reverend, no less! What an unusual and provocative combination?' Brooding for a long moment with his fingers entwined and thumbs revolving slowly. Then he took the cigar from his lips and said malevolently, ‘Maybe I can down those two birds with a single shot!’

Pleasuring this thought he lost interest in the scene outside and rose from his chair and moved across to the gleaming dinner table to pour a glass of wine. Sniffing appreciatively at the bouquet he glanced down at the large dinner plate and his smile was pure evil as he said:

‘My favourite meal: especially when the lobster is one of Rudd’s!’

12

Marching up the roadway like a fleet of ships of the line three abreast and four deep: and from the din of chatter, with all cannon blazing. All armed with brooms and buckets and a sense of importance evident in their bustling demeanour and he stepped hastily aside as they bore down on him, then came to a shuffling, uncertain halt.

Blanche Tremaine leading the platoon. Her unruly hair was tied back and an all-embracing pinafore hung loose about her ample frame. The rest of the work force were attired in similar garments but of varying colour and on their heads perched bonnet-like caps of white muslin bound with ribbon and tied under the chin with streamers of black ribbon, the one exception being Miss Agnes Plympton who wore the bonnet without which she was never seen. It was a shiny affair of dark blue with a lacy fringe overhanging the front and a faded cluster of imitation carnations on one side. Miss Plympton kept the accounts in order for the local trades people and was reputed to be of gentle origin.

'Good morning, ladies,' he greeted warmly, 'so good of you to give your time in this way.'

'Only doing what's right and proper,' said Blanche, 'something we should have been doing before if you ask me, it's a disgrace that we have allowed the church to become so dilapidated.' Then she smiled and her voice softened. 'You've no idea what it means to have an energetic and likeable minister in the parish. We all feel that you are going to make a great difference to our village life and you can rely on the Ladies of the Committee to help in any way we can.' This statement had the Ladies nodding in concert.

'I'm most grateful for your support.' Then, hesitantly, 'I'll return with you to the church.'

'No need,' said Blanche, 'we know what to do and don't want you nosing about and getting in our way.' The Ladies murmured agreement and she looked at them approvingly, before adding, 'Anyway, Reverend, I'm sure you have more important matters to attend.' They were looking at him as if impatient for him to move away and let them get on about their business and he forced back the chuckle that threatened to shatter the solemnity of the occasion.

As they gathered themselves and prepared to move off, he said, 'Mrs Farquasan is already in the church, and she has water heating and some other items ready that she thought might be useful.' Then, casually, 'Perhaps you'll allow me to look in on you later?'

Blanche was the self-elected spokeswoman and none of the others had anything to say and they just waited, somehow respectfully, yet the approval on their faces as they saw the smile that spread the corners of his mouth, was apparent and suddenly warming to him. 'We're wasting time, Ladies,' announced Blanche He half-expected her to order the troops to quick march but instead they took off in formation behind her. 'See you later, Reverend.' Her words drifted back and he watched as they proceeded in the direction of the church gate. Relieved of the presence of their minister the chatter soon resumed its former voluble din.

'Phew!' Shaking his head in wry humour he resumed his way down the road into the village heading for the rear entrance to the *Blue Lugger* and seeing the kitchen door ajar he knocked twice and walked in.

Janie Ralston had promised to make up some light refreshment for the working party. The kitchen hosted a fragrant aroma of freshly baked bread and there was a tray of small, savoury pasties cooling on the table and she looked up from her work as he entered.

'Madam,' he said with mock formality, 'your kitchen is a delight to the eye and a torment to nose and stomach.'

She saw the boyish glance he gave the pasties. His face was mischievous and hopeful, and with a look of studied coolness she murmured, 'Need someone to try a pasty before I dare offer them to the ladies. Wonder if I can impose on you to taste one for me?'

He cocked an eyebrow at her and she could no longer hold herself in check and laughter bubbled. Her face was flushed from the oven and her nose and cheeks were smudged with flour, and with an answering smile he stepped closer to look down into eyes sparkling and vivacious with laughter. Then he touched her on the nose and he held his finger up before her and she saw the pale white of flour and her eyes widened in concern with the laughter dying on crestfallen lips. 'Oh!' she gasped, 'I must look terrible!' Lowering her face as though to hide it from sight but he lifted her head with gentle hands.

'You look good enough to eat and, like your kitchen, a delight to the eye.'

His complimentary words brought a pleasing sensation, then she said accusingly, 'Did that on purpose!'

'Couldn't let you get away with such cheek.'

'You won't taste my pasty, then?'

'Only if you promise not to laugh at me.'

'I'll try hard not to.'

With this light-hearted exchange he took a pasty and stood warming his back to the cooking range. The pasty was delicious and hot and he drew a quick breath to cool his mouth. He had seen her often in these last few days, calling at the *Blue Lugger* in the early evening and spending a pleasant half-hour with a jug of ale and deliberately choosing a time when the tavern was quiet and before the customers arrived in numbers and when he hoped she would have a few minutes to spend in conversation. Never staying long at the Inn, suspecting that Glyn Ralston might not approve of a restraining influence on his free-spending customers. So he would drink his ale and enjoy Janie's company for a short while and they soon established an easy and comfortable relationship and she more and more appreciated the compelling, gentle courtesy of this man who had so recently taken a place in the centre of village life and found herself looking forward to his evening visit.

In return, Mathieson had come to rely on the judgment of this strangely mature young woman. Especially when he needed to enquire on some intimate detail of the community, some matter perhaps that could only be judged from experience and stranger that he was, there were many such details. As he enjoyed the pasty he sensed Janie to be of unusually serious demeanour and now the good-humoured exchange was over she seemed to have difficulty meeting his gaze, and he opened conversation with. 'If you had been cook on my last ship, the *China Star*, I don't think I could ever have left her.' A deliberately provocative comment that succeeded in bringing her eyes back to his face.

'Sometimes wonder about that,' she said in musing tone, 'you always seem more like a seafarer than a man of the church?'

'You're prejudiced because you are well aware of my former life.'

His voice held a quiet authority that seemed to reach out and embrace her, but she continued with her train of thought to state, 'You and Jonathan are so alike in many ways, and yet . . . ?' Hesitating as though confused, and he thought that whatever troubled her this morning had much to do with Rudd.

'I haven't seen Jonathan or your Simon for a few days,' he said, 'or the other crewman, Jake,' adding, 'your brother and Jonathan appear to be very close friends as well as shipmates.'

'Simon worships and tries his best to be just like him.'

'Quite a remarkable man is Rudd, outwardly carefree and nonchalant yet with great qualities of understanding and integrity.' Scrutinizing her face that just then betrayed a tell-tale flush but her eyes evaded as he said, 'I can easily understand how Simon admires him. Something to do with the manner in which Rudd lives his life because such buccaneering style has always been envied and imitated.'

'He seems to have changed of late,' she said, 'in a way I cannot explain but almost as though he is finding life dull and restrictive.' She spoke in a questioning tone that puzzled him and he looked at her for a long moment.

'The Jonathan Rudd's of this world,' he said at last, 'often find everyday life restrictive for they are by instincts adventurers and explorers who need the stimulus of fresh horizons and the challenge of finding new worlds. This is life itself to such men and while they themselves find it reward enough, I fear it is a very private course they sail and one that can be heart breaking for those who seek to love them in the kind of demanding way which can only bring sorrow and loneliness.'

Sensing again the strange melancholy that occurred when speaking of his former life, she commented, 'You have very cleverly switched the conversation away from yourself.'

'Only because it seemed to be what you wanted, and because I need to find out just what troubles your mind today. Tell me, Janie . . . are you afraid he has the need to look for these new horizons? Is this the thought that brings the cloud to your pretty face this morning?' As he said this he remembered Rudd's declaration of intent about Janie when aboard ship, and she thrust her hands into the pockets of her apron and looked uncomfortably at him.

'Something like that,' she said in sotto voice.

'Are you going to tell me about it?'

'Don't know if there is anything to tell.'

‘Are you in love with him?’

This query brought sudden and disconcerting conflict. She idolised Rudd and since her early teens had never given a passing thought to another man. Not until recently? He stood there in easy stance, so relaxed and somehow comforting in this wonderful communion they so often shared. Then she said candidly, ‘Think I have always loved him.’

‘Perhaps it is the thought of him leaving here that bothers you.’ Looking at her as if trying to read her mind, he said, ‘I begin to see, he has asked you to sail away with him.’

‘Not quite in those words,’ her eyes never left his and they were piercing into his innermost thoughts as she added, ‘but he is going to.’

‘Would you leave with him?’

‘He hasn’t asked me yet, I don’t know!’ She seemed confused and her face was flushed and he looked at her but said nothing because he didn’t know what to say, but she raised her head to look back at him and plaintively ask, ‘What do you think I should do?’

‘It’s not for me to influence you.’

‘Help me, Richard, I can’t decide on my own!’ It was a cry from the heart that shook Mathieson to the core and he strode across and took her by the hands.

‘Listen to me, Janie.’ His voice was commanding and he gazed deep into her eyes and said firmly and with every word measured. ‘Decisions!

So momentous that they will affect you for the rest of your life can only be made by yourself . . . because it is your life and you alone must decide on the course it will take and only time will tell whether your judgment has been proved wrong: but if it so proves, then you must be able to face the stark fact that the decision was yours, for at such a time it is all too easy to abdicate responsibility and lay blame on the shoulders of anyone who may have influenced such a decision.' Clenching his fingers tightly over her wrists he said in distraught tone, 'Oh, Janie, can you not understand what I am saying?'

'Not really!' She looked at him and he looked back because she spoke in a pensive sort of voice he couldn't understand and her look intensified as she went on to say, 'But then I'm a woman and cannot think as a man and I haven't the strength to make such a decision on my own. I need someone with your understanding to lean on.' A hint of urgency appeared in her voice and her eyes were wet with starting tears as she pleaded, 'You could guide me, I trust your judgment more than you realise . . .' Hesitating, she went on in questioning tone. 'If you were to ask me to stay?'

'You are not being fair. How can I presume to interfere? It is up to you alone to balance what you have here against the kind of life you would have with Jonathan.' The thought was provocative and he added, 'I think somehow that sailing with Rudd would never lack interest or excitement more than you will ever find here in Perranwithick, but the one sure thing I do know is that you would leave an undeniable void in me if you should decide to go.'

'But you won't ask me to stay?' her voice was too calm.

'It is not my decision.'

'Then if Jonathan wants me I'll sail with him to the far corners of the earth!'

She was defiant now, and challenging, and he remained silent for a brief moment, then said, 'Only if desire is strong enough can a way be found and your decision will eventually follow whichever of your desires is the stronger.'

'So be it, Reverend!' Mood broken she turned from him and began to fill a basket but her hands were fluttering-busy and her brightness artificial. 'Think your ladies at the church will be getting hungry.'

'Janie!' He couldn't leave it this way and spoke in so distressed a voice that she had cause to regret her outburst.

'Don't look so worried,' she remonstrated, 'you can't carry everyone in the village around on your shoulders.'

'Feel that I've disappointed you in some strange way I don't know about.'

'No! It was hardly fair of me to embarrass you.' Smiling, more like her normal self. 'Come in to-night,' she said, 'and I'll pour you a glass of wine to make up for my childishness.'

Far from convinced, he said, 'Sounds good to me.'

But his mood remained one of deep reflection as he regained the roadway and walked slowly up the long slope. Through the lych gate and up the gravel path then pausing at the open door with the basket in his hand. There was a difference about the old building, a sereneness that intrigued and excited. Moving through the vestibule he eased through the double doors.

The transformation was complete and overwhelming! Gone were the cobwebs and dust that had festooned the windows. The floor shone and the little chairs gleamed in straight-backed and uniform rows. The flaking patches on the walls were almost hidden from view by hanging baskets of flowers. Indeed! Flowers everywhere: great bowls of brilliance. The red and gold paint of the carved ornamental woodwork of the rood screen shone bright in newly found splendour and a ray of multi-colour light streamed from the high, stained glass window to illuminate the whole nave and, wonder of wonders? Sinking to his knees as the slow, stately chords of a church organ began to flood the ancient building with heavenly sound. Tears filled his eyes and he raised his head.

The crippled figure of Thomas White looked almost beautiful as he sat at the organ. His one good hand moved with delicate grace over the keys and the gnarled fingers of the other hovered with sure knowledge on the ivory stops and the musician was lost in his work, oblivious to everything about him and as the music soared up into the barrel-vault ceiling the church resounded with a glory that sent Mathieson's head down on to his knees. The music finished with one last glorious chord then died away and he rose in the embrace of silence to focus on the organ as Thomas moved from his stool and turned to face him. Mathieson saw not the deformity or the twisted side or the hunched shoulder but only the look of exquisite rapture on his face, and as Thomas looked at him, he could see unshed tears in the soft eyes then the little man sat down again at the organ and a sob shook him and his head drooped on to his hands in silent prayer.

Mathieson's eyes were burning and with his gaze misted over as he turned to find the Ladies of the Committee kneeling in unison and tears were streaming down every face and he looked over their bowed heads. 'Ladies,' he said in a voice husky with humility, 'what can I say in thanks? You have transformed this humble House into a chapel of colour and brightness. You have filled it with glorious light and we have been blessed with wondrous music, and for this one moment I thank you!' He then said in reverent voice, 'Glory be to the Father.' Holding them thus, he then bade them rise and wiping the back of his hand across his eyes. 'Should have given me some warning, for a man doesn't relish being caught so unprepared.' Then, remembering the basket of food. 'Perhaps we can take refreshment together, courtesy of Janie Ralston, but if you will first excuse me, I must thank our musician.' The ladies moved away with their voices mute and wondering.

Thomas White sat slumped over the organ keys and Mathieson placed his hands on the hunched shoulders and raised him up. 'Thomas, that was so wonderful . . . music of such beauty for which I cannot begin to thank you.'

'This old church is coming back to life, Reverend, so I wondered? Hoped? If I might help in some small way.' The soft eyes held a glow of serenity and a smile played on the sensitive mouth as he rose unsteadily to his feet. 'If there are to be any thanks?' he said, 'I am the one to offer them.'

Mathieson couldn't believe, or take his eyes from the sudden pride revealed on the face of Thomas White. His head was held high and reflected light from the gable window seemed to linger on him as though in welcome and as though in greeting then he started to shuffle away but turned back. 'Reverend,' he said through trembling lips, 'you have helped me to come alive again, kindling hopes in me I thought were long dried and as dust in the bitterness by which I was consumed. Yet? You seek to thank me!' Shaking his head in disbelief he began to move his ungainly body forward.

‘Thomas, will you take refreshment with us?’

‘Let us not embarrass the ladies.’ The voice was calm and the harshness that once characterized his tone had disappeared as he stated, ‘Today has been more than sufficient, for a start back at least.’

Joining the ladies in the vestry, Mathieson helped himself to a sandwich. Mrs Farquasan looked at him as if she had something to say but turned hastily away without saying anything. All voices were hushed and muted in the confines of the vestry and with a quizzical glance he enquired, ‘Why so quiet, ladies?’ One of them whom he knew as Mrs Rose Endacott, offered the thought that seemed in all their minds.

‘Think we’re all overcome by the revelation we have encountered today, and also much bewildered by the man who played the organ so magnificently.’

‘Thomas White . . . I feel sure you all know how long he has been here?’

‘For several years,’ agreed Mrs Farquasan, ‘and yet we didn’t even know his name.’

Blanche Tremaine seemed to concur with this sentiment as she murmured, ‘We’ve never had reason to suspect he was such a talented creature . . .’ hesitating on the last word, she then added, ‘he’s always seemed so wild and frightening.’

‘Never mind what has been,’ he said sternly, ‘I think and hope that he is going to find a place in our village community in future and I’ll be looking to you, ladies, for help in bringing him out of this recluse-like existence with which he has surrounded himself.'

'After today,' said Rose Endacott with feeling, 'and after listening to his music I'll do anything you ask of me and I'm sure I speak for us all.'

Unanimous nods of agreement and he began to hope that the cripple's days of loneliness would soon be over and he made a little speech to thank them once more after which Blanche assumed control again and mustered her troops for departure. 'The next job is to paint the church,' she said with emphasis. Eyes hardening at the thought, she promised. 'We'll get the men organized for that, just leave it to me, Reverend.'

He followed them out and as they gained the entrance he noted that the flowers on Agnes Plympton's bonnet were covered in grey dust and impulsively choosing a white bloom from a nearby bowl he tucked the flower into the band of her bonnet. 'Such a lovely hat, Agnes, deserves the colour of fresh flowers.'

Miss Plympton's hands fluttered like two frightened birds, then she relaxed and said shyly, 'Thank you.'

Bidding them farewell he walked back into the glory of his church.

13

Closing the door behind him Glyn Ralston stepped out into the rear courtyard of the *Blue Lugger*. Then he strode out on the highway and making without sound towards the church. It was the hour of two in the morning. No moon: not a glimmer of light to illuminate his way and darkness wrapped him in an all-embracing cloak as he strode cautiously up the slope. His head turned constantly to make sure there was no one about to observe his movements but at this hour every window was shuttered and all decent, law-abiding folk were in bed and fast asleep.

He stole past the churchyard and crept around to the rear hedge. Then, moving aside a section eased through and pulled the hedge together behind him. Now in the graveyard he moved slowly between the rows of brooding headstones. A bat swooped low out of the black night sky, startling him, an owl hooted in eerie association and he shuddered in distaste. 'Enough to scare a man silly,' he muttered. Pausing at the double headstone with the two dancing cherubs he squatted with his head cocked in listening pose then reached into a vest pocket for his watch but it was too dark to see the fingers so he replaced it with disgust. Minutes passed and still he crouched, waiting. Then he heard a furtive sound from below the marble slab. Came a muffled knock, repeated three times. Ralston straightened and reached for one of the cherubs. It was carved from local stone and heavy but his powerful hands lifted it with ease. The base had been chiseled into a deep collar and placing the cherub on the grass verge he plunged his hand into the empty socket. A click came from the depths of the grave and the marble slab began to tilt and lift without sound on balancing weights to rest upright against the headstone.

A dim glow from a shielded lantern revealed a set of stone steps and the tousled head of Jonathan Rudd emerged. 'Flamin' cold down there,' he said with a shiver. Cold it may have been but his brow was wet with perspiration and spreading patches of damp had formed on his shirt below the shoulders. .

'Don't hang about,' growled Ralston, 'this place is too creepy for me.'

'Better men than us have used this route over the years.' Glancing down Rudd said in whisper, 'Ready, Jake?'

Jake Ward now appeared bearing a wooden cask that he hefted over to Rudd then reached down to where Simon was ready with a similar cask. They brought up a total of eight casks and these were stowed in a row on the damp grass. The three who then emerged from the grave were dressed in long flowing shirts of deathly white that seemed to give off some strange phosphorescent glow. Rudd handed a similar garment to Ralston and they stood by the grave like four ghouls out of some fearful horror story.

'Don't see why we have to wear these robes?' grumbled Simon.

'Tradition, lad,' said Rudd in suitably weird tone. 'If any of our brave villagers should see us they would run for their lives and the legends of the graveyard and the ghosts will circulate freely again.' His laugh resounded macabre in the darkness as he said, 'Many desperate men have walked the graveyard in this ghastly garb . . . would you have us break faith with their memory?'

Without further ado Ralston again worked the controlling lever and Rudd eased the slab into place over the gaping tomb. He spread soil around the edges of the slab and with the gravestone rearranged to satisfaction the four men each took two of the heavy casks and forming a silent line crept around the graveyard and through the accommodating gap in the hedge into the roadway beyond. They moved with great care but with no real fear of discovery for the scary reputation of the graveyard made certain of seclusion on so dark a night.

But this night was different! A lean figure eased from behind the cover of a nearby gravestone and moved with ghostly quiet in the wake of the smugglers, a further apparition that surely must have made the any curious onlooker flee in panic. Mathieson had dressed in dark clothes and his feet were bare to prevent any giveaway sound and he paused for a speculative look at the cherubs before resuming pursuit. He had kept vigil in this manner for the last two nights, because keen observation of Rudd's movements, together with the mystery of the double grave and the stories of the churchyard haunting, had caused him to seek confirmation of his suspicions.

As the party halted for a rest under the shelter of an overhanging bush, Rudd queried, 'Hope Will's expecting us?'

'Course he is, though he's grumbling about having to stay up so late.'

'You know we dare take no chance of the new minister being about. Said only the other day that the less he knew the better would be his peace of mind.'

'Will's taking out the brandy in the morning under a load of hay.' Ralston then counted aloud. 'Two for Sandford Barton and one each for Jack Trevelyn, Peter Farnweather, Smethurst and Richardson.'

'Pay's better than fishing,' said Rudd cockily.

Mathieson had achieved all he had set out to do and quietly retraced his footsteps while the other four made their laborious way to the farmhouse of Will Perryman.

The following morning: chill north easterly blowing with boisterous force through the village whipping the strewn leaves of autumn into swirling maelstroms against any sheltered corner. A troop of four horsemen trotted up the lower end of the main street, reining to a halt outside the *Blue Lugger* and dismounting. Leaving one in charge of the horses the others marched to the Inn doorway. As was customary during the hours of daylight the front door stood open and without knocking the three men pushed into the entrance hall.

Glyn Ralston was behind the bar polishing glasses. Hearing the sound of forced entry he was about to investigate when the bar door crashed open. Over the years Glyn had learned to control his temper but this kind of visitation aroused immediate anger and throwing down his cloth he stormed to confront the intruders. 'You'd better have good reason for this outrage!'

Faraday, waving an official document in his face, said bluntly. 'This warrant is reason enough. We're here to turn you over and if you know what's good for you . . . co-operate!'

'Bloody Excise are all the same! Can't leave

a man to run a decent hostelry without always looking to make trouble! You'll find no short measures in my house so get on with your turning over!'

'I'm not here to look for your cheating short measures,' replied Faraday disdainfully, 'at least, not today, such a pleasure I'll reserve for another time. No, Mr Suspect Ralston, today I'm looking to perhaps find a somewhat larger stock of brandy than expected in such a miserable tavern.' His tone was contemptuous and the deliberate provocation brought added fury to Ralston. The *Blue Lugger* was his pride and joy and enjoyed the justifiable reputation of being the most popular hostelry in the area.

'I run a fair house, Faraday,' he growled, and moved as if to bar entrance to his tap room in a stance that stopped short when Janie came hurrying in and a look of dismay clouded her face as she saw the unmistakeable signs of confrontation.

'What is it, father,' she said in startled voice, 'why are these officers here?'

Faraday smiled at her and bowed courteously. 'Miss Ralston I presume, had no idea such a lovely young woman resided at the Blue Lugger or I would certainly have called on you much earlier.'

Janie wasn't impressed by his smooth manner. She had heard much about the Excise Officer from her brother Simon, and nothing to his credit. Regarding him apprehensively, she replied, 'And you are Captain Faraday.' Realising that no advantage could be gained by antagonizing so powerful an officer she took his outstretched hand to smile sweetly at him and say, 'How nice to have such a gallant officer here in Newlyn.'

Ralston frowned in puzzlement at the soothing note in her voice but Faraday took the compliment as being no more than his due 'This visit is going to be more interesting than I had envisioned,' he said. Keeping her hand captive he felt a flush of pleasure when there was no immediate attempt at withdrawal and her cheeks flushed as his gaze traveled with covert scrutiny over the curves of her body, then he gestured in the direction of his men 'With my deepest regret, Janie,' he said in smooth tone, 'but we are here to check your father's stock. Purely as a matter of routine of course and only in the line of duty would we seek to intrude on you.' This young woman was having a peculiar effect on Faraday: her flushed and lovely face almost causing him to forget he had come with the express intention of discrediting her father. Then the persistent, nagging memory of Rudd returned and his calculating mind took over and he relinquished his hold on her hand. 'I have a warrant to search this hostelry from top to bottom.' Gesturing impatiently and two of his men straightaway trooped behind the bar and began to check the contents of the kegs of wine and spirits, tasting each keg to ensure the contents were as labeled.

When they came to the cask marked "brandy" they drew a small measure into a clean wineglass and placed it on the counter for Faraday's inspection. Lifting the glass to the light he sniffed at the bouquet before tasting, then rolled it round his tongue in practiced manner. 'Didn't realise you stocked Spanish brandy?' he said with deliberate query.

'Don't try your devious ways with me, Faraday,' scorned Ralston, 'you know damn well you are tasting French cognac!'

'Take it you can show a receipt for this – er – cognac?'

'I can!'

'I'll see it then?'

'Bring in the brewery file and the accounts ledger, Janie please.' Ralston glared at him as he said this, but his scrutiny was returned with equally cold eyes. .

'In the meantime,' said Faraday, 'I will inspect your cellar.'

'I've nothing of interest to you in my cellar.'

'We'll soon find out,' said Faraday.

The Excise man in the street outside pulled up the collar of his greatcoat and shivered. Wind plucked at the tails of his coat and blew icy cold around his thin legs and while the horses stamped restlessly at the roadway a heavily laden cart lumbered down the street from the direction of the church, drawn by a shire horse of deep golden colour with its mane tossing in the wind.

Will Perryman loved his horse and much of his time went in grooming the giant mare and in polishing the leather and brass work of her harness until it gleamed. The shire seemed well aware of the interest taken in her appearance and always stepped out in noble fashion with great legs pumping in a rhythmic gait of pure majesty. Perryman's nose glowed red in the chill of the morning. The stub of a clay pipe protruded from the thick, wiry beard and moustache that hid his mouth, and the soft cap that always adorned his head was pulled low over his forehead. Such of his face as could be seen was dark and inscrutable.

'Whoa, girl!' Stopping his hay cart outside the Inn he wiped his nose with a red-spotted handkerchief. 'What brings you out here, John Agget?'

'Mornin' Will,' said the Excise man. Leaving his charges for a minute he stepped out into the roadway and stroked the shire's neck. 'You're looking very smart this morning, Joanna.' The shire tossed her head in agreement and Agget grinned at her then, nodding towards the doorway of the Blue Lugger, explained, 'Captain's inside with three men, he thinks there is some smuggled brandy about and suspects Glyn of receiving.'

Agget managed to sound sympathetic and Will

grinned as he said, 'Your Captain seems to enjoy wasting his time,' leaning back against the bales of hay that towered behind, he added, 'Glyn won't be too pleased to be rummaged over.'

'Probably not, but Faraday is determined to catch someone out.' Lowering his voice as he stated, 'Too bloody high and mighty for my choice, thinks he's far too good for the likes of us!'

'He'll soon tire of chasing straws in the wind.' Will stuffed his unlit pipe between his teeth. 'Can't spend all morning hanging about, I've a long way to go.' Looking down from the driving seat he said, 'Why not come over one evening, John, I've a jug of home brew I think you'll enjoy,' adding slyly, 'long as you don't tell your Captain about it?'

'It's not your home brew he wants to get his hands on. Thanks, Will, but with Faraday in his present mood we're all on twenty-four hour call. Ask me again later.'

'Better hurry, it's too good to last!'

Will spoke quietly to his shire. The mare's shoulders hunched into her work and the laden cart trundled away from the *Blue Lugger*. Looking back with a grin, Will murmured to himself, 'Now what was it Glyn said? Two for Sandford Barton and one each for Jack Trewelyn and the others.'

* * *

The Excise man kicked down the flap of the trapdoor leading down into the cellar and announced, 'Clean as a new pin!'

Faraday was studying the accounts book brought in by Janie and he now looked at Ralston. 'The last receipt from your brewery for brandy is dated two months ago,' he mused, 'yet yonder cask is still half-full.'

'Don't get many spirit drinkers in the *Blue Lugger*,' replied Ralston bluntly, 'my customers are mainly poor folk who can't afford such luxuries.'

Glancing at him and then at Janie as though satisfied, Faraday said, 'I won't trouble you any further this time.' Handing the accounts book to her with a flourish. 'You write a very neat hand, my dear.'

She smiled at this, pleased at the compliment and by the way his brusque and frightening manner had disappeared. He took her hand. His fingers were soft and moist and she resisted a wild impulse to snatch away from his grasp as he bowed low over her hand. 'May I perhaps have the pleasure of calling on you again?' Beckoning his men to leave, he said, 'Purely in a personal capacity of course, for I wouldn't wish to pursue the thought that the proprietor of the *Blue Lugger* could be involved in contraband . . . especially when he has such a lovely daughter.' Sibilant tone, that had Ralston starting forward but Janie moved between him and Faraday.

'We'd be most pleased to have you call on us in your leisure time, Captain,' she said, 'and will look forward to your next visit.'

Faraday bowed his head to her and his heels clicked in salute and, regarding her with calculating eyes. 'Your servant, Janie,' he said in gallant voice. 'May I further hope that you might call on me at my office when next in Newlyn?'

This was more than she had bargained for and she hesitated in the face of this invitation: she was getting in deep water! Then her shoulders straightened and she said, 'I seldom have time to spend in Newlyn, but my father and I will be glad to call at your office when we next have occasion to be in town.'

'I'll be waiting, with impatience!' With these expectant words he wheeled and strode away and as the Excise noisily departed Ralston glared at his daughter.

'Never thought to hear my Janie making up to a monster like Faraday?'

Admonishment in his voice and she replied heatedly, 'Perhaps you'd rather I spat in his face! Do you think he would have given up so easily if he hadn't got his eye on me instead of on his business? We can't afford to have him as an enemy, even if it means I have to be nice to him.' Smiling in self-satisfied reflection, she added, 'I found him quite charming and you must admit, the Captain has a certain style about him.'

To which Ralston replied heatedly, ‘If he so much as lays a wrong finger on you he’ll find that charm and style are of little use to a dead man!’

14

Engrossed in the accounts of his vast estate Sir Harry Sedgewick gloomily realised that the annual loss incurred would encroach even further into his private income and the foul mood brought on by this confirmation increased when Hawkins the butler entered to announce, 'Captain Faraday to see you, sir.'

'Hell!' Pulling hard on a clay-stemmed pipe and glowering at the butler as though it was his fault. He had no liking for Faraday, even less for his smooth, condescending manner and, not wishing to entertain him alone, snapped, 'Show him in, serve coffee, and ask her Ladyship to join us.'

The footman scurried away and after a polite knock, Faraday strode in. Resplendent in dress uniform with epaulettes of gold at the shoulder the Captain seemed in a mood of anticipation and greeted his host with a robust:

'Sir Harry, I bid you good morning!'

'You've had a long ride, Captain, before we discuss the reason for your visit may I offer a glass of wine?'

He poured ruby wine and Faraday took a glass and sipped appreciatively before saying, 'I had hoped to have the pleasure of again meeting with Lady Sarah and your lovely daughter.'

Sir Harry winced inwardly at the suave tone. 'Sarah will be here directly,' he said, 'but Cassy is out riding.'

'I here she sometimes rides on the beach.'

'Why the devil do you say that? My daughter rides anywhere she pleases!'

'Just a passing observation,' said Faraday in sly tone. Just then the butler appeared with a silver tray that exuded a fragrant aroma of coffee and preceding Lady Sarah.

'Good to see you, Captain,' she said, 'and how splendid you look this morning.'

'Charming as ever, my Lady,' he said, bending low over her hand

Her Ladyship welcomed gallantry, a commodity much lacking in her normal daily routine, and completely ignored her husband's grimace. She poured coffee and they stood for a few minutes making polite conversation, then Sir Harry interrupted to say, 'I imagine this isn't merely a social call.' He wanted to get back to the mystery of his accounts and his tone bordered on impatience.

'Now, Harry,' admonished Lady Sarah. 'Let us just enjoy the pleasure of the Captain's company for a while longer before I have to endure your boring talk of business.'

Her hospitable tone pleased Faraday. 'Don't think you will find the reason for my visit so tedious,' he said with confidence evident in his tone, 'for the information I have for you has been acquired through much effort on my part.' Allowing this observation to register he went on with. 'You will certainly agree that I have acted diligently on your behalf, and in return,' he added significantly, 'I would hope that if you are ever in possession of information that may assist my own investigations you will do all in your power to bring the facts to my notice.'

'Wish you'd get to the point!'

Sir Harry couldn't envisage any likelihood of providing such information and Faraday's eyes narrowed at the brusque tone then reaching into his pocket he brought out a long envelope bearing an official seal on the closure. Pausing for a moment in anticipation of the interest this action would create, he announced, 'This letter, from an acquaintance highly placed in the Port of London, is in reply to my enquiries about your Reverend.' He then prompted. 'You may recall that I mentioned the name of Mathieson to be familiar.'

'For God's sake get on with it!'

Sir Harry's irate tone brought a flash of

irritation to Faraday's face. He didn't appreciate being on the receiving end of his own demanding mode of address and thought his host needed a lesson in manners and thought he was about to get one. Regarding the sheet of notepaper he had removed from the envelope he said arrogantly, 'It would be simpler if I read this communication directly to you.' Receiving no acknowledgement he looked keenly at them and began to read out.

'My dear Captain Faraday,

In reply to your recent letter I forward the following information.

It appears that one Richard Mathieson sailed for some considerable time on the clipper *China Star* owned by the Far Eastern Trading Company. My enquiries reveal that Mr Mathieson resigned his position as First Mate following an incident on a return voyage from Hong Kong during which a member of the crew met an unfortunate death. No action seems to have been taken about this incident and I have encountered much difficulty in obtaining further information but my untiring efforts on your behalf leave me in no doubt that the unfortunate seaman met his death at the hands of the said Richard Mathieson.

Hoping this information is of value . . . I remain.

Yours faithfully, etc.'

'I don't believe it!' Cathryn Sedgewick in the doorway glaring accusingly at Faraday as he folded the condemning letter and replaced it in his inner pocket.

'I assure you that these details are from an impeccable source,' he said in disdainful voice.

'No matter how impeccable,' she flared back, 'this allegation is false and completely untrue and I would like to know what purpose you have in bringing this foul lie before us!' Eyes flaming as she demanded, 'What gain can there be in this for you?' She was dressed in riding habit and with whip in hand flicking against her polished boot and her fiery posture giving the distinct impression that she would welcome a chance to use it on Faraday.

'Steady now, Cassie', remonstrated Sir Harry, 'I did agree with the Captain's suggestion that he check on Mathieson, though I never imagined we'd be confronted with a statement like this?'

'Could be another Mathieson,' interrupted Lady Sarah. Moving across to Cathryn and joining with her in a stare of worried consternation at the Excise officer, she stated. 'I agree with her . . . Richard is a fine and gentle man and I cannot believe him capable of killing someone.'

'How do we know what he was before he came to Perranwithick?' replied Sir Harry, 'but more important! What are we going to do about him?'

Appealing to her mother, Cathryn anxiously stated, 'If we allow such a vile story to circulate it could ruin any hope Richard has of settling here.'

Her distress was obvious and Lady Sarah

placed her arm round her daughter in support. 'She's right, Harry,' she said in worried voice, 'we cannot lend our support to such a monstrous allegation.'

In the face of their combined appeal Sir Harry didn't know what to say and running a perplexed hand through his hair he looked at Faraday in acute dilemma. 'We have our duty to the people of the village,' he said doubtfully, 'but until we can be sure of his past we must be careful to keep this to ourselves.'

'I do not share your regard of Mathieson.' Faraday spoke directly at Lady Sarah and, as if to emphasize his statement, said blandly, 'I happened to observe him only this week carousing on Newlyn dock in association with the unsavoury Rudd and his motley crew, hardly the company in which I'd expect to find the rector of your church.' Then, with an indifferent shrug. 'In any event, I fear the matter is probably out of our hands for very few letters arrive on my desk without their content becoming known to the ever inquisitive men of the Excise.'

'You are despicable!' snapped Cathryn with uncontrolled venom in her voice. 'You deliberately let them have a sight of your letter!'

Her outraged manner brought much satisfaction to Faraday. He had come with the express intention of discrediting Mathieson, and now maliciously thought she may inadvertently be assisting his cause. Foul work accomplished he made ready to depart. Facing them in conceited posture he said, 'I only do my duty as an officer of The Crown. Now, if you will excuse me, I will leave you to think about your very unusual Reverend,' bowing his head in arrogant pose as he added, 'don't bother to show me out.' Clicking his heels in mocking salute he stalked out the door and Lady Sarah looked at her husband in dismay.

'Harry! Whatever have you done?'

'Never cared overmuch for Mathieson,' he blustered and more perturbed than he cared to admit. Not for Mathieson's impending downfall but for the condemnation in the eyes of his wife and especially in those of his daughter. Glaring after the departing figure of Faraday, he growled, 'There goes a man who calculates his every move but what can he hope to achieve by bringing Mathieson into disrepute?' He took Cathryn by the shoulders none too gently to demand, 'Why are you so upset? Has he been trying to see you again without my permission?'

'No, he hasn't!' She was almost at screaming pitch and she squared up to him and cried in tormented tone, 'He's far too honourable to go behind your back!'

'So you have been meeting? On the beach, when you were supposedly out innocently riding!' Blast Faraday, he thought. Where does he gather his information?

'Enough, Harry, leave her alone!' Lady Sarah

took an angry step forward and Sir Harry stood in astonished silence, for she had never spoken to him in such a commanding way. Then she told him to. 'Stick to your horses – you seem to understand them much better than you do your daughter!' Eyes sparking fire as she confronted him and announced in blunt tone, 'No matter what Richard has been in the past I know him to be a wonderful person and would welcome him with open arms should he choose to call on Cassy.' Turning from him, she added scathingly, 'After today I begin to wonder if we are worthy of him.'

Sir Harry was feeling bad enough already but this last attack brought on flaming rage and he shouted at top voice:

'Call on Cassy! I'll see him in hell first!'

15

Reins slack in his hands allowing Mistral freedom to amble leisurely along the narrow path that wound across the lower fields of Sandford Barton. He was returning from a round trip among the outlying farms and cottages, a visit primarily to make sure everyone knew the church would re-open for service on the coming Sunday but the notice had not been received quite so warmly as he had expected after the enthusiasm shown during the past few weeks. It appeared his parishioners were all so heavily committed to their workload that they could find no time for worship: a unanimous refusal that puzzled him deeply.

Morose thoughts. Even Cathryn seemed to be avoiding him. She never rode to the beach to see him and their relationship had taken on a dismal aspect of stalemate and though he still thought the fault was his own and could understand her reticence, why had everyone else rejected him?

Autumn surrounded him in glorious colour. The trees were shedding the last of their copper foliage and Mistral's hooves made barely a whisper through the carpet of fallen leaves and he rode with shoulders slumped and his mind hovering gloomily on the strange dismissal he had encountered this day. Then a flush of pleasure drove away melancholy as he caught sight of her Palomino stallion tethered under the spreading branches of a huge oak tree, close to a barn-like building, the stallion's coat blending so discreetly with the background it was almost undetectable except from close to. Dismounting with anticipation he walked around the barn and finding a rear door open moved quietly inside hoping to surprise her then an urgent rustling in the hay behind a wooden barrier brought apprehension. Revolt! And surging disbelief!

They lay amidst the hay: and with a gasp and with a pain that was a knife thrust in his chest he saw the matt of fair hair on the lower back of the man whose buttocks jerked rhythmically and with controlled force into the white thighs that spread wide beneath him and in this devastating moment he also saw the long, chestnut hair cascading over the creamy-rounded shoulders of the woman writhing ecstatically on the couch of straw. Then her eyes opened and a look of horror flared and at the same instant the man realised their passionate embrace had come under scrutiny and the animal jerking stopped short but Mathieson turned from them with a sob wracking uncontrolled from the depths of his being and his eyes seemed without sight as he reached out for support onto the low, dividing structure.

Scrambling to his feet Jonathan Rudd muttered awkwardly, 'Sorry you had to see this, Reverend.'

Mathieson gripped the hard oak partition with an intensity that made his knuckles show white and his head drooped down on his hands for an unbearable moment then, forcing upright, he turned reluctantly to face them. Rudd's shirt now covered his upper legs but his trousers concertinaed about his ankles so he jerked then up and tight-buckled his belt but Mathieson's gaze riveted only on her as she sprawled face down as if hiding from sight, and the stark emotion on his face was reflected in Rudd's voice as he blurted. 'Don't blame Cassy! Sometimes feelings of passion overcome all other consideration.'

'What consideration do you place on feelings of friendship and respect?' Mathieson's words spat dire menace, then he growled in accusing voice. 'You couldn't resist the chance of getting your groping hands on her!'

Shrugging at this, Rudd casually replied, 'Have it as you will, Reverend.'

His nonchalant manner brought the white heat of anger as Mathieson demanded, 'Are you asking me to believe this roll in the hay was just a passing thing, that you met here by accident?' He couldn't keep from trembling but knew with a certainty which shattered that Cathryn was a consenting party to Rudd's passionate embrace and in no way being forced to prostrate herself in the dirt and straw of this miserable barn..

'We've met on previous occasions,' admitted Rudd, 'in a need we both had to satisfy.'

'A need such as yours could be satisfied in any waterfront brothel.'

His pain had turned into the dull anguish of despair and the words were deliberately cruel but Rudd had recovered some of his normal cheeky composure and said, though somewhat shamefacedly, 'Gather my pleasures where I can and never yet have I had to buy them.' Adding very quietly, 'I know how she feels about you, Reverend, you are the one who should have been down there with her.'

Mathieson faced him with eyes brooding and his hands a tight ball at his sides, then. Devastation! Betrayal! Agony of mind! All exploding in his brain and for one uncontrollable second he was back! Mate of the *China Star* taking water from no man and meeting violence head on and his fist blasted into Rudd's cocky face and pounding his mouth into a gory mess of blood and battered lips and the sheer force of the strike sent him sprawling into the barrier wall where he lay prostrate with his legs limp on the dirt floor and blood pouring from nose and mouth and trickling down his shirt. Mathieson sagged, made as if to depart, then turned abruptly and went to her. 'Come, Cathryn, I can't leave you this way.' He pulled her unresponsive body upright and straightened her disheveled clothing and he brushed the hair from her cheeks and lifted her face with gentle hands but she shook him off with angry gesture.

'Leave me alone!' she snapped through contorted lips. 'Your charity makes me feel ashamed.'

'Ashamed to be making love with him or just ashamed that I was the one to find out?' He couldn't keep the bitterness from his voice and the way he said this brought a defiant:

'I gave you the same opportunity: blame yourself!'

He knew she could be arrogant but this acid and cold rebuff struck like a cannon ball exploding amidships and he fired back, 'You well know my reasons, and also how much I love and wanted you!'

'Not enough to take me! You weren't man enough!' Embarrassment had given way to spiteful annoyance and she snapped in biting tone, 'The noble-minded Reverend, keeping himself pure and under control but whose breeches were to bursting every time he touched me!'

Her words bore the cutting edge of truth and had him immediately defensive as he retorted, 'I told you once before that this couldn't be the way of things between us. Scorn me if you will but realise also that I have not the freedom of a Jonathan Rudd.'

'You talk so grandly about measures of love,' she said heatedly, 'but just what is your own measure of love? I know you're a man with desires and needs like every male animal. I remember how it was with you. Knew the passion of your embrace! Arousing . . . only to put me down in frustration!' Her voice took on a sly note as she goaded, 'Surely there can be no sin in the fulfillment of this great love you profess to hold for me?'

Vindictive words, but echoing many of his own doubts, and the tone of her voice caused him to state in rebuking tone, 'We have also been endowed with a quality that places us above the animal. The ability to think and to maintain honour and self-respect and to also know the vast chasm between love and naked passion.'

'Dedicated as ever!' The reply had only served to infuriate and she scorned contemptuously, 'But it is all too one-sided because the sacrifice has been mine alone and brought only unhappiness! How I have lain awake night after night longing for you and for the communion of our bodies?' Hereditary Sedgewick instincts in revolt against this seeking to justify were evident in the rising tone of her voice as she cried, 'But no more! I can no longer exist in this ivory tower of yours . . . I'm a woman, not a pedestal puppet! A woman with a need to be loved! Someone for the touching and the taking! I tried so hard to make you aware but you failed me when I most needed you! Jonathan at least has no such inhibitions and took me for what I am.' Her voice faltered, then rallied once more as she stated, 'And he's the only man I knew who could even begin to compare with you.'

He had no defence and knowing the truth in her words and sensing the conflict within her, said dolefully. 'Oh, Cathryn! Such a terrible waste and what a fool I have been: to you and to myself.' He made as though to touch her but she shook him off.

'Don't blame yourself too much, for you have no fault here.' Finding composure enough to face him squarely now she continued in quieter tone, 'I hoped to submerge these desires in the warmth and comfort of your strength but I finally succumbed, and worse, because I took your love and returned only dishonour.' Her shield of arrogance re-appearing, she concluded icily, 'But understand this, Richard Mathieson, I do what I want to do without apology or inviting any outside judgment on my actions!'

Too consumed with self-accusation he hardly heard her. 'Should have hammered on your father's door!' he cried, 'made him understand how we felt about each other.' Despair shadowing deep in his eyes and on his face and bringing great feeling to his voice and she could no longer hide behind the veneer of pride and arrogance and she knew she had betrayed his love and could not face him ever again and ran out the door before the tears betrayed her! Then immediately, from outside, could be heard the frantic, pounding hooves of the stallion. There came a rustle of hay and Rudd got to his feet and he wiped the back of his hand across his mouth and looked at the smear of blood.

'Few men have hit me like that,' he said through bruised lips, adding wryly, 'and been left standing on their two feet.'

'You're not the only one with passions that can be aroused like a wild animal,' said Mathieson in utter weariness.

'I deserved it,' grimaced Rudd, 'you are worthy of better treatment than I just dealt.'

'Feel more bitter, perhaps, if I didn't realise that Cathryn was equally responsible. As you have already pointed out, you could have just been fulfilling a need.'

Rudd looked at him and the look was one of concern and also of consuming sadness, and the conciliatory words and the reasoning behind them encouraged him to quietly ask, 'Dare I hope we can still be friends?'

'I need to respect a man before I call him friend and you have just forfeited any right to respect.'

'Perhaps one day you will have need of me as a friend.

‘Such friends I can do without. Keep well away from me, Rudd, for every time I see your face I’ll think of you and Cathryn here in the hay on this barn floor and I couldn’t remember this day without wanting to smash you down again!’ He turned away without another word and stumbled through the barn door and not seeing Rudd slump against the rail in defeated posture but he wasn’t the only person left at the scene for outside the barn peering through a knothole in the boarding crouched a ferret-faced figure with a very satisfied expression on his face. Samuel Westlake, labourer on the Sandford Barton estate, again had something of importance to report to Captain Faraday who had promised to be generous on receipt of information pertinent as this and Westlake could already anticipate the delights of the Newlyn taverns with coin to jingle in his pockets. He scurried away and disappeared in the undergrowth.

Back in the barn, Rudd dusted himself down, glanced around, and then said out loud:

‘Reverend Richard Mathieson: you have no idea of the service I have done you this day!’

16

Looking at his congregation with a sense of terrible dismay. He had not expected the church to be full but this lack of response devastated. Service was due to start at eleven but now, only five minutes before the hour, there were just nine people sitting before him.

Janie in the front row, Mrs Farquasan in the second with her back ramrod straight and her mouth in an angry line. An elderly couple he knew only slightly, sat huddled close together halfway up the aisle and close to a group of four strangers whom he assumed to be visitors to the area. Even the Ladies of the Committee had deserted him, with the exception of Agnes Plympton who sat alongside his landlady wearing her little blue bonnet and adorned with a single, fresh cut flower. The morning was fair, no reason for people to stay at home and he just couldn't understand why so few had chosen not to attend his opening service. If nothing else, he thought that curiosity would have brought a reasonable number and he wouldn't have questioned their motives if only they had thought enough of him and their church to come to this new beginning.

Dismissing his morbid train of thought he moved to the doorway of the screen that partitioned off the Altar. Then a smile lit his face and a sudden overpowering warmth filled him within as a shambling, crippled figure came hobbling through the open front door and without looking to left or right shuffled slowly up the aisle with his leg dragging clumsily behind. Mathieson strode to meet him, noting with surprise the badly fitting suit and the polished shoes that Thomas White had found from somewhere.

'Came in by the front door this time, Reverend,' said Thomas. There was an air of calmness and composure about him not previously seen and, unable to speak for a moment, Mathieson turned and walked back with his arm around the thin shoulders.

'You have never been more welcome,' he then said.

'I felt you could use a little support.' Thomas had heard the note of sadness and his eyes reflected deep concern and he said with contempt in his voice. 'I watched and waited and when I realised they weren't coming, I knew the time had come for me to stand up beside you!' Then he announced proudly, 'I'm going to make music for you such as people have never heard, and no more will I bow my head in shame or hide away from the eyes of such an uncaring world.' Halting at the altar threshold to look back at the vacant seats. 'What empty fools these people be!' He sat down at the organ and a great chord thundered and rang out, one of soul-stirring beauty that reverberated back from the domed ceiling, then died away to a low, embracing murmur and he turned and said, 'I'm ready now.'

The Reverend Richard Mathieson turned proudly to his congregation.

'Will you please kneel and join me in prayer.'

They said prayers and sang hymns together and somehow the fact that there were so few didn't matter any more because the music of Thomas White throbbed and soared with great passion around the tiny church and the singing grew in volume as though the singers were themselves inspired by the magnificence of the music flooding up and round and over all. He mounted the pulpit and every face raised to his. The notes he had made were in his hand. He looked at them and crumpled them into a ball and let them fall at his feet. 'The sermon I had prepared seems far too long, and yet not adequate enough.' Looking into every face in turn before continuing with, 'How can I begin to thank you all? You have, today, brought with you the finest gift you possess...the gift of yourself and of your time.'

Though spoken softly the words penetrated into the furthest corner of the little chapel. 'Time,' he then said, 'is a dimension that should not be discarded lightly, but savoured, with every single second being used and treasured, for the span of our lifetime on this earth is so short that we cannot afford to squander any of it in idleness.' Pausing, and a tender smile lit his face, then he went on:

'I'm not suggesting you fill every moment in work, and I do ask you to accept that there has to be something more in life than working for a living. We work to keep fit and well and to pay our way in the world outside. This we must do because a human being needs to be able to live with pride and dignity and in pursuit of this . . . work is a noble and honourable thing.' Breaking his narrative to look down at them, he then stated, 'But leisure time is something of your very own for this is part of your life where you can decide for yourself just what you are going to do with this most valuable of the gifts the Good Lord has bestowed on us.' He slowed his address to emphasize more clearly his next penetrating words. 'I ask you again not to look on this gift lightly but to savour every single second and to grasp it firmly in both hands in a constant search of how to use your precious time wisely, for the furtherance of your own being and for the continuing benefit of the loved ones who already enrich your life.'

Faces raised and every eye on the preacher. Here was no fire and brimstone but a vibrant and commanding voice that had them entranced and reaching into the very depths of emotion. He said again, 'Time . . . this terrible dimension that must eventually devour us? Hold on to it tight but with ever open hands and so be not afraid to relinquish your hold. For in the knowledge that you have taken the span of your life on this earth and dispensed it with compassion and to its entirety, then goodness and mercy shall surely have followed you all of your days and you will come to dwell in the House of the Lord forever!'

They waited, in silence,, but he broke the spell and came down from the pulpit to stand before them. The sermon was over, or so he thought, but they wanted more: and weren't moving! The organ began to throb. Light from the high window streamed in glorious multi-colour illumination down the centre aisle and the church at Perranwithick at that time truly became a House of tranquility and worship.

He spoke again and his voice was consumed with surging emotion as he humbly said, 'You sang so beautifully, would it be too much to ask you to join in one last hymn with me?'

The music soared from behind and they rose as one and sang their hearts out for him and the hymn they sang was "All ye who hear: now to His Temple draw near: joining in glad adoration". The organ played a last diminishing chord, reaching out as if into the heavens then died away into a silence that was awe-inspiring.

He stood waiting as they came slowly out the main doorway and he offered his hand to every one of them. The strangers lingered with him. 'That was one of the most moving hours I have ever known, Reverend,' said one in warm voice. 'The music, the singing and that wonderful, penetrating sermon!' Looking around in amazement, he enquired, 'What kind of people live here that can be so blind to the devout beauty which is offered in this lovely old church?'

Mathieson appreciated the sentiment, he was in dire need of support just then and, after a moment for thought, said in reply, 'They are people who are free to choose, without prejudice and without us finding cause to seek fault.'

They bade him a fond goodbye, and then Mrs Farquasan rushed past touching his arm as she fled. The elderly couple held his hand in close couple then Thomas White shuffled out followed by Miss Plympton and Janie.

'What can I say, Thomas?' Taking his hand and shaking it warmly. 'Your music was wonderful.'

'Wonderful,' echoed Agnes, 'I have never been so enraptured in my life.' Looking at Thomas she suggested in a voice somehow both hoping and vulnerable. 'Could I ask you to share Sunday dinner with me, Thomas?' She added his name in soft and shy tone, and alarm flickered in his eyes.

He looked at Mathieson in a silent plea for support but received no response. It had to be the cripple's own decision and Mathieson couldn't help him in this, but the hesitation wasn't lost on Agnes and her head drooped, and as she walked away she said, 'It would have been so nice to share a meal with someone.'

Thomas stared after her retreating figure with a look of yearning in his eyes.

'Miss Agnes!' Cry tearing from trembling lips and stopping her as she was about to pass through the lych gate and she turned with uncontrolled eagerness as Thomas said, 'Wait for me then!'

Agnes moved towards him, but noting the proud and stubborn lift to the hunched shoulders she stifled her instinctive reaction to help him down the steps and instead reached out in invitation. He looked at her and the look was one of appreciation and there was wonder in the look and he shuffled down to her and his fingers closed on her welcoming grasp and they walked arm in arm through the old gateway and Mathieson's heart seemed about to burst as he murmured, 'There goes a happy couple.'

'You seem to have a wonderful and moving influence on other peoples lives, Reverend,' said Janie, 'but what of your own life?' The last words were delivered with deliberate query and caused his brow to furrow as he glanced curiously at her. Then she asked, 'Have you any idea why the village folk stayed away this morning?'

Shaking his head: the lack of support again bringing conjecture but he had nothing to say in reply and taking a deep breath, she blurted, 'It is being said that you left the sea because you killed a man! They think you are a murderer who can have no rightful place here in the church.'

'So that is the reason?'

His eyes were suddenly vacant and his face was barren and dismay apparent in the slump of his shoulders, in a posture of dejection that she couldn't bear to see and she took his hands and held them tight. 'If only they knew you as I do' she cried, 'they would never be able to countenance so monstrous an allegation,' adding forcibly, 'Richard! You have to stand up and expose this shameful story for the untruth that it is!'

The paleness of his face sent a shock wave through her. The light that had been in his eyes while he watched the union of Agnes and Thomas White had been replaced by dull hopelessness.

'It isn't a lie then?'

The despair in his face confirmed the awful thought 'No,' he said, 'what they say is true!' He freed his hands and held them out. 'I took a man's life with these hands.' Shuddering, as if consumed by the memory, then regaining some vestige of control that allowed him to explain in calmer voice. 'Thought I could hide away in this remote corner of the land. That I might find redemption in the church and by so doing would be able to make amends before the details of my former life became known. A man cannot hide away forever, this I also know, but I just needed a little time.' He tried to smile but failed as he stated, 'Time for redemption, I suppose.' Looking into her eyes as he repeated, 'Time, Janie my love . . . there is never enough time . . . for I surely know it is always too late!'

Her emotion was uncontrollable and her eyes brimmed with tears. 'I know you better than you realise,' she sobbed, 'and I also know you could not take a life so easily. Whatever you have done, I will not accept that you are capable of a cold-bloodied killing?' Her words came quick and angry and indignant now. 'Tell me about it! Let me explain to the village folk so they can have a chance to understand you as I do. So that they too can be judged: by their actions. Oh, Richard, I have to know, for my sake as well as yours!'

Taking her gesticulating hands in his own, he replied, 'One day I'll tell you . . . one day when the pain has gone and it no longer seems to matter. But not yet! I will not erect a barrier of explanation around me. If I am to be judged then let it be fairly and on what I am and what people know me to be.'

'You can see by the way they have ignored you today that you'll never be given the chance to prove yourself and every day will be wasted, just like this one!' She couldn't believe he was so oblivious to public opinion and frustration was evident in the way she said this, but a smile warmed his pale, barren face.

'For once you are wrong,' he said, 'this day is far from wasted. For we have just seen the coming together of two lonely people, joined by an overwhelming need and a compassion that instinctively understands those needs, each for the other. No, Janie, in no way wasted, for today we have been witness to the workings of the Lord in all His infinite wisdom and mystery'.

Moving words that shattered all inhibition and churning deeply into the very depths of her and she wanted to throw her arms round him, and she stared at him wide-eyed and said in trembling voice, 'I love you, Richard!' Blurting out the words: so unpremeditated had been her declaration and she turned away in extreme embarrassment but he straightaway gripped her hands and brought her face to face.

'Oh, Janie,' he said in a voice consumed with tenderness, 'such a capacity for love should not be wasted on one so unworthy.' Drawing her nearer as he added humbly, 'I first have to prove myself before I can accept such a love and before I can return it in equal measure. Can I ask you to give me a little more time to find my place here?'

'Is it not yourself who has said there is never enough time, that it's always too late?' Her cheeks were flaming red but she persisted in her plea. 'Come with me, out into the streets, together we will show them how wrong they are!'

‘They will have to decide for themselves without outside influence. The choice must be their own.’

‘People need guidance,’ she cried insistently, ‘you have to give us some help!’

‘Before I can give such guidance I have to seek my own.’ He turned from her and walked back in the church and his head was down and his whole posture one of defeat and she couldn’t stand it and ran off through the lych gate and down the road towards home but couldn’t see where she was going because her eyes were blind with tears.

17

Autumn lingers late in the temperate climate of West Cornwall but finally and inexorably winter descended on Perranwithick and the ports of Penzanze and Newlyn. The days when the fishing fleet could put to sea became more and more infrequent. Ships lined the dockside with their sails furled and tied down against the fierce gales of winter. The fishermen were mostly idle and as a result short of money, a condition that soon spread through the surrounding townships. The shopkeepers extended credit where practical but their shelves began to run empty and stock difficult to replenish. Even the taverns and inns, usually the last outpost of the free-spending seafarers, felt the effect of the empty pockets of their customers, and apart from the occasional weekend carousing, were hostelries where peace and quiet reigned supreme.

Christmas came and went with its normal flurry

of merry-making and then the cold of January began to bite deep. But the log fires burned with cheery warmth in the open hearths and the light from the tiny cottage windows shone bright over the frost-girdled ships with a glow that seemed to say it all.

"Do your worst, winter, we've weathered your misery many times and you haven't beaten us yet!"

The fishermen took up their trade at every possible chance and braving the terrible winds and seas so cold that the hope of a man surviving an involuntary immersion in its icy clutches was reduced to a few fleeting minutes before his body froze into irresponsiveness and the cold waters took him for their own. Death sailed side by side with such men: a dark angel of sombre shape with arms outstretched and beckoning.

The church at Perranwithick had gradually become a venue for popular Sunday worship. The magic created by the embracing presence of Richard Mathieson, whose sermons were listened to with deep feeling by all who attended, and the devout and moving beauty of the music created by his organist, proved of compelling appeal and the tiny building filled to capacity on every occasion. But still the people of the village ignored their minister, refusing almost unanimously to accept him, and the wonder that was before them in his church went unheeded in their blind refusal to disregard the story of his past: a story that grew more terrible with every malicious telling.

But if they could not accept the wonder so humbly offered others could and did so, and on a Sunday morning the roadway by the churchyard began to be crowded with vehicles and horses. Carriages of all types and of all classes and people from many differing walks of life sat down side by side on the rows of little chairs, for no distinction could be found in the church of Richard Mathieson. The people crowded in their eagerness to hear him speak of the Works of God: and to listen to Thomas White play the organ.

Mathieson would be waiting for them by his open door. Clad confidently now in his robe of office and smiling his gentle smile and as the people came to him they would be warmed by his presence and welcomed by him and by the sound of the organ playing from the depths of the church, a sound that reached invitingly and so very movingly into each and every being who sought to give their time in worship. But the people of the village: his own people? Chose to shut him out of their lives!

Inevitably, such growing acclaim would be found desirable to others and there came insistent requests for Thomas White to play for larger and more influential parishes and Mathieson brandished one such offer as he strode down the centre aisle.

'How would you like to play in the great church at Truro?' he said excitedly.

White's dark eyes lit up but he made no response.

''Tis a mighty organ, Thomas!'

'Do they want you also?'

'My work is here.'

'So is my music.'

Mathieson shook his head wryly and looked at Thomas with affection as he said, 'Seems the whole of Cornwall wants you to play your music for them.'

'Then Cornwall will have to come here to Perranwithick.'

Gazing round the tiny building, Mathieson smiled and said:

'Do you think we can get them all in?'

At the same time there was another confrontation taking place in the library at Sandford Barton. The fire crackled and flamed in the open-hearth fireplace but brought no warmth to the atmosphere as Sir Harry roared, 'You are what!'

Facing him without flinching Cathryn repeated, 'I am with child.'

Sir Harry lurched sideways and his legs seemed unable to support him and he sagged against the oak beam above the hearth. 'God, no!' Clenched fists hammering on the hard wood he turned on his wife and thundered, 'Did you know?'

Lady Sarah recoiled before the accusation in

his voice but found composure enough to admit. 'For some weeks . . . but her condition cannot remain unnoticed for much longer.'

Sir Harry's eyes were filled with pain as he looked at the beauty of his daughter's slender figure. 'Who is he?' he asked with a growl deep in his throat.

'I cannot tell you,' she said quietly.

His response surprised them. Thrusting his arms round Cathryn he pulled her close. 'Don't be afraid, Cassy,' he said, 'you're not the first young girl to be used in this way.' Looking down at her and sorrow softening his words. 'But I must know who is the father.'

His voice was gentle and persuasive and she sagged into his chest. 'Don't ask, Papa, what difference can it make?'

'Makes a lot of difference to me!' Grasping her by the shoulders and his voice held a grim note as he demanded, 'It's Mathieson isn't it?'

'No! It is not Richard Mathieson!'

'Did he take you by force?'

His initial shock had given way to outrage but Cathryn said firmly, 'Nobody took me by force.'

'Then who else but a smooth talking rogue like him could charm your legs open?'

'I tell you again, the father is not Richard Mathieson,' a sob shook her, 'I only wish it were!'

'No good you trying to shield him! Sir Harry remained unconvinced and needing an outlet for inflamed and suspect raging smashed his fist into the palm of the other hand and snarled, 'I'm going to run that murdering, seducing minister of God so far from here that he'll never be seen again.' Eyes vicious and like two pits of hell-fire. 'When I've finished with your Reverend Richard Mathieson,' he stated determinedly, 'he'll be glad to run back into the sea from whence he came.'

'Tell him, Cassy,' said Lady Sarah.

Looking at her mother in amazement she gasped, 'You know?'

'Not really, but I am sure that Richard isn't the father.' Then she pleaded, 'You must tell or you'll be the finish of him.'

Cathryn hesitated, but Lady Sarah's words were very convincing and she confronted them both and said, 'Jonathan Rudd is the father.' The quietness of truth was in her statement but the words were stark in their ears and both registered instant dismay.

'Rudd!' roared Sir Harry. A terrible and unreasoning anger swept him and he shouted in fierce and blinding rage. 'That foul-living scoundrel! How dare he lay hands on my daughter!' Eyes narrowing he stated in out of control voice, 'He'll be made to regret he even so much as looked at you.' He couldn't believe this, and torment and anguish blended into accusation and he looked at her as though she was something despicable and snarled, 'Couldn't have brought more disgrace to yourself and to us if you had deliberately tried!'

In no mood for chastisement she retorted in equally harsh tone. 'What you really mean is that though he is good enough to keep you supplied with cheap liquor he's not nearly good enough for us to associate with.' Her father's tirade had inflamed and incited rebellion and there was venom in her voice and she stood erect and faced him down and fired heatedly, 'At least he's his own man and a sight larger in stature than the simpering over bred idiots that you and your society friends seem to think suitable for me to settle down and live happily ever after with.' Her lip curled as she added scornfully, 'Jonathan is worth a dozen men like these.'

'You have said enough, Cathryn,' admonished Lady Sarah.

Looking at her for support, Sir Harry said, 'She cannot possibly have the child here'.

'My loving father! The grand county squire! You're all puff and wind Sir Harry! Never mind how I feel as long as you aren't embarrassed before all your fine cronies at the Hunt meetings.' Spitting mad and increasingly defiant as she screamed at him. 'Who needs them? They're just hangers on after the free brandy with which you shower them, brandy that Jonathan risks his all to bring across the sea so you can buy your friends with it!'

He reared and his face was livid as she lashed into him and exposing the posturing vanity of the man and causing Lady Sarah to step hastily between a father and daughter so alike in volatile temperament that if left alone they would destroy each other. Taking control of the dangerous confrontation she snapped. 'Now enough, the two of you! My sister in Bath will look after her until the child is born. This will give us all time to adjust and to be able to think more clearly.'

Cathryn had the last word as she stalked out of the library.

'Send me away now I might never come back!'

Sir Harry made as if to follow but Lady Sarah put out a restraining hand. 'Leave her be! We are all much too upset for rational behaviour.'

Alone now in the library he paced to and fro with restless and burning energy and a face like thunder. 'Rudd!' he kept on repeating and the name was like poison on his tongue. Daylight began to fade: the short winter's day receding unnoticed into fast gathering dusk. Still he paced with mind racing and his thoughts a tempest of regret and sorrow and of impending disgrace and with a wild anger that ravaged all reason. Then he stopped in his tracks and a look of determination showed bleak on his face and he sat down at his desk and, picking up a quill pen, started to write.

"Dear Captain Faraday" . . . The letter soon finished, he rang the bell and when his butler appeared, Sir Harry glared at him. 'Send that sneaking fool Westlake to me,' he growled, 'I have an errand for him to run!'

18

The grey light betwixt dark and dawn: *Rose of Endau* beating into the bay against a strong off-shore wind and making little headway on each tack before having to come about again but every short board earning more valuable yards.

'Ready about! Let go and haul! Lee-oh!' The shout repeated over and over and the sweating crew would again heave on the sheet ropes, hauling the sails round and sheeting home before they filled on the opposite tack. Hard work, but the dark cliffs were becoming closer.

Simon glanced warningly back at the steering position. They had delayed overlong on that last tack and he had seen the ominous swell of water over a submerged rock close under the bow as she came about. But picking up smartly the *Rose* ploughed into safe water. Even when they got close enough to drop anchor, thought Simon, they were in for a wet ride ashore with the surf running so strong. Bringing the ship about once again Rudd ran her almost parallel to the shoreline. 'One more board should do it!' Senses tuned to the movement of ship through water and watching the surface with alert eyes and, as they came in close, a startled cry came from Jake Ward amidships.

'Coastguard cutter to larboard!' The shout brought consternation akin to panic as from behind the bend of rocky coastline sped a sleek craft under full working sail. Must be *Intrepid* the new Revenue cutter from Penzance! No time for thought, or conjecture. Rudd had heard she was a fast ship and reacted instinctively.

'Stand by to come about!' The wheel spun and her head came up to seaward bringing the wind almost directly behind and Simon paid out the main sheet until the huge mainsail stood square over the starboard side and the standing rigging of the mast cut deep segments into the full body of the sail. All deceptively quiet now they were running downwind, with the ship surging on the wave crests.

'We won't get round her,' jerked Simon. Sailing at speed the coastguard cutter was taking up a position to intercept: and board!

'Let's see how they like shallow water?' Rudd steered towards the shelving side of the bay but the cutter covered his move with a quick alteration of course and narrowing the angle between them and closing fast. 'It'll be a tight squeeze but have they the belly for it?' said Rudd with a determined set to his mouth. Steering the ship closer to the towering cliff side and Simon stared in horror at the rocks close under the bow. The restless waters surged and foamed at the base of the cliffs. The higher waves covering the tips of the reef then receding in a menacing swirl to expose jagged granite.

Simon jumped on the ship's rail thinking he would be more able to guide his skipper from a higher vantage and his hands closed for support on the stout rope work. Eyes glued to the rocks, he shouted, 'We've only about two yards to spare!'

'She's come about!' Jake's shout came back from the bow and Rudd took a quick glance at the coastguard cutter. He fancied he could see the figure of Wilder Faraday in the wheelhouse. There were certainly several Excise men lining up on deck with long-barreled muskets in their hands

'How the devil could they know we'd be here at this hour?' he said out loud. The cutter had the advantage and he wondered what they would do next. If he could just squeeze out through the narrow gap they might reach the safety of open water and in the half-light of dawn he was confident the *Rose* would outrun the Excise men and even though their situation was perilous he couldn't help but be fired by the excitement of the chase. His ship was moving fast now and as she came out of the lee of the mainland the wind freed and pushed her surging along before it and so smooth and quiet that he could hear the lantern swinging just below the companionway: such is the way of a sailing ship when running before the wind.

A crackle of musket fire came from the cutter as her men fired a volley. But a rolling deck makes for poor marksmen and the musket balls only splashed tiny waterspouts in the sea.

'We're going to do it, skipper!' cried Simon jubilantly. Still perched on the rail with his gaze focused on the rapidly nearing headland he knew that if they could just weather the point the cutter would see only the stern of the *Rose*. A wild shout tore from his mouth. 'Come on my beauty, we'll beat them yet!'

They were almost abeam of the cutter and his words heralded another volley of musket fire. Their aim proved more accurate as the range decreased and a sharp splintering sound came from the bulwarks.

'By the time they reload,' said Rudd hopefully, 'we'll be out of range.'

Aboard the coastguard cutter Wilder Faraday was beset with rage and frustration.

'By God, Gillard,' he snapped, 'if you let Rudd sneak away from me this time I'll see you are held directly responsible! You'll rot in prison for insubordination and cowardice!' Clenching his fists in a tight ball he thrust his face at Gillard. ‘I’m ordering you to board the *Rose of Endau*. Ram her if you have to but I want that ship stopped!’

Lieutenant Charles Gillard was a young man slight of build with a mop of red hair and just now with a worried look on his finely drawn, freckled face. Then his mouth set in a tight line as he said, ‘I cannot put my ship at risk.’ But resolve soon vanished before the sheer power of Faraday as he raged:

‘If you refuse to obey my order I’ll have you court-martialed for disobedience and for aiding and abetting this smuggler Rudd! Further more! ’ Real threat came with the next statement. ‘I’ll have to suspect that you are in league with the smugglers and will also charge you as their accomplice and that only your cowardice allowed them to escape when we were in such a commanding position. I think these facts will put an end to any career you may have in the Service.’ He then snarled, ‘If Rudd gets away I promise you will never again command one of Her Majesty’s ships!’

Gillard began to waver. Only recently appointed to this tiny cutter he took pride in his command. There were literally hundreds of Naval Officers paid off and living from hand to mouth and any reflection on his own ability could result in him being similarly cast down, with a future that could only be described as non-existent.

Gloomy thoughts: compounded by Faraday's abrupt. 'Make your decision, Gillard, or I'll take command myself!'

Still uncertain: but the bleak determination on Faraday's face? Knowing the man would break him without the slightest remorse he cast doubt aside. 'Ready about!' he ordered. 'Stand by to board!' The cutter's head came round smartly and her sails filed on the larboard tack. A responsive craft she gathered way in easy surge of motion. Her mainsail taught with the force of the wind she heeled rail down and cut through the water on a course that would surely intercept the fleeing *Rose*. The Excise men loaded their muskets and awaited the order to fire.

'She is closing fast,' cried Simon, 'looks as if they're going to ram us!'

Rudd seemed relaxed and his mouth spread in a broad grin. 'They're going to be in big trouble directly. Yon skipper's a fool and ignorant of these waters.'

Sailing this area all his life Rudd knew that the narrow channel through which he was steering had been formed over the centuries by the scouring action of the tide that ran so strongly around the headland, and that this same scouring had caused a bank of mud and shingle to heap up in a long, submerged shoal beneath the surface on his starboard side and lay in silent invitation to the unwary and inexperienced sailor.

The two racing ships came steadily closer and it

became obvious that the cutter's captain intended to ram the *Rose* and stop her by any means he could and they could clearly see the Excise men as they steadied themselves against the bulwarks with muskets at the ready. A bow cannon fired from *Intrepid*, a vain attempt in such tumultuous seas, and the ball disappeared into the heavens but the percussion brought a grimace from Rudd.

'Didn't know they had cannon aboard?' Their position began to look fraught with danger, the cutter's bow wave like a bone in the teeth as she came roaring at them. Eighty yards! Sixty! Fifty yards only separating them: and bringing anxious comment from Jake Ward.

'Hope they don't start shooting at this range?'

'Hold firm, lads, she'll strike any second,' said Rudd. Confidence confirmed as the foaming white water at the bow of *Intrepid* suddenly subsided and there came a mighty crack from the doomed ship. Her bow reared high and her hull slewed drunkenly sideways and her bilge showed black and obscene then her forward rush halted as though some huge hand had reached out to hold her tight. Her mast snapped off at the deck to fall forward across the bow and hang there held only by the sturdiness of the standing rigging. Relieved of the press of her sails the stricken ship righted herself and her keel sank deep into soft mud and the sails ripped and tore into shreds and fell over the side in a mess of rope and canvas and all on deck hurtled forward with the momentum and there wasn't a man left standing. Faraday went sprawling over the cabin top and down into the waist of the ship and his upper arm smashed with all his weight against the stump of the shattered mast. Gillard was left hanging over the binnacle with all breath driven from him and with a solitary spoke from the steering wheel still in his hand.. Dragging upright he stumbled forward to help his crew who were already cutting frantically at the ropes holding the heavy mast then a wall of water curled over the listing hull and came rushing inboard.

'Get that mast cleared,' screamed Gillard, 'or she's going to fill!'

A cheer rang out from the *Rose of Endau* as the crew saw the chaos aboard the cutter. 'They'll be too busy to bother about us now,' said Jake.

Savouring the humiliation of Faraday had brought loss of concentration on their own course and as just then the *Rose* cleared the headland a beam sea rolled her gunwhales down and Rudd sensed his ship in trouble. 'Simon!' he shouted urgently. 'Ware gybe!' He was too late and could only watch in suspended horror as the steep roll brought the wind across on to the forward side of the mainsail. The head of the sail fell away and the towering mainsail gybed itself on the opposite tack and flew across the deck bringing the heavy boom screaming with it and gybing all standing and fetching up with tremendous impact against the rigging and mast and the great swinging boom caught Simon across the head and shoulders scything him straight over the side.

'Watch him every moment, Jake!' Tearing his horrified gaze away from the swinging boom. The wheel responded in his demanding hands and spun with an urgency that brought the ship round in a tight circle and head up into wind with all way off her. Looking back along the line of Jake's frantic, pointing finger he saw an inert shape among the waves some fifty yards away and he ran aft. 'Get all sail off,' he called, 'and drop the hook before she drifts on the rocks!' Wresting off oilskin and sea boots he dived over the stern. The first iciness enveloped him in its grip and his breath seemed to leave his body then, breaking surface, he set off at a fast stroke towards the spot where he had seen Simon. He caught a fleeting glimpse of a dark head before it disappeared under a foaming crest, and struck out more strongly. Reaching the approximate vicinity he trod water, worriedly scanning for a sight, for he knew there was little hope of Simon being conscious after such a blow. Eyes boring into the murky depths then, with a flash of relief, he saw a trailing mop of hair rise to the surface then go under again. He dived after it and his groping hands found the descending body and clutching him round the waist he kicked powerfully for the surface. Gasping for air he held Simon's mouth and head clear of the water but he drooped lifelessly in his hands and a trickle of blood oozed from the corner of his mouth. Turning him so that Simon's back was against his own chest, Rudd clasped him firmly and began to swim backwards to where the *Rose* lay at anchor but Simon was a dead weight and acting as a drag and impeding his stroke and his strength and Rudd made little progress and the tide that had served so well before now exerted an unfeeling and merciless pressure on the man struggling so desperately for survival and the strong undertow began to sweep Rudd away from his ship and out into the grey waters of the English Channel. He tried to shout but a wave instantly filled his mouth so he concentrated all his efforts to keep himself and his helpless burden afloat. Jake Ward stared unceasingly and in growing despair towards the area where Simon had fallen overboard but the time spent wrestling with the heavy gear and the anchor had caused him to miss Rudd's unwilling passage out to sea.

On board the cutter something of order had been restored. Still hard on the mud bank but with the mast cut away and lying alongside she lay almost on an even keel and Gillard had the situation under firm control. The stopping of the headlong rush of the fleeing *Rose* had not gone unnoticed and Gillard focused on the anchored vessel to query. 'Surely they haven't stopped for us?'

'Someone in the water!' cried an observant seaman.

Clapping a telescope to his eye, Faraday announced, 'Rudd and one of his crew and they won't last much longer if the tide has its way with them!' Closing the telescope with a snap he turned a mocking look on Gillard and his laugh was pure evil as he sneered, 'Seems he has been too clever for his own good . . . what a perfect story-book end to Jonathan Rudd.'

'Ship's boat over the side!' commanded Gillard, 'I want two men on the oars and one on the bow.'

'Why bother? Let the sea have him, the man's a thief and you'll only be saving him for the hangman!'

Gillard looked at Faraday and the look was one of contempt and one of distaste. 'Lower away men,' he ordered.

'A little too late to assume command, Gillard! You've already lost your ship by incompetence and stupidity so why attempt the rescue of the one person who got you into this mess?'

'Captain Faraday, I'll thank you for no more interference in the running of my ship! Those are seamen out there and no English seaman leaves another to drown: not while he has a decent thought left.' Turning angrily from Faraday he jumped into the longboat, the crew pushed off from the grounded cutter and rowed with all strength towards the sighting.

'Ship oars . . . two men in the stern for hauling aboard!'

Rudd grabbed hold of the stern transom, relinquishing his grip on Simon as willing hands lifted the youth into the boat. Then strong arms heaved him out of the water but Rudd was so exhausted that he could only just manage to prop against the centre thwart where he sprawled with his breath coming in great gulping mouthfuls. The two near-drowning men aboard, the longboat came around and headed back to the cutter and the rescued pair were soon hauled aboard into the waist of the ship where Rudd sat shivering with his back against the bulwark and his head slumped on his knees. Simon was inert on the deck planking and his face was deathly pale and his lips a ghastly dark blue and Gillard stooped over him to confirm. 'He's still breathing.'

Seamen stripped away the sodden clothing and toweled the unresponsive body with a rough towel. A dark bruise showed on his neck while his shoulder and arm lay in grotesque angle from his body.

'On your feet, Rudd!' Hard-toed boot kicking his upper thigh, and from his near horizontal position Rudd's eyes opened to see two booted legs straddling the deck by his side. The boot raked him again as though he was dirt and as he eased onto his knees and then to his feet slow rage began to kindle and help to drive fatigue from his tired mind then came an ominous click and he stared at the pistol cocked in the hand of Wilder Faraday.

‘Make no mistake.’ Pistol pointing suggestively and with menace. ‘One sudden move and I’ll shoot you down!’

‘Thought you’d rather save me for the public hangman,’ gasped Rudd. The effort brought a sharp rush of seawater in his nostrils and a bout of coughing. The spasm raked his aching stomach muscles and he had to resort again to the bulwark for support and Faraday’s eyes portrayed immense satisfaction as he surveyed Rudd’s discomfort.

‘I’d have left you to drown,’ he said malevolently, ‘you and your wretched crew together if it hadn’t been for this fool Gillard?’

Rudd shivered without any hope of control in the cold morning air and Faraday for the moment became obscured by the Lieutenant and one of his men bringing warm clothing. They stripped and toweled him vigorously then helped him into a warm shirt and oversize trousers and all the time watched like a hawk by Faraday. Oblivious to the thrust of pistol Rudd knelt to hold his ear against Simon’s chest then rose to say to the Lieutenant, ‘He’s barely alive and needs medical care without delay.’

There was anxiety in his voice which the Lieutenant found strangely moving and he looked at him and said, ‘You could have sailed away to freedom, yet deliberately stopped your ship just to save your comrade even knowing that your own life might be forfeit.’

'Captain,' said Rudd with his eyes holding those of Gillard in a look of appreciation, 'how could a man live with himself if he left a shipmate to drown?'

Gillard felt a surge of association for the man before him. Realising that in his own quiet way Rudd had just given thanks for saving him and his crewman from the cold depths of a Channel grave but Faraday was looking on with hawk-faced impatience, so he stated in officious tone, 'I am placing you in irons and taking your ship in custody. The only way we can place your man ashore is to sail the *Rose of Endau* to Newlyn.' Looking at Rudd with compassion and not a little sorrow, he then said, 'Thought for a while you had hove-to in order to assist me.'

Looking him straight in the eye Rudd said with a cocky grin, 'Not likely! You were in no immediate danger on this mud bank and I would most happily have sailed away and left you to reflect at stranded length on your impetuosity.'

'You're a damn clever seaman, I grant you that,' replied Gillard, 'and I'd like to hope that one day we might match ships again, but perhaps out in the open sea where you won't have the knowledge of local waters to place me at a disadvantage.'

'Get on with it,' growled Faraday, 'and don't waste our time in idle speculation! Rudd is going to hang from the gibbet. His sailing days are well and truly over and, I suspect, yours also if you don't soon create some order out of this incompetent chaos!'

'You forget, sir, it was your command that forced me to take such a risk and that you held the threat of court martial over me if I failed to obey, and I am trusting you to assume responsibility as an officer and a gentleman.'

'Gentleman!' repeated Rudd scornfully. 'The man's a monster, and make no mistake, Lieutenant . . . he'll sell you short if it serves his own cause.'

This observation was greeted with disdain as Faraday attempted to sooth the Lieutenant. 'There is no cause for us to engage in dissent,' he said. 'We have caught the smugglers in the act and this fact alone justifies any decision you had to make under duress.' Looking at his prisoner with intense satisfaction as he added, 'You can rely on me to bring this satisfactory conclusion to the notice of your superiors.' His injured arm was held supported by a cloth sling which showed a patch of blood and while in considerable pain the only emotion he showed was one of being highly pleased with himself, coupled with impatience to get back to Newlyn with his prisoners.

With Faraday looking irritably at him, the Lieutenant said to Rudd, 'Will you give me your word that you won't attempt to escape?'

'Until we get Simon ashore. After that,' Rudd shrugged and said, 'I think Faraday has plans of his own for my future'

'Throw the blackguard in irons! His word holds no value. I want him under guard every second and will tolerate no more of this leniency!'

Gillard's dislike of Faraday showed in his voice as he replied, 'We need him aboard his ship if we're to make a fast passage back to port.' Then, to Rudd, 'In the circumstance I regret that I must tie you up.' Ordering rope to be brought and two of his men bound Rudd's arms behind him and so tight that even Faraday appeared mollified. Gillard then divided his personnel into two sections, one to stay aboard and attempt to re-float her on the next high tide, the remainder to take the longboat across to the *Rose* where a prize crew would board and the longboat return to assist the stranded *Intrepid*.

'Better let me go first,' suggested Rudd, 'Jake is still aboard and there are likely to be some sore heads if you try to board without counter instruction from me.'

Transferring to the *Rose* without further delay. Simon lay inert as he was hauled aboard in a net that was then slung fore and aft, like a hammock, in a quiet corner of the stern deck where his injuries would not receive any disturbance or aggravation, but Jake's relief in their safe return was premature and turned to dismay when he was locked below.

With Rudd directing from behind the wheel the *Rose* soon cleared the headland and stood in for

Newlyn where a crowd gathered on the waterfront as she came in with her prize crew rampant, and a disgruntled murmur started from the engrossed onlookers as the prisoners were thrust ashore. Rudd and Ward were tightly bound and with their feet shackled together at the ankles so they could only progress along the quay in ungainly shuffle. Faraday marching arrogantly at the head of his squad and oblivious of the angry clamour that accompanied them along the harbour front and into the streets of the town and he hastened pace to cause the prisoners as much discomfort and humility as he could and deliberately flaunting his triumph as the two men were dragged along stumbling and nearly falling as their manacled feet scraped barefoot over the rough surface.

Jake staggered and fell pulling Rudd down with him and the party halted momentarily while they were yanked upright, then the squad moved off at a brisk pace. Jake was writhing violently at his bonds and Rudd looked at him with concern. The big man was raging mad and his eyes were fierce and burning into Faraday's back. 'Steady, Jake lad,' cautioned Rudd, 'don't let him see you in such a state! This is the very thing he's aiming at so that everyone watching will come to fear him.'

Jake's normally unconcerned expression had been replaced with one of ferocity and, ignoring Rudd's attempt to calm, raged, 'I'll get my hands on Faraday's filthy neck one day no matter what the cost!'

'Forget it, Jake, that sadistic sod belongs to me!'

19

Jonathan Rudd's been taken! The news spread like wildfire! Janie came up the street at a run with skirts flying and her hair blowing in the wind. Charging through the lych gate into the churchyard and almost bowling Mathieson over as they met at the corner of the church. He caught her in his arms as they came forcibly together and his stomach muscles contracted at the incredible softness of her body as she clung to him. 'They've arrested Jonathan and Simon has a broken shoulder and all three are in prison in Newlyn!' Choking the words into his chest and her shoulders heaving in anguish. 'They're going to hang as smugglers!'

'Smuggling is not a hanging offence these days,' calmed Mathieson.

'Captain Faraday found weapons aboard and he's going to charge them with being armed and dangerous!'

‘They can’t convict without a trial and that will take months to organise.’

‘Faraday will make it soon! You know he will!’

She appeared out of control and some of the urgency began to communicate, but after a moment for thought, he enquired, ‘What happened to the *Rose of Endau*?’

‘She’s in Newlyn dock with a writ nailed to the mast and an armed guard watching her. Father went in to town as soon as we heard but Faraday refused to let him see either Jonathan or our Simon even though he’s been injured.’

‘Is he badly hurt?’

‘At first they thought so but when he recovered consciousness it seemed that excepting for a sore head he’d only suffered a dislocated shoulder.’

‘Hardly think even Faraday can deny you access to your brother.’

‘Would you take me to see him, Richard, they surely wouldn’t refuse you permission?’

‘Of course I will go with you, and I’ll wear my best parson’s neckband. It’s surprising how much influence Sunday dress can exert on reluctant officials. Give me a minute to finish up here then we’ll see what Mistral thinks about going between the shafts of your trap.’

The grey thought very little of it and cast a jaundiced eye on him at the feel of the unfamiliar harness but he spoke soothingly in her ear and led horse and trap out into the roadway. Mistral soon accepted the strange rig and her ears began to prick up as the miles sped by. 'Didn't know there was a prison in Newlyn?' said Mathieson as they approached the waterfront.

'It's just an old stable behind the Customs House.'

Driving round the building he halted the trap outside the gaunt looking prison block indicated by Janie. A rating in naval uniform looked at them warily as they approached on foot.

'You'll have to see the Lieutenant,' he said in reply to Mathieson's request for admittance, 'he's in Captain Faraday's office.'

Moving quickly across the roadway they approached the entrance just as the door opened to reveal Faraday and the Lieutenant. The Captain's eyes narrowed and he looked at Mathieson as if he was an irritant wasp worth only stamping underfoot then, pointedly ignoring him, addressed Janie in suave voice. 'How pleased I am to see you again, my dear Miss Ralston . . . even if the reason for your visit is not exactly the one I envisaged.'

Mathieson replied for her, but directly to the Lieutenant. 'We need your permission to see Janie's brother.'

'I'm in charge here,' snapped Faraday, 'and have given strict orders that the prisoners are to see no one. However . . . I have no objection to Miss Ralston seeing for herself how we are taking good care of her brother.'

'I would like your permission for the Reverend to accompany me.'

Her distressed manner brought a calculating glance and, after a brooding moment, Faraday commanded, 'Lieutenant, escort Miss Ralston and the Reverend to the prison office and have the prisoner Ralston brought to them.'

'I have a basket of food,' said Janie, 'may I give it to Simon?'

'Only after the contents have been examined, the Lieutenant will see to it for you. Come to my office afterwards, Miss Ralston, there is much we have to discuss.' With a pointed look at Mathieson he snapped, 'Alone!'

'What devil's brew are you working on now, Faraday?'

'From what I hear of you, Reverend, you are more than familiar with the devil's work?'

Gillard stepped in with hasty. 'This way, Miss Ralston.'

'Stay with them, Gillard, I want no private conversation between my prisoner and Miss Ralston: and the not so Reverend Mathieson!' His tone was deliberately offensive and Janie moved quickly to intervene.

'Please, Richard,' she implored, 'we have more than enough to worry about already.'

Mathieson allowed himself to be shepherded away but not without a rueful thought of what once would have been his immediate and violent reaction to such blatant provocation. But his dislike of Faraday increased with every abrasive encounter. Leading to a small office-like room in the prison Gillard ordered that Simon be brought to them. While they were waiting in uncomfortable posture he enquired, 'Are you the Mathieson who served as mate on the *China Star*?'

'It seems public knowledge but certainly not put about by me.'

'When Faraday gets his hook into someone, or something,' said Gillard, 'he doesn't easily let go!'

The sympathetic reply brought enlightenment and Mathieson realised that only a person with Faraday's authority could have commissioned access to shipping company records. The knowledge served to further inflame antagonism and the frowning resentment on his face caused Gillard to query, 'What did you do to make an enemy of him?'

'More probably something I said. Faraday seems to delight in making life difficult but perhaps inadvertently he has done me a service, at least I have no need for secrecy about my former life.'

'One of my men aboard *Intrepid* claims to have sailed the clippers to the Far East,' adding with a smile, 'before he was – er – persuaded to join the Navy.'

'Like to meet him one day, we should have much in common.'

The dialogue ended as the door opened and Simon entered. He looked thin and haggard and his right arm was thrust inside a sling of soiled linen but he was glad to see them and greeted Janie with a cheeky grin. She went to embrace him but drew back as Gillard shook his head. 'Don't look so worried, sis,' said Simon, 'I'm not as bad as I look. We're all fine but I'm so glad you've come. They told us no one would be allowed in before we are taken for trial.'

'How did they manage to take you?'

'Damn strange really! They were waiting for us as though they knew where we'd be.' Simon's face registered shame as he went on with. 'Even then Jonathan out-sailed them. We were in the clear with the coastguard cutter aground on a mud bank. If I hadn't been so stupid and let the boom smash me overboard? So Jonathan stopped the *Rose* and came in after me, though I didn't know anything about it at the time.'

Nodding in confirmation, Gillard said. 'We pulled them out of the water just as they were both about finished. It's true though, Rudd would have been safely at sea if he hadn't stopped to save Simon.' Smiling ruefully as he added, 'You've got to admire Rudd, he's a bloody fine seaman, begging your pardon, Reverend.' Looking at his watch. 'Sorry, Miss, but I cannot allow you further time.' Then, noticing her move towards her basket of food. 'Leave it here, I'll make sure they receive the contents.' Thoughtful for a moment, Gillard had a word with one of his men before requesting, 'If you will please follow the sentry, Miss Ralston, Captain Faraday is expecting you in his office.'

Mathieson watched her being escorted away by two ratings and showed intense concern as he turned to Gillard. 'That man's an unscrupulous fiend!' he said in hard tone.

'Perhaps so,' replied Gillard, 'but his position here is unassailable. I'm subordinate to him and he doesn't miss a single opportunity to remind me of the fact.'

'What do you think he wants with Janie?'

'No idea, but I neither like nor trust him and I've instructed a sentry to remain on guard outside Faraday's office door…and no harm will come to her with my man nearby.'

Doubts stifled, Mathieson said, 'I wish to see Rudd.'

'I have orders not to allow anyone to see the prisoners.'

'My orders come from a Higher Authority, can you deny these men their right to spiritual guidance?' This uncompromising statement brought worried speculation and uncertain lines formed on the Lieutenant's brow.

'Perhaps not,' he said, 'but you'd better make it quick while the Captain is occupied.' Turning abruptly. 'This way.' He led along a bare stone corridor and down a wooden stairway that spiraled into the depths of the building then into a small ante room protected by a door of studded oak.

Gillard knocked twice and the door opened to reveal a dark alley running along a diminutive cellblock with a ceiling so low that Mathieson had to stoop as he entered. Only one window, small and iron-barred in the end wall with no glass in the opening and which apparently overlooked a stable yard because a strong smell of manure penetrated the prison to blend overpoweringly with the odour of stale bodies and foul air. There were only two cells on this floor with the first occupied by Simon and Jake. As he approached, Jake's face appeared in the iron grill set high in the door. 'Come to take the helm again, Reverend,' he said, 'don't suppose you've a jug of ale with you?'

'No, Jake lad, but maybe next time.'

'Better make it soon.' His hands were gripping the bars of the grill and his downcast manner brought immediate concern.

'Try not to despair, Jake,' said Mathieson. Moving on to the other cell he peered through the grill but all was so dark and foul that quite a few seconds passed before his eyes could penetrate the gloom.

'Sorry I can't get up to greet you,' said Rudd from the depths. Gesturing down to his feet and at the heavy iron band around his right ankle and the metal chain that secured the band to a hoop of iron built in to the stonework. With several days growth of stubble on his chin he looked dirty and unkempt but his eyes sparked fire at Mathieson's scowl of outrage and concern. 'This is Faraday's doing! He wants me to look a disreputable rogue in case my clean good looks should influence the court.'

'Does he have to keep you in chains also?' fumed Mathieson.

'Steady, Reverend, your temper's showing. Faraday's afraid I might break out if he allows me half a chance,' then, with a reflective grin, 'and I did manage to knock a sentry down before they brought us in here.'

After a pause for thought, Mathieson asked, 'Did they find contraband aboard the *Rose*?'

'No! Jake dumped everything overboard just like we had planned should occasion arise, but one of the casks had enough air in it to stay afloat and the Excise fished it out of the water. Other casks drifted ashore at low tide and were picked up on the beach by the men on the stranded cutter.' Rudd then stated in a voice that held a distinct note of conjecture. 'The way they were lying in wait for us was too much of a coincidence. I've been squatting here chained like a wild animal and wondering how they found out where and when we'd be landing.' He broke off as if troubled with thoughts alien and confusing, then said, 'Only two others knew our schedule.'

'Doesn't matter much now.' The stench from the adjoining stable appalled and Mathieson's eyes flicked around the dingy cell and back to Rudd. 'Your dreams about sailing to romantic islands seem far removed at this moment.'

'Permanently if Faraday has his way.' Staring

into the face framed in the door grill, Rudd said with uncertainty apparent, 'Listen to me for a minute, Richard, I know I have lost your friendship . . .' after uncomfortable hesitation he added, 'a friendship that I ask you to believe I held most dear, and I ask nothing for myself but Simon and Jake are in this only because they chose to follow me and I'd do anything to keep them from the gallows.'

The despair that tremor-ed in his voice caused Mathieson to hopelessly reply, 'Wish there was something I could do but I am just a minister of the church and a very discredited minister to boot. As for friendship, you seem to regard it in very strange manner?' Without premeditation the memory of the stark scene in the barn brought bitterness flooding but the desperate plight of Rudd and his crew fastened again on his mind, driving such thought into insignificance and, looking sadly at the prisoner he said, 'The only help I can offer is of the spiritual kind.'

'Is the *Rose* still in Newlyn?' asked Rudd with deep yearning in his voice.

'The Navy has two armed men on twenty-four hour guard.'

'Look out for her, Richard. Promise you won't let them sell her off.'

Mathieson couldn't shatter Rudd's last despairing hope of salvation and, releasing his hold on the door grille, said, 'You have my word that I'll keep tight watch on the *Rose* for you.' With these words he turned away but with the expression on Rudd's face burning into his soul. Then he came back to urgent reality with the thought of Janie in Faraday's office. Brushing past Gillard he raced up the spiral stairway.

'May I offer a glass of wine?' asked Faraday, rising to his feet as she entered.

Declining with a shake of her head she straightaway said, 'What will happen to them?'

'Come, my dear Janie, have we no time for pleasantries before discussing such disturbing matters.' Pouring wine in casual manner then, realising she was in no mood for social grace, he said, 'The situation is no longer in my hands for I only apprehend wrongdoers – what happens afterwards?' He said this with a shrug and leaving the words suspended between them but not even Faraday could remain unmoved before the gaunt-eyed distress of Janie Ralston. 'I am truly sorry,' he said, 'but when men set themselves against the laws of the land they must expect that sooner or later retribution will be exacted.'

'Retribution sounds so terribly final,' whispered Janie in fragile voice.

'The penalty for such offences usually is final.' Trying to sound regretful but elation at success managed to creep into his tone. 'There is no doubt that Rudd and his man Ward will hang,' savouring this thought then, with a covert glance, he added, 'but your brother is just a youth and perhaps the court will view his case more kindly.'

'Simon would be haunted for the rest of his life if they were to hang!' Confronting him with a desperate look on her face she blurted, 'You know that Jonathan would be free today if he hadn't stopped his ship to save Simon . . . surely this fact will influence the court to leniency because they virtually gave themselves up rather than let him drown.' Directly to him now with eyes huge and dark-shadowed and moist. 'If you were to present the facts to the court just the way it happened . . . ?' breaking off despairingly.

Elegant as always: shirt of finest silk with a ruffle of lace at the throat, tailored uniform coat of dark blue in contrasting harmony with slim line white trousers, Faraday was in complete control as he raised a sardonic eyebrow to ask, 'What reason have I to render assistance to a thief and smuggler such as Rudd?' With these words his tongue crept like a slimy snake over his lower lip and his eyes roved obscenely over her as she stood in dejected pose. Into his mind came the picture of her young body submissive in his arms and he was suddenly inflamed with a tormenting passion. At that moment Faraday was nearer to love than ever before in his life, for Janie Ralston had been the subject of his brooding since the day he had first met her.

There had been women, of course. He was a compelling figure of a man with an animal vitality that many found exciting. But to Faraday love meant possession! A rapist by instinct he found satisfaction more in the pursuit. His courtships were frantic and the final conquest violent and the women who had fallen prey to his maniac sex drive usually remembered with horror and pain the fouling embrace of Wilder Faraday as their bodies were taken without a shred of tenderness then thrust aside and out of the way of his all-consuming need: the one lasting desire of his existence . . . lust for control and absolute power! In this quest for personal advancement he was insatiable and any finer feelings he may once have had were long since trampled underfoot in his unrestrained drive for recognition. But now the young and desirable Janie had been suddenly and so provocatively placed within reach of his eager hands. A stir of anticipation started a slow rise in his loins. His eyes had the baleful, slant-eyed look of a tiger ready to pounce and with the snarl on its mouth already tasting blood. How fortune had so unexpectedly smiled on him. But then again, he thought, lady luck favoured only the bold, and Wilder Faraday had never been anything less than bold.

His suggestive stance brought the chill of icicles feathering across her shoulders and running cold down her back but she faced up to him and questioned, 'Do you need a reason for presenting the truth in a plea for clemency?'

'My dear Janie, I find your naïve manner so

refreshing!' Faraday was smirking at the thought of clemency, but the tone of his voice was evil and repellent as he went on to state, 'Every situation in which we find ourselves has eventually to be evaluated as a personal loss or gain. My duty has been carried out to the full and I don't see any need for further involvement . . .' Pausing to allow time for this to be absorbed, then with a searching glance. 'Unless of course you have a suggestion of your own?'

Janie might be naïve – unworldly! But as the full implication struck home her cheeks flushed crimson as she replied, 'What are you trying to say?'

'Just that I would need some very personal reason to place my considerable weight behind a plea for clemency.' Clenching his hands behind his back he surveyed her arrogantly before suggesting, 'There may be a small chance that I could sway the judgment of the court.'

'And the price for this cooperation?'

The tremulous query made him laugh out loud. 'I see no price,' he said, 'and would be only to happy to be of service. If you will remain here and dine with me this evening we could discuss in more detail just what together we can do to remove the sentence of *death* my prisoners are facing.'

He placed emphasis on the word *death*. Pressuring her into submitting to his evil designs, and effective as she faltered, 'And – after dinner?'

Faraday's eyebrow raised and he said, 'Who can foretell the delights the future may hold for us.'

'Captain Faraday,' she pleaded, 'do you want me to beg? Do I have to go down on my knees to you?' Clasping her hands together as she said this she sank down in supplication before him. 'Please, sir, I implore you to save then from the scaffold!'

'No! Not on your knees!' Reaching for her in a grasping swoop, his injured arm forgotten, he clutched her with brute strength, forcing her into him. She was deathly afraid, mute and powerless in his fierce embrace. His arms about her, one around her waist, the other pressing her hips into his. Her soft body brought raging desire and, almost beside himself, he hissed passionately, 'I want to breath fire into you. Feel the warmth of your body under mine . . . vibrant and alive! For such a delight I could be tempted to break down the very walls of the prison with my bare hands!' She recoiled as he buried his mouth into her neck and throat. Aflame with passion he gripped her tight and growled in her ear, 'A few minutes of your time seem little enough sacrifice for the lives of your precious Rudd and his two men.' His arms seemed to be squeezing all resistance from her and his eyes burned into her and they were the eyes of a jungle predator and his fetid breath was in her face and she recoiled in horror and anguish with her body writhing as she sought release from the intensity of his sensuous embrace.

Came a scuffle in the corridor outside, the door crashing open with Mathieson's full weight behind it and a sentry in outraged pursuit. A dramatic entry that brought instant release for Janie as he shouldered Faraday aside with force and stood between them and looked about to strike. 'Touch her again,' he said threateningly, 'and I swear that I'll smash you down!' His eyes were flaring wild and his shoulders hunched in menace but Faraday was completely unmoved and he straightened his dress with a casual brush of fingers.

'Such violence from a man of the cloth,' he scorned. 'Really, Mathieson, even your sorry reputation doesn't do justice to the viciousness of your temper. Miss Ralston and I had finished our little talk before you so typically burst in. Just what did you expect to find here, some scene of terrible seduction? Looking at him with infinite contempt, he concluded, 'Me and Janie now understand each other perfectly.' Ignoring Mathieson as if he wasn't there he said to her. 'I think you are wise not to decide immediately. Such decisions are better made when the mind has had time to absorb all the relevant details. But just remember that I am here at your pleasure and waiting only to serve you, as always.'

She fled from him out the door but Mathieson wouldn't be contained and turned again on

Faraday. 'There is something about you!' he raged, 'something so despicable and evil that it makes my flesh crawl just to be near you.' Seizing the silk waistcoat he half-lifted him in unrelenting grip and Faraday's face turned livid and his eyes flamed murder

'If you interfere once more,' he snarled, 'I'll have you thrown into prison alongside your friend Rudd and, from what I hear, no one would give a damn!' His contorted features floated before Mathieson. He fought to regain control and thrust Faraday away so forcibly that he fell sprawling against his desk, then followed after him with his fists clenched and every nerve screaming for a strike. To belt him one just for the hell of it: and because he wanted to: then stopped in full flight while still towering over him. Then he turned abruptly away to follow after Janie rushing down the stairs and into the refreshing cool of the street.

She was silent for much of the ride back to the village and eventually he reined to a halt and took her hand. 'Are you going to tell me about it?' he asked.

'Nothing to tell.'

'Something has happened to take the bloom from your lovely face.' The caring tenderness in his voice made her eyes mist over and she leaned into him for support and she bit her lip to keep at bay the flood of explanation and her manner so downcast that he demanded, 'Just what has that devil said to upset you so?'

'It isn't Captain Faraday,' she denied, too quickly, 'I just despair to see Simon in that awful place.' Looking at him pleadingly as she asked, 'Can you do anything to get them out?'

'I cannot set myself up against the law of the land.' The words were bitter in his mouth and the more so because he could feel her anguish reaching so desperately for help, but the torment in his voice and on his face brought realisation of the unfairness of asking him to become involved in any way with rescuing the condemned men, for his already tarnished reputation would be irrevocably ruined in the violence that would surely occur. In that moment she made up her mind. What other choice had she? It seemed the only chance the three men had of escaping the hangman's noose lay in her submitting her body to Faraday's foul desires. Hopeless thoughts churning inside, for in her sheltered life she had little knowledge of men. Her body had been a sort of shrine nurtured and cared for and to keep inviolate until the day when a union, blessed in church with someone she loved dearly, would complete her emerging womanhood. A dream that had occupied her thoughts more and more of late, but please God: not Wilder Faraday! Shuddering inwardly at the memory of his hands on her but couldn't for shame's sake reveal the extent of his demands because she knew Richard would surely confront him and bring ruin to any hopes of saving her dear ones. She had to do this on her own and said with cold composure. 'Sorry, Richard, I had no right to ask that of you.' Surprised at the change from pensiveness to assurance he looked at her curiously but she merely said, 'It's just that I am so unhappy to think of what is to become of us.' Her manner of speech brought uncertain conjecture but she brushed aside any questions to murmur:

'Please, no more. Let's go home.'

20

Evening fell as he tried to relax in the cosy sitting room but his racing thoughts allowed no rest and kept returning to the plight of the men imprisoned in that foul-smelling hovel. All the bitterness and revolt at the relationship between Cathryn and Rudd had faded before the desperate situation facing the three men. They had been in captivity over two weeks and he couldn't help but question why Faraday kept them so long at Newlyn. Those searching eyes of Rudd stabbed at him and caused him to stir uneasily in his chair, and Mrs Farquasan looked at him with concern. He hadn't been his normal tranquil self for days and she had a fair idea of what troubled him. 'Jonathan Rudd,' she said waspishly to herself, 'folk around here, especially womenfolk, seem to think he's some kind of hero. Serve him right, if you ask me? Knew what he was doing, took the risk and can't blame anyone but himself if he was caught?' She wasn't in charitable mood. Anything causing this much concern to her Reverend invited instant condemnation and he's plenty enough trouble of his own, she concluded, without Rudd and his crew adding more. He seemed unusually restless tonight and she worriedly surveyed the frown that deep-lined his forehead and the concern in the eyes staring vacantly into the book in his hand.

'Supper will soon be ready, Reverend,' she said in an attempt to break his sombre mood but he replied only with a reluctant smile so she shrugged and moved away into the kitchen just as someone hammered on the front door. Springing to open it he found Glyn Ralston on the threshold. He had been running and was breathless and straightaway said:

'Can I speak with you?'

'Come inside, Glyn.'

Declining to enter Ralston said urgently, 'Need your help!' Twisting his cap in his hands as if he was wringing it dry. 'It's Janie,' he blurted, 'she's gone to Faraday!'

'At this hour of day!' '

His voice lunged at Ralston, who replied in faltering tone, 'She claims he promised to help Simon and the others if . . . ? Reverend,' he cried, 'she's going to offer herself to him!' His hands weaved tormented patterns and, as Mathieson stared dumfounded, he jerked, 'We found out today that they are going to move the prisoners to

London . . . to the Old Bailey! She said if no one else would make any effort she knew of a way to influence Faraday.' Ralston seemed close to tears as he went on to say, 'I begged and pleaded but she said that three lives were worth a little sacrifice.'

'Surely you could have stopped her, man!' Glaring at the burly inn-keeper as though he couldn't believe what he was hearing but Ralston answered with downcast eyes:

'I tried, but she raised her whip to me, then asked which was more important, my son's life or a temporary violation of her body? God help me, Reverend,' he cried, 'I almost agreed with her!'

'How long since she started?' demanded Mathieson as he wrestled into his riding coat.

'About five minutes! After I realised what I had done I knew you were the only person she might listen to . . . so I came running.'

'I want to see you when I get back. Assemble three or four reliable men and wait for me at the Inn.' He then snapped, 'Did you bring my horse?'

'How could I? You might not have wanted to interfere! But she's saddled ready.'

Mathieson flew out the door and ran down the road at top speed.

Mistral sped through the fading light as though aware of the urgency, horse and rider in perfect, demanding rhythm and going like bats out of hell.

'Faster, Mistral,' he urged, 'we have to catch up

with her!' Racing through the little township of Marazion. Lights in the windows: glowing warm. Cloistered! The residents cosy within and probably responding with curious interest to the sound of urgent motion outside, but wanting no part! And as they came abreast of St. Michael's Mount causeway his windswept eyes caught a glimpse of Janie's trap along the low road. Mistral seemed to see it too and the big grey fairly hammered along the last few hundred yards separating them.

Janie turned in alarm at their fast approach but her mouth was a hard line as he grabbed the reins in an iron fist. Her face was pale but wore a very determined and defiant expression and she glared angrily at horse and rider. Mistral's flanks were steaming and vapour jets puffed from her flaring nostrils. Mathieson also was breathing hard and had difficulty in speaking, but Janie's whip rose in threat as she snapped, 'Get out of my way!'

'Would you really use that?' He finally had the trap under control and wheeled Mistral to confront her.

'If you try to stop me?' she said harshly. She had dressed in deliberately wanton manner. Her hooded cloak had slipped away to reveal the rounded splendour of her neck and shoulders and the dark velvet gown that plunged deeply in the front. He gathered the cloak once more about her shoulders but his solicitude brought only embarrassed irritation and a defiant, 'I know why you are here but keep out of this! My mind is made up and I'm going to help Simon in my own way, for Captain Faraday has promised to do all he can to get them off with a light sentence if I go to him.'

'Should have realised: suspected?' Cursing himself inwardly, he then said in hard tone, 'The very nature of such a suggestion shows up the man as despicable.' Attempting to take her hand but she evaded his grip. 'Janie! Janie!' he pleaded, 'he'll use you for his own pleasure and most probably with no intention of helping his prisoners. Capturing Rudd in the act is the chance he's seeking to return to London with distinction and he would never risk jeopardising this opportunity.'

His voice surged dramatically as he sought to persuade but she just shrugged him off. 'It's a risk I'm prepared to take,' she said haughtily, 'and perhaps you underestimate the effect I have on the Captain. He's only a man, after all, not the fire eating dragon you are all afraid of.' Glancing covertly at him she snapped in waspish voice. 'He seems to find me more desirable than some others I know.' The snide comment registered but he made no reply and her eyes hardened at his lack of response and she said, 'Surely you don't think I would do this unless it was the last chance we would have.' Despair broke through and she cried, 'Nobody seems to care any more but I've thought about all these things you speak of and

I'm convinced I can handle Captain Faraday, he won't get my favours so easily as you imagine!' She was confident again and the way her eyes held his without wavering brought deep concern.

'Maybe not,' he said at length, 'but please don't sell your body to him for such a vague price.' Looking away from her for a moment, out to sea and into the distance. The moon had risen and hung suspended and huge and lovely and turning the still water into a sheet of shimmering silver and shot stars into Janie's eyes as she glared at him and, taking advantage of this brief respite, he mounted the trap beside her but she icily resisted his attempt to take the driving seat. So he tried persuasion again, saying, 'Noble gestures are wasted on a man so evil. He'll take your body without any intention of giving you the support for which you are sacrificing yourself,' gripping her hands tight and his voice was fraught with concern as he added, 'and for someone so normally shrewd I find it surprising that you haven't taken your thinking further and tried to calculate the final consequence of this liaison.'

'What consequence?' Impatient now.

'Can't you imagine what would happen if Rudd ever learned of the reason for Faraday's unexpected leniency?'

Chilling words that hung between them and she recoiled with a look of incredulous understanding. 'He would go after him?' Answering his question with a wondering one of her own and Mathieson nodded and said in confirmation.

'There would be no place on this earth where Faraday could escape Rudd's final and ultimate vengeance and all you may thought to have accomplished would be wasted because now his plight would not only be worse, but his life ruined irrevocably and far beyond reach of further help from you or me!'

She slumped in despair as the full implication registered and her eyes held the dull sheen of hopelessness as she sobbed, 'Then what are we to do? I felt my way was the last and only chance for them.'

'There may be another way.' Looking at her and the intensity and appeal in the look shattered and broke down her resolve and he knew he was winning. 'Will you trust me,' he said, 'to try in my own manner to help them? Promise that you will never again think of approaching Faraday.'

Her eyes searched his face and she looked at the lines of tension etched deep around the sensitive mouth. 'It doesn't seem fair that you should have to become involved,' she said with growing concern.

She churned with a mixture of emotion and with her sense of reprieve contrasting bitterly with despair for the future of Richard Mathieson, but he didn't seem to care as he shrugged and said, 'I don't know what's fair any more. But the thought of you in Faraday's clutches makes my blood run cold and I could never allow this to happen: no matter what the cost.' His relief as she yielded was obvious, and mutual, and she linked her arm impulsively through his and squeezed it tight. Their faces were close together for a breathtaking second and her eyes shone tender in the moonlight's glow and they were dark and moist and very lovely and he re-arranged the hood of virgin white lambs wool like a halo about her face and his lips touched her pert nose, and he said:

'Let's go home!'

Four men waiting in the back room of the Blue Lugger as he strode in from the stable. Glyn Ralston, Will Perryman, the blacksmith Jan Coggeshall, and an inshore fisherman named Brian Hartland.

'How many more can you rely on, Glyn?' asked Mathieson.

'Many as we need in Newlyn,' said Ralston, 'there are scores of fishermen who would relish a chance to unseat Faraday.'

'How about fast horses?'

'The only fast horses around here are up at Sandford Barton,' said Will Perryman with a negative but convincing head shake.

Mathieson looked very troubled as he said, 'Not so good! Perhaps I can persuade Sir Harry to lend us a few.'

He spoke with a distinct lack of confidence,

and Jan Coggeshall broke in to say. 'The Sedgewick family have been quiet of late. I was up there in the week shoeing one of their stallions,' smiling at this as he added, 'had to show the brute who was in charge, but I didn't see anyone except the stable lads, which was most unusual.' He then said in conspiratorial tone, 'They told me the two women had gone away.'

This remark brought conjecture. 'Looks as if that side of it is up to me,' said Mathieson. Glancing at Ralston he queried. 'We are going to need some explosives? Just a couple of small charges but enough to make a nice loud bang.'

Ralston pulled at his lower lip but Brian Hartland spoke up. 'Friend of mine works as blaster in the tin mine.' Brian didn't waste words. 'How much do you need?'

The four men gathered close around the table.

The following morning Mathieson rode out to the sprawling estate of Sandford Barton. It was now Friday and he had only the weekend left in which to work his plans and keep his pledge to Janie. Just forty-eight fleeting ours before the chance would be irretrievably lost. Cursing his past indecision and apathy, and his thoughts were sombre and self-condemning. Men were the same no matter what their way of life. No matter how angry or determined they always needed someone to take charge. Someone to lead and organise: someone to follow! He had hoped in vain that he could have stood aloof from such an involvement; one he knew well could completely ruin his already precarious position here and bring a swift end to his chosen work. Thoughts in desolating turmoil as he cantered into the courtyard to where Sir Harry stood examining one of his horses with a groom by his side. They glanced up from their scrutiny as he approached and Sir Harry seemed in foul mood: not improved by the sight of his visitor.

'What the hell do you want?' The two had not faced each other since the night of the ball at Sandford Barton and his tone was far from cordial.

'I need your help,' answered Mathieson as he dismounted. Sir Harry's eyebrows came together at this unexpected request then he gestured to the groom who straightaway led the big chestnut back to the stables with a briskness that indicated he was removing himself from the line of fire, and Mathieson felt far from confident as he explained, 'You once said you'd let me have the use of some of your men.'

'A long time ago! You've a damned nerve, for much has happened since I made that suggestion.' Sir Harry looked at him with a definite lack of interest and in a manner suggesting he didn't much care about anything. 'How many and for how long?' he asked with a shrug.

'I need three discreet riders, three good horses and a fast coach and four.'

'Discreet! Fast horses! Just what the hell are you up to?' Sir Harry seemed in shock then his eyes narrowed with refusal evident. 'Is this anything to do with that foul seducer named Rudd?' he then demanded.

The venom with which he jerked the words gave confirmation to Mathieson's suspicions. 'Better if you don't ask for reasons,' he replied cautiously.

'I have no need,' retorted Sir Harry, 'your friendship with Rudd is common knowledge. But why now and with such urgency?'

'Because the prisoners are being transported to the Old Bailey early next week and will be far removed from our reach.'

This information visibly shook Sir Harry and served only to increase his foul mood. These last few days had seen the domestic bliss of Sandford Barton shattered, for his routine and home comforts were in total disarray without the guiding hand of Lady Sarah. He had been badly hurt and his nature was such that he needed to strike back, no matter at whom, and he looked calculatingly at Mathieson. 'Just how much does this mean to you?' he asked in sly tone.

'A great deal! To me, and many others. Will you help?'

'I might, on one condition.' Sir Harry's face held the glow of early morning indulgence with liquor and he surveyed Mathieson with a look of bloated anticipation.

'Condition?' asked Mathieson with sudden foreboding.

'I want your mare, Mistral.'

The grey stood at his shoulder, the reins still in his hand. Mathieson looked at Sir Harry who was maliciously waiting for capitulation, and the agony in his look transferred to his voice as he said forlornly, 'Do you always have to win?'

The hopelessness in his manner penetrated even the triumph of his tormentor and Sir Harry glanced uncomfortably from horse to rider and his conceited pleasure in the situation began to turn sour. 'Why else should I help Rudd and his motley crew?' he blustered.

Mathieson in dejected pose: he was risking his all in this quest, and now he was about to lose Mistral. Was it ever worth it? Then, despair and outrage combined to dismiss all thought of diplomacy, and he turned on Sir Harry. 'Perhaps because your own action proved the initial cause of them being taken,' he snapped, 'and one that may cost them their lives!'

'What the hell are you talking about?' The stark accusation had Sir Harry on the defensive and he couldn't meet Mathieson's probing glare.

'Only two men knew the place and time of Rudd's return from Roscoff . . . Glyn Ralston and you!' He spoke in scathing tone and his eyes were like blue steel in the granite of his face.

‘What possible reason could I have for wanting Rudd taken?’ growled Sir Harry. The alcoholic veins on his nose had deepened in colour and his eyes were downcast.

‘How about the outraged father?’ probed Mathieson. The wild look appearing on the face before him justified the allegation and without waiting for reply he queried, ‘I don’t see either Lady Sarah or Cathryn about this morning, may I enquire as to their health?’

The change of attack had Sir Harry reeling. ‘None of your damn business!’ he snarled.

‘I have to think that the health of your daughter has everything to do with the predicament in which we now find ourselves and that this is the reason you stoop so low as to inform on the whereabouts and cargo of the *Rose of Endau*, an enterprise in which I believe you were involved and even financing?’ Accusing words that further shattered Sir Harry but the Squire of Sandford Barton wasn’t easily put down and anger brought the fire of defiance in his eyes.

‘Serve him damn well right! Rudd needs to be taught that he can’t have his way with every virgin in the county, though I didn’t reckon on them being sent up to London for trial.’ Sir Harry seemed in a dilemma as he added in more thoughtful tone, ‘Faraday’s a calculating sod, and probably realises that a jury of Cornishmen would never bring in too severe a sentence on their own kind.’ He needed a few seconds to accept this development, then said, 'Don't see why you should feel responsible when it was Rudd's action that broke up any possible relationship between you and Cassy? Wish now that I hadn't been so intolerant of you in the past. Perhaps?' He broke off and his eyes met Mathieson's squarely for the first time. 'You're an unusual man, Reverend,' he said, 'and I haven't met your like before. You befriended Rudd and he took your friendship and defiled it. Aye,' he growled, 'and my little girl as well! Yet still you seek to help him and even have the damned nerve to ask me to do likewise.' Anger reared again and the sting of bitterness appeared. 'When I think of him and Cassy wallowing together,' almost at shouting pitch as he added, 'after all the plans and ambitions I had for her!'

Mathieson sensed the genuine anguish under the facade of rage and he thought that Sir Harry couldn't cope with the knowledge that he might have to accept a share of blame for his daughter's fall from grace. 'Young people are too vulnerable,' he said, albeit carefully. 'They don't always wish to follow along the paths others have chosen for them and parents can sometimes be too demanding, no matter how much devotion is bestowed with their ambitions.' Speaking with deliberation and striving to reach out to Sir Harry as he went on with. 'Perhaps it was inevitable for two such intense and reckless souls as Cathryn and Jonathan Rudd to come together and neither you nor I are capable enough to sit in judgment upon the ways of loved ones who insist on living life in their own demanding way. In fact,' he said insistently, 'after the initial hurt and disappointment begin to fade I cannot help but wonder if we ourselves might be found wanting in our relationship with Cathryn and even accept some responsibility for this situation.'

'You put my deepest thoughts into words and my actions to shame.' Sir Harry regarded him with strange assessment, before asking, 'Do you know she's carrying Rudd's child?'

There was naked pain in Mathieson's eyes and Sir Harry found himself in the unusual position of being moved to sympathy for someone other than himself. His condemnation of this man had been created mainly by a blind refusal to accept that his strength of character more than equaled his own. Then, acceptance of mutual grief brought strange association and a degree of compassion crept in to his voice as he stated, 'When I accused Cassy that the child was yours she flared back at me and said she only wished it were! Think now I also share that wish.'

'Perhaps we are both the losers?' said Mathieson, then his face brightened. 'A child of Cathryn by Jonathan Rudd,' he said excitedly, 'this will be an infant to behold!' A smile started and his eyes lost their sombre look as he declared, 'I believe, Sir Harry, that this grandchild will prove a great source of delight and that very soon you'll discover endless joy growing from the unhappiness that surrounds you at present. I implore you, sir, not to allow bitterness to overshadow your love for Cathryn or to exert unfair influence over your judgment.'

There were definite signs of moisture in Sir Harry's eyes as he absorbed this moving indictment of his actions and he needed a long moment before he could answer. 'I have done you a great wrong, Reverend,' he said in vibrant voice, 'and my values are being adjusted perhaps a little too late. Even worse . . . I turned my back on Cassy when she needed me most, damn it!' Remorse and self-condemnation added a biting edge to his words as he said bitterly, 'I sent her away, thinking only of position and stupid pride, but not any more because she's coming back home forthwith, and if my fancy friends don't like it they can go to hell!'

Turning to face his stable block. His shoulders squared. He stood proud. 'Take my best riders,' he instructed, 'as many horses as you need and don't hesitate to call on my further help in any way you need.' His manner and tone had taken on some of the urgency Mathieson had brought with him, but though he had achieved his purpose more fully than he could ever have anticipated his feet were positively leaden as he began to move towards the stables.

'Don't forget your mare.'

He stopped in his tracks, glanced back, asked quietly, 'What about your condition?'

'Keep tight hold of Mistral, Richard Mathieson, your love for her does you credit: and is greater than mine could ever be!'

21

They came to Newlyn: pilgrims on a journey and a quest they considered worthy. Last to arrive was Will Perryman with his shire horse. He needed the cover of darkness more than the others because Joanna was too well known and, succeed or not, it was essential to avoid recognition if they were to resume normal life afterwards.

Hiding with Mistral behind a sea-front building, Mathieson looked at his watch in some anxiety. The daylight was reluctant to let go its hold and the last rays of sunset illuminated the roof of the Customs House in vulnerable glow. A light glowed in the window of Faraday's office. He was no doubt planning for his evening's entertainment. Uncertainty and trepidation: perhaps it wasn't such a good idea to allow the Captain to expect her tonight. Her note to him had been couched in desperate line and he would surely be in a mood of lewd anticipation. Shrugging aside morose thoughts. At least they knew the whereabouts of Faraday, which was the purpose behind this subterfuge. Checking his watch again. Five minutes before Glyn Ralston would set off the first of his charges and still the daylight refused to give way.

The light in Faraday's window flared bright, indicating that another lamp had been lit. He began to move nearer followed by two shadowy figures. They were all heavily laden and a bulky package lay across Mistral's broad haunches. Her hooves were padded and she made scarcely a sound as he led her carefully along. Nerves tingling with suspense because he alone had planned this rescue attempt and responsibility lay heavy on his shoulders.

Ralston lit the first fuse. Long and slow burning and connected to a small charge that lay harmlessly on waste ground just up the steep hill from the harbour. He watched it fizz and spark, making sure of ignition, before moving away and down to the harbour front to take up his second position in an old, disused wood shack. A pungent smell of oil pervaded the derelict shack where the floor had been stacked high with old sacking and driftwood and as he set about preparing another charge a group of three darkly dressed men crept along the quayside towards the *Rose of Endau* where the sentries just starting the first watch stood grumbling to each other about this never ending vigil on the impounded vessel.

Mathieson and his escort had halted about fifty yards from the Customs House. Daylight had finally begun to fade but they could clearly see the armed guard patrolling outside the prison block and the light in the window behind him. Pulling a woollen stocking over his face he gestured to the other two men to do likewise. The heavy wool stifled and he adjusted the breathing hole around his nose and mouth. His eyes peered through the slits and he couldn't hold back a chuckle at the bizarre appearance of the others. Tension building all the time: this night was fraught with danger!

Whoomph! Explosion rent the night as the first of Ralston's charges blew a shallow hole in the dirt. Blasting across the gloom the noise brought instant activity as the prison door flew open and Lieutenant Gillard flew out into the street with two ratings behind him. They were fumbling hastily with muskets and outer clothing and staring around in alarm. Nothing moving! Then the sentry joined them and Wilder Faraday rushed out of the Customs House. Dressed impeccably in full dress uniform he seemed in no mood for distraction and scowled questioningly at Gillard.

Will Perryman brought his shire up the back street leading to the stable yard behind the prison. After the din of explosion no one would be concerned about the movement of a single horse. Gaining admittance to the stable yard. He knew the place well and led into the cobbled square that housed neither man nor beast at this hour. Slipping a bag of oats over the shire's head to keep her quiet he began to prepare the heavy harnessing and chain work that had ridden in front of him all the way from his farm dwelling.

Whoomph! The explosion was much louder this time and a sheet of flame lit the sky over Newlyn. The waterfront shack was burning fiercely and illuminating the harbour with its crackling flames and causing the two ratings guarding the *Rose* to exchange alarmed glances. One of them moved uncertainly in the direction of the blast but as he passed a mound of gear between two mooring bollards rough arms grabbed him and held him immobile and tore the musket from his grasp. The musket was then fired high over the head of the other guard and the shot blazed into the sky adding further alarm and confusion to the bemused sentry by the *Rose*. His own piece was leveled ready but he could see no intruder to aim at so he jumped hastily aboard ship to take shelter behind the bulwarks. Ralston poured oil on the fire and flames whooshed skyward. The streets were alive with people all alerted and curious and men came running towards the harbour in concern for the safety of their own vessels. Fire! Dense black smoke! Confusion and panic! Hubbub on the packed waterfront! Everyone in uproar! A rumour started:

'*Rose of Endau* is being taken away!' Growing in volume as the cry was taken up and travelled like grease-lightening along the waterfront and the harbour was a bedlam of noise and the flames lit the night sky and reflected eerie shapes onto the ballooning black and dense oil-smoke and a shrill cry penetrated the dark street between Customs House and prison. 'They're moving the *Rose* from Newlyn!' A convincing cry that produced reflex action.

'Get down there Gillard,' ordered Faraday, 'but leave two men on guard here. I want that ship kept in Newlyn even if you have to torch her!' Following which command he grabbed a pistol from the belt of one naval rating and waved it in the air. 'Move, Gillard, damn you! At the double!'

The Lieutenant snapped orders and four ratings formed up, then turned as one and set off at brisk pace up the alley.

During the confusion Mathieson sneaked through the front door of the Customs House and together with his two companions crept up the stairs into the office of Wilder Faraday. Elaborate dinner table: gleaming silver and cut glass and two candles burning to give an atmosphere of seductive intimacy to the lush room, a sight that made him even more determined.

The three men straightaway emptied the

contents of their bulky packages on the floor. These were mostly of heavily oiled and tarred paper that they spread about in hurried piles. He set them alight with one of Faraday's fancy candles. The oil and tar ignited reluctantly, then fire took hold and spread and filling the room with black, overpowering smoke. Then they scurried down the stairs and out the front door. Peering round the corner again he saw Faraday pacing up and down pistol in hand, in a conceited posture indicating he would soon brush aside this minor distraction. Smoke billowing from a window above their heads. One of his men pointed to it with a shout. Faraday's face was a picture of outrage as he screamed. 'My office!' Rushing into the building followed by all the men of the Excise, leaving just the two naval ratings on guard at the prison entrance. The two were already in a state of bewilderment as they stared at the dense smoke mushrooming out the window.

'Water! More water!' Came the scream from the office. Running to the doorway Mathieson opened the door. 'Guards,' he roared, 'in here, quickly! We need help!'

The Navy men moved away at once from their station at the prison door and disappeared into the Customs House. He heard them run up the stairs then closed the door behind them and sped out into the alley, placed two fingers in his mouth and whistled, a shrill sound that was instantly drowned in the rattle of a fast moving carriage that swept down the alley behind a team of four horses and, with a clatter that deafened in the confines of the alley, the rig screeched to a standstill and two figures jumped down from behind the coachman driver. A heavy, long handled sledgehammer smashed the prison door to pieces with a few blows and with noisy deliberation. Everyone was calling out in maniac voice, the horses rearing in fright at the proximity of fire and stamping iron-shod hooves on the ground. Sudden shouts from behind the closed door of the Customs House but Mathieson held it tight against all attempt to thrust open and almost choking in the acrid, surging smoke. Then he called out in a voice that soared hoarse above the frightening din.

'Jonathan! This way! Simon! Jake! Get aboard!' Moving away from the door as shadowy figures scrambled into the carriage. The horses surging forward even as Faraday's men flooded out of the Customs House and the coach and four gathered speed down the alley-way. One of the sentries aimed a shot after them and Faraday fired his pistol as the coach turned into the roadway at the bottom of the alley. Incredible panic! Flames from the office window reflected eerily through the densely hovering smoke and Faraday's bewildered stare took in the shattered door of the prison and the disappearing carriage with its indistinct figures crouched in the back.

'They're getting away,' he screamed, 'to horse and after them! Reward of a hundred guineas to the man who brings me Rudd: alive or dead!' Hysterical! Unbelieving! Face blackened with smoke and his uniform in sorry state with great smudges of oil and tar staining the white of his tailored trousers.

The horses of the Excise men were stabled at the rear end of the Custom House and the animals were screaming wild as they smelt the evil of fire. Amidst all the panic it was some time before they were saddled and spurred after the coach and four. First in the saddle, Faraday dug his heel viciously into the flanks of his frightened mount and rode at furious pace with his men trailing behind and, with their departure, quiet descended on the dark alley.

In the stable yard behind the prison Will Perryman backed his shire up to the tiny barred window. Hooking a metal grapple behind the two bars he gave a quick tightening to the chain leading from the heavy shoulder harness, then speaking softly into Joanna's ear he led her forward. The mare's stride faltered as the chain tautened, the metal bars of the window bent outward but remained intact and the chain stopped Joanna in her tracks. 'I'm surprised at you, Joanna?' scolded Will into her face. 'Don't you remember how your mighty ancestors rode into battle with noble and valiant knights on their backs? Are you getting so fat and lazy that you must shame the memory of such great deeds by being defeated by this miserable window?' He tutt-tutted in disdain and the mare's ears lay back and she looked at him with pained eyes. 'Now we'll try once more,' he said, 'and this time do it right!' He backed her a pace or two then urged her forward and as the chain came taut he slapped the shire smartly on the rump. She surged in disbelief at this summary treatment and her shoulders flowed into power and the full force of her strength and indignation came onto the grapple at the bars of the window. They held in the iron framework but the whole structure of the wall burst outward in a cascading mess of stone and powdery mortar and brought down a section of the roof: and worm-eaten roofing spars sagged drunkenly over the hole and a shudder ran through the roof structure and an ominous crack appeared in the stonework. By this time Mathieson and Jan Coggeshall had come to lend support and Mathieson stared astounded at the sheer power of the shire then hastily back at the crumbling structure before groping over the rubble and by the dim glow of a solitary oil lamp hanging awry made his way to the cell occupied by Simon and Jake. The heavy shoulders of the village blacksmith swung the sledgehammer and the lock shattered with a single blow.

Simon stared without comprehension at these apparitions but there was no time for explanation. 'Simon and Jake,' commanded Mathieson, 'outside!' Moving on to Rudd's cell. Smashing the lock from the door and the two men thrust inside to find him crouching on the floor and pulling with all his might at the chain and staple that bound him to the wall. The wide crack in the masonry had already freed the iron staple and it needed but a further strong wrench to un-tether Rudd..

'Figured it was you out there, damn near had us buried alive,' he said with a typical grin, then with a glance at the hooded faces he added, 'Doesn't do much for your looks, Reverend.' Holding out his hands. 'Can you get these chains off?' Mathieson shook his head, all the while urging him out of the shattered prison. The roof cracked and groaned as it sagged even more and the walls began to spread outward and they pulled him clear just as the building slid sideways and down with a rush of dust and stone. Will Perryman had already led his victorious Joanna from the stable yard and now four horses appeared in the lane outside with Mistral stamping amongst them. Mathieson turned to the blacksmith.

'Well done, Jan,' he complimented. The blacksmith's eyes shone through the slits in his mask, then he nodded and strode away.

'Can we make a dash for the *Rose*?' asked Rudd eagerly.

'No chance: had to use her as a diversion.' Urging them towards the horses. The dust streaked faces of Jake and Simon were too astounded to allow of any questions. Unexpected freedom was explanation enough and with an incredulous glance at each other they mounted with alacrity but Rudd wasn't so easily quietened.

'If not the *Rose,*' he asked, 'then where else?'

'Somewhere Faraday doesn't know of.' Ripping off his stocking mask with a sigh of relief. 'You might almost say you're about to exchange one prison for another.'

The pointed meaning in this statement registered. 'You knew about the cave all the time,' said Rudd wryly.

This is the last time it will be used, in any manner, but until we can find a way to get you all out of danger?' He had to help Rudd up on the last of the horses because his chains hindered him. 'There's no time for explanation,' said Mathieson, 'because we have to get you hidden before Faraday and his men come looking.'

Rudd's eyes narrowed at the name. He'd spent long days with nothing else to think of: or brood upon. Sitting his horse without moving he declared, 'I want Faraday before I go anywhere!'

Not about to tolerate a display of temperament Mathieson glared at Rudd as if he was some kind of idiot. 'A great number of men have placed themselves in jeopardy to free you,' he said angrily, 'and to do it without unnecessary bloodshed. Any further stupidity from you, Rudd, and I will personally chain you back to that prison wall.

Now show sense and gratitude and thank the Good Lord that you are out of there and for once in your life do as you are ordered!'

Rudd didn't like it! Then he looked at Simon and Jake and their supportive stance brought the sobering thought that they would follow only where he led. Then, he shrugged, and something of the old grin softened the severity of his face.

'Lead on, Reverend!'

The village of Perranwithick had all the appearance of normality the following morning and everyone went about their normal daily routine as if nothing had happened, a typical calm, rural scene innocently greeting Faraday as he rode at furious pace through the village and up to the church. He and his men had already ransacked the *Blue Lugger* in a frantic search for the prisoners and his frustration and weariness after his unceasing vigil of the night before only added fire to unreasoning rage.

Anticipated Faraday's arrival, Mathieson was working apparently unconcerned in the embracing peace of his churchyard when Faraday thundered through the lych gate and stormed up to confront him. They stood either side of the double grave with the two cherubs gazing on them in stony silence.

'Where are they?' snarled Faraday.

He looked awful! Dirty! Unshaven face smudged with oily soot and his eyes wild and bloodshot. His coat was unbuttoned and his breeches filthy and Mathieson eyed him with distaste. 'How should I know?' he asked.

'Are you denying knowledge of the fact that Rudd and his crew escaped from prison last night?'

'It's the talk of the county his morning, everyone knows of their escape.'

'I know this was your doing!' Faraday's face flamed and his eyes held a maniacal aspect as he stormed, 'the whole business of diversion was much too elaborate for any of these simple minded peasants around here.' Stepping on to the polished stone slab in his eagerness to get closer he thrust forward with fists clenched as if ready to strike. 'You've given me trouble from the very first time we met,' he said in a voice heavy with menace, 'and I know only too well who organised the chaos of last night. I also know they are hidden somewhere about here.' His boots scuffled on the stone slab and Mathieson fervently hoped Rudd wasn't underneath and listening to his arch-enemy sounding off. Then Faraday looked at him with eyes evil with intent. 'I'm going to turn your church over,' he announced, 'and heaven help you if I find so much as a suggestion that they've been in there.'

Mathieson folded his arms and stood directly in the way. 'Look in the church if you must, but if you defile or desecrate one single item you must stand prepared to answer to a Higher Authority than any you will encounter in this life.' His voice was brittle-hard and the threat sent a shudder through the men of the Excise who were lined up within earshot. They looked askance at Faraday but he brushed away reluctance with a snap of his fingers.

'Top to bottom!' he commanded harshly.

'I will have no weapons taken inside,' said Mathieson in firm tone. He had preceded the search party and now stood before them in the church doorway. The Excise men hesitated then one laid down his musket and pistol on the ground and entered. The others followed his lead but Faraday wasn't carrying any visible arms and shouldered Mathieson arrogantly out of his path and stalked inside. In the church Thomas White sat playing the organ and the tune wavered for a second, then continued. The music charged the atmosphere with quiet dedication and one by one the men removed their hats and appearing most ill at ease, but not Faraday who snapped. 'Get on with it!' The command came brusque and unfeeling, and the men sped about crashing chairs and moving any obstacle without care or consideration. Scrutinising every remote corner. Rummaged the vestry. Climbed up the bell tower and even brushed aside the altar display and all the while the organ music increased in crescendo as Thomas grew more and more incensed at this desecration and the church reverberated with mighty sound.

Eventually, Faraday had to be satisfied and his relieved men fled from the church. The thundering of the organ died away to a murmur but still challengingly audible to those outside but the frustration of Wilder Faraday was an obvious and tangible thing and brought him to screaming point as he looked wildly around.

'I know they are here somewhere! But I'll soon flush them out because I am offering a reward for information that will lead to their re-capture.' Turning abruptly and, after a last piercing look, said with demoniac, sneering intent, 'There's always a Judas to be tempted by easy money.'

22

Four weeks passed and gradually the search became less frantic. Armed columns of men still searched the countryside and patrolled with regularity through the village, but with less enthusiasm and with dwindling hope that the escapees were still in the area. Rumours circulated freely that they had been seen in such places as far apart as Plymouth or Torbay, all calculated to confuse the men of the Excise and also the local armed militia who had been drafted into the search throughout the county.

He knew the time had come to work the last part of his scheme to get the men away. In addition, it was becoming more and more difficult to restrain Jonathan Rudd. Weeks of imprisonment and of hiding and of soul-destroying inactivity were taking heavy toll of his patience and Mathieson could sense that the final escape attempt must be soon before Rudd completely lost control and broke out of the cave. The news that *Rose of Endau* was shortly to be sold at public auction made the decision even more urgent. She was a good ship and bound to be knocked down at a cheap price and many would jump at the opportunity. Rudd was no longer around! Memories and loyalties quickly eroded with the chance of a bargain. All of this not revealed to Rudd and his crew because Mathieson realised this was the one thing that could finally snap through the fast disappearing restraint of Jonathan Rudd. It had to be now, if all was not to be ruined!

23

Darkness shrouding Newlyn dock: the quiet of night hanging damp over the fishing vessels moored along the wall. A distant clock striking the hour of twelve as, with a clatter of boots, the Navy guard on the *Rose of Endau* was relieved and two fresh men took up their position. The middle watch, from midnight until four in the morning, always seemed the longest of all, especially on such a chilly-damp night. All the Navy men were fed up to the teeth with this never-ending guard duty and would be glad to see the back of the bloody *Rose*! Cursing their bad luck they pulled up the collars of their greatcoats and settled disgruntled to their lonely vigil. A solitary light hung suspended in the forward rigging, casting a dull illumination over the still waters of the harbour as movement along the quayside alerted the nearest sentry who instantly thrust his musket to the ready and challenged, 'Who goes there?'

'Wouldn't shoot a lady would you, sailor?' Into the lanterns glow strolled the figures of Rudd's girl friends, Kathleen and Susan. They sidled in close to the suspicious sentries. Each of them had a cloak over her shoulders thrown wantonly open at the front and the sentry's eyes riveted on Susan's figure and feasting on the deep cleavage between her full breasts..

'What are you doing here at this time of night?' asked the second sentry curtly.

'We thought you might be glad to see us?' Kathleen moved toward him and the cloak fell away from her soft arms. Producing a bottle from behind her back she added, 'I've brought something to warm you on such a chilly night.' She spoke in suggestive tone but the sentry glared at her as he said importantly:

'You know we can't drink on duty.'

'Who's going to know?' asked Kathleen coyly.

Placing his arm round Susan's waist the other sentry had no such inhibition and gazed with lewd admiration down the neck of her gown. 'Pass the bottle,' he said eagerly, 'I don't mind sharing a drink with so tempting a maid.'

'We have one of our own.' Susan brought out a bottle from under her cloak and whispered into his ear, 'Never mind those two, we'll have a very private party.' The sailor was easy game to the luscious Susan, and couldn't believe his luck.

'Come on down here then!' Pulling her into the shelter of a nearby bollard he sat her on a heap of netting and sprawled down beside her and raised the bottle to his mouth. The other sentry, being the senior and of more responsible nature, said brusquely to Kathleen:

'You haven't said just what you are doing at the dock so late at night?'

'Just looking for a good time.' Her soft bosom touched his chest and the smell of her perfume seductively eased his suspect thoughts as she said, "There's been little fun with you men since Captain Faraday arrived and we get so bored when we have to spend very evening alone.' She caressed his arm and thrust her bosom closer and raised her face invitingly, and the musket dropped from his hands as he reached for her.

'Why not?' he leered. 'Like a bit of fun myself.' Taking the bottle and helping himself to a hearty swig before handing it back to her insistently. She tipped it back and allowed a few drops to trickle through her full lips.

'Only one thing better than rum for keeping a girl warm,' she murmured in his ear.

Excited now he grabbed the bottle and drank with abandon. The fiery liquor burned his throat and fired passion, and breathing fumes of strong Navy rum into her face he cried, 'Give us a kiss, me-beauty!'

* * *

Into the harbour entrance swept a long, powerful rowing boat: six men on board but only two rowing. The oars were padded and the rowlocks greased and the blades bit into the calm water without sound. They shipped oars as the longboat smoothed across the dock towards the *Rose*. Sure hands seized the iron ring inserts in the stone of the dock wall and the craft came to rest against the granite steps. Four of the crew crept barefoot up the steps, paused warily for a moment before moving up the slime-covered lower steps onto the verge where they crouched in a waiting stance. One of them inclined his head in a positive gesture to the others aboard and they responded by working their way among the mounds of gear and fishing nets that littered the wharf, and creeping cautiously towards the guard's position. 'It's alright,' said Susan with a chuckle. 'They've gone!'

Four men converging to where the Navy guards lay sprawled in a state of drugged unconsciousness and the leader of the longboat crew raised a sentry's head and peered at him and let his head down again. 'Fancy the rum from the Landfall is more potent than usual,' he said, 'so let's be at it, mates!'

Placing the unconscious sentries back to back against a bollard. They were soon expertly roped with gags thrust in their mouths and, with them secured, Susan looked along the jetty and gave a low whistle, greeted by the appearance of

Mathieson and Janie Ralston who joined the group, and after a quick look at the inert sentries, he took the two women by the hand. 'Kathleen, Susan, you have done your work well and without us having to resort to violence. Now away to the warmth of your beds.' Looking at them warmly as he stated, 'You have done Jonathan a great service this night.'

'Newlyn won't be the same without him,' replied Kathleen, 'tell him we'll be watching for his return.'

The two women exchanged a look of conspiracy and satisfaction then ran off at speed, and Mathieson turned back to the four men with a look of surprise. 'Thought you had no liking for Rudd,' he said, 'now I find you risking your own welfare to help him get away.'

'Don't like him at all,' scowled Curt in reply, 'but I like Faraday even less and I'll not see a good fisherman go to the gallows while I'm around and able.' He then stated immodestly, 'Need men for a job like this.' Gesturing now at his crew, and they began to untie the warps mooring the *Rose*.

Leaping on board, Mathieson helped Janie up, then went forward to lower a long, stout rope down from the bow to connect with the rowboat. The men on the quayside gave a concerted heave at the bulky topsides and the ship eased away from the confines of the harbour wall. She was heavily built and cumbersome, but a well-found ship moves easily through the water. The crew scrambled back into the longboat and now, with four men at the oars they leaned powerfully into the stroke and the *Rose* gathered way.

'Need you on the bow as lookout, Janie, just to larboard where I can see you.' Mathieson at the helm, he had steerage way on and conned the ship into clear water. The men rowing were sweating freely but the *Rose* followed ponderously after the longboat with the towing warp alternatively slack, then taut, with each forward surge. The harbour entrance loomed high and Janie gestured urgently, signaling Mathieson to steer more to starboard. The ship seemed to poise in motion but too close to the larboard wall and he hurriedly left the wheel and fended off with a wooden scull, scraping and crunching against granite and bringing a warning grumble from the longboat, but already the towering masts were moving out and away and clearing the entrance. Now the pull of the fast-running ebb could be felt and eased the labours of those rowing and Curt's stroking count lengthened and the shoulders of his men relaxed into a smooth-flowing pattern and the harbour entrance opened up behind as the *Rose* gathered way on the tide.

'You're on your own, Reverend.' Curt cast off the warp and the longboat pulled aside as the ship bore down on them.

'Pull in the warp, Janie.' Leaving the helm he leaned over the bulwarks as the longboat came alongside and they lay together for a moment. 'My thanks to you, Curt,' he said, 'and to the men of *Barracuda*.' With these grateful words he beckoned Curt closer. 'I'm concerned for Susan and Kathleen, their services tonight may be held against them by the Navy men.'

'Doubt it! Not when I've had a word in their ears!' Eyes flashing at the thought, Curt seemed to be relishing his role as a Good Samaritan. He was dressed in a black oilskin coat and the woollen stocking hat covering his baldpate lent an almost angelic look to his barren face. 'Reverend,' he announced, 'I've not felt this good for a long time!' His tone held a note of satisfaction blended with embarrassment and Mathieson looked deep into his face.

'The personal reward for a good deed and proudly done,' he then said, 'remains with a man for the rest of his life. It could well be, Curt my friend, that in risking your safety to help another you'll find something of yourself that will forever enrich you, and those who sail with you.'

Curt looked at him as if he didn't know what the hell he was talking about. 'Come off the soapbox, and don't try to make more of me than I am… you'll have me going to church next!' His crew were watching, and enjoying this. 'What are you grinning at me for?' he snarled. 'Cast off, you scum bags!' Though the words were harsh some of the old venom seemed to be missing and his crew responded by pushing ever so casually away from the ship and preparing oars for the long pull back against the tide. As they pulled away Curt looked back. 'Come and have a drink with us at the Landfall sometime, Reverend,' he jested, 'promise not to serve you any of Susan's specially prepared rum.'

Might just do that, thought Mathieson as he regained position at the helm. Now carried by the tide with no grip on the rudder to give steerage-way he began to worry in case they should drift out of the fairway channel and on to the mud shoals lying either side, so he called, 'Take the wheel for a minute, Janie!'

Scurrying aft she gripped the wheel with nervous apprehension. 'What do I have to do?' she asked. The dark dress she was wearing reached almost to the ankles, and around her shoulders she had a warm woollen jacket with the collar upturned and he thought she looked very trim but was the most unlikely looking seafarer he had ever sailed with.

Placing his arm around her he raised her face skyward. 'See that star shining so brightly,' pointing to the star as he added, 'the one below the funny shaped cluster.' The night sky was like velvet. All the stars in view and sparkling in bewitching brilliance and she looked into his face and a straying lock of her hair brushed his mouth and the fragrance of her was all about him and words surged without premonition inside but he bit them off almost savagely, and turned away from the appeal on her face. 'Yes, Janie,' he said, 'the star that beckons like some far off beacon. Steer your course always towards that one, guiding star.' Securing her hand on the wheel, holding on briefly, then he ran forward and unrolled the foresail that lay secured on deck. It rose like a pale, fluttering gull's wing and set in a lovely curve as it filled in the offshore breeze. The wake bubbled and lit up with a soft glow of phosphorescence as wind in the foresail brought life to the drifting vessel and she felt assertive pressure on the helm. He hoisted the inner staysail and the ship ghosted over the ebb tide with new purpose and she knew sudden content as confidence grew and she steered the bow towards her guiding star. With two foresails set and working, the wheel gave positive response and after a few, initial gyrations, the ship's head settled on course. Returning aft, making no attempt to take over. 'Well done, Janie,' he congratulated.

She flushed with pleasure at this demonstration of his confidence and she looked up at him and his eyes were focused on the curving foresails, and with a smile of content, as if he was back, in his own environment, and she began to appreciate the compelling love he had for the sea and for the beauty of the ships that sailed the magic waterways. The growing emotion she felt for this gentle yet so utterly self-sufficient man surged into the very fibres of her being and caused a tremor, an almost nervous flutter inside. The change in his mood a few minutes ago had left her bewildered and, seeking to recapture the tenderness of that fleeting encounter, she looked at him with speculation rife. 'Richard,' she asked, 'what was it you started to say before you went forward?'

'Something about steering us towards a star.' Smiling, as if he knew she was probing, he placed his arm round her. 'First rule aboard ship is not to distract the helmsman, not that I have ever sailed with so disturbingly lovely a helmsman as you.' Brusquely removing his arm as he added, 'Jonathan and the *Rose* will have to cope with some very erratic courses with you on board.'

Retreating from intimacy, as he had done before, and she could have stamped her feet in childish tantrum. For a moment she thought she had reached close to him and now this change of attitude brought frustration. 'Richard Mathieson,' she cried, 'you can be a most irritating man!'

'Have you known so many men?'

'Not like you,' she said with feeling, 'with such bewildering change of mood.'

Moving away to perch on the cockpit side-coaming, he looked at her. 'Only because the nearness of you tends to make me forget the purpose of our being here,' he said, 'and the urgency of the task before us.'

'Are you always so dedicated?' This remark had been said to him on a pertinent occasion once before and a shadow crossed his face and she could have bitten off her tongue. 'Sorry, Richard, I shouldn't have said that.' Regret was obvious, then she went on to outline her feelings. 'It is just so puzzling when I feel you are close only to have a barrier raised between us.' The twin foresails fluttered in the fitful wind and the sky was becoming clouded over. 'Can't see the star!' she cried in panic.

'It will come into view directly.'

He took the wheel and Janie stood in the shelter of the hatchway with her back against the bulkhead as if for support. She had something to get off her mind. Something to say and didn't know how to say it and he looked at her in that understanding way as if he knew and was inviting her to reveal whatever was troubling her but he wasn't prepared when she stated abruptly, 'I know what happened on the *China Star*.' She said this in a voice almost defiant but obviously with more to come and though taken aback he held her gaze but his brow was furrowed and his eyes cloistered as he waited for her to continue. Taking a deep breath, she was in dangerous waters and it was none of her business but, committed now, she blurted, 'The coxswain of the Coastguard cutter sailed on a sister ship and knew all about it and Lieutenant Gillard thought I would be interested to hear what happened aboard your clipper.'

'Only I know what truly happened.' His face

had gone deathly pale and distress showed in the slump of his body over the wheel.

'Oh, Richard!' she said, 'I don't wish to intrude into your past life or probe into such secrets.' Eyes afire and entreating as she explained, 'This man, Jackson, told me what he heard from one of your crew and there was nothing he said that was to your discredit. He also said that there was no man aboard who could have done what you did.'

'Just what did I do?'

'You helped a man to die because he was too terribly injured to survive and because his pain and suffering was unbearable.'

Her face was very young and full of earnest appeal as she said this but Mathieson's mouth formed a bitter line and he reached out two open palms and looked at them as though they were the instruments of infinite shame. 'I took a man's life with these hands, held them over his nose and mouth until he stopped breathing.' Voice breaking as if reluctant to tell it but had to, he said in desperate tone, 'But that awful moment when he tried to draw breath! That terrible struggle when even his pain wasn't torture enough to let him want to die!' Shuddering in extreme anguish he said huskily, 'I couldn't allow him to linger in agony but that last, dying appeal, will tear at me as long as I myself shall live.'

His face was drawn and the pain in his eyes and in his voice was more than she could bear and she flew to him and flung her arms round his waist.

'Why do you torment yourself this way?' she sobbed. 'You did nothing that wasn't brave and honourable! I know from Jackson that the man begged you to end his agony: what else could you have done?'

'If only that was all?'

He was calmer now, but speaking with a finality that struck a deathly chill and she looked at him to entreat, 'Tell me, Richard, allow me to share this burden and perhaps help to make it easier?'

He looked into her pleading face and his tender smile returned: only to be extinguished. Then his eyes left hers and searched the sky and focusing on the guiding star that was once again in view and the *Rose* rolled impatiently and the wind sighed a soft lament in the rigging as if they too were waiting with baited breath to hear the story and, as he stared into space, in his mind flashed a searing picture of a lovely tropic lagoon and a sea of blue crystal and the pale sand visible below the great clipper and the cantenary of the anchor chain showing through the clear water. The boats filled with near naked man. Bronzed and fit as they laboured at the oars bringing sweet water from shore to fill the ship's empty barrels. The scene was one of glorious colour and warmth but his mind and body were cold as death as he began his narrative.

'We were on our way home across the Pacific but, in need of water, called at an island we had been to before where the natives were always friendly and welcomed us like visiting royalty.' In hushed and reminiscent tone he then told of the beauty of the island and the music of the drums and the natives dancing in happy rhythm around the great cooking fires burning on the beach as evening fell, and Janie's eyes mirrored pleasure and wonder as his words painted the picture in her mind, but his mouth was a hard line. 'It was the pearls,' he said bitterly. 'Pearls . . . and my own greed!'

'You found pearls?'

The eagerness in her voice brought a look of remonstrance. 'We knew where the oyster bed lay in the lagoon,' he explained, 'for the natives showed us some small specimens they had fished up, but they wouldn't dive for us. They were afraid and told of a giant octopus that inhabited the deep-sea bed and coral of the reef, said the place was voodoo! But we dismissed this at superstition and took our own boat and rowed out to the reef.'

'How many of you?'

'Just him and me.' He had difficulty framing the words and she sensed reluctance to give a name to the other man as he went on to say. 'He was a fine swimmer and could dive almost as well as the natives. Can see him even now, with long fair hair and his body tanned the colour of mahogany by the tropic sun. I could follow his clean shape as he dived into water so clear it was almost transparent, and brought up oyster shells by the dozen. They didn't all contain pearls but we soon had a half-dozen good looking specimens.' The colour had drained from his face and she noted the vacancy of despair in his eyes. 'He was tiring,' Mathieson then said, 'but suggested one last dive. He had seen a cluster of shells a little deeper on the reef and wanted to try for them.' Posture slumping and hands clenching on the wheel. 'Knew we should have given it best there and then,' he said in tormented voice. 'We had enough! But my judgment was distorted by greed . . . for more!'

'What happened then?' She had to know and probed mercilessly into his grief and pain.

'Insisted he had a line round him this time.' Hands to his eyes as if to shut out the vision and the memory. 'Didn't see the shark until it struck and until I felt the terrible struggle through the line. I yanked him to the surface but the blood was coming up with him and the shark savaging and shaking his body like a rag doll.' Voice hoarse with the self-destructive blame of remorse. Shoulders heaving as he stared at her in gaunt-eyed appeal. 'How can I ever live with that memory!' His anguish was so great that he couldn't continue, then he found voice enough to carry on with, 'I speared the shark and it sank away with the spear sticking out of its gaping, vicious-teethed mouth but I knew it was too late! It's always too damn late! He was still conscious when I brought him aboard the longboat but his body was mutilated beyond belief.' She buried her head in her hands as he droned on, 'Right leg gone below the knee and there was a gaping hole in his side where the shark's teeth had tore into him and I was trying desperately to hold the wound closed with my hands.'

'No more! Please: no more!' she moaned in real horror but he went on as if unheeding and as if to let it all out of mind and memory.

'My feet were treading in his blood. He didn't appear in any pain, think his body was numbed. In shock!' Mathieson needed a moment to regain control. 'Janie,' he then said in a whisper, 'he held his hand out to me and in his palm was the biggest pearl you could imagine . . . black and glowing lustrous in the afternoon sun and he gestured me to take it.'

'Did you?'

'I had to, you see.' Note of finality in his voice as he explained. 'He knew he was finished and, in some way, I think that in giving me this priceless treasure he seemed to feel that his sacrifice was worth while. As he lapsed unconscious there was a smile on his face and I knew he had found some satisfaction.' He stopped speaking and the silence was almost unbearable and she gazed at him in deep compassion, then his mouth twisted cynically. 'The rest of the story you already know,' he said as if in shame. 'When I got him back aboard ship he had recovered consciousness and the pain was driving him out of his mind.'

Shrugging in a mode of helpless torment, he concluded, 'I couldn't let him live in such monstrous agony, even if only for a short while, so I put my hands on him and held him tight until it was over.'

'Richard! Oh God, Richard! You had to!' Shedding unashamed tears as she finally managed to speak but there was infinite sadness on his face as he looked down at her.

'The crew of the *China Star* were gathered in a circle about us,' he said sadly, 'and there wasn't a man without tears on his face, for the boy was loved by everyone aboard.' Trying to smile, but failing, he then said. 'He was the golden boy. Tall. Clean-limbed: and so handsome. Without a care in the world or fear of anything or anyone.' His head sagged and his voice faltered as he added, 'Such a waste of a wonderful life.'

'But it's over! Finished! You can't live out the rest of your own life accepting blame for what was virtually an unfortunate accident!'

'I have to accept sole responsibility, because it was due to my own greed that he dived for the pearls and, in the final reckoning, it cannot be denied that I was influenced by lust . . . for more!.' Looking directly at her in unqualified yet explanatory manner he then stated, 'This is why never again will I exert influence on the personal and private life of another human being, because the penalty for false judgment is unbearable.'

The insinuation struck home but something in

the way he had told the story puzzled Janie. 'You seem strangely reluctant to put a name to this boy?' she asked, 'yet you must have known him well?'

'His name,' he said, so very quietly, 'was Adam Mathieson. He was my brother.'

She couldn't cope with this and her face characterised his own agonising guilt and her mouth distorted with words she could not speak then her hands reached out and they grasped his in a need for mutual comfort and he looked at her and took strength from her support. 'Even the most bitter memories fade as the years go by,' he said, 'and though you have re-opened old wounds tonight I have to admit that talking it through with you makes me feel a great weight has been lifted from my mind and perhaps some of the despair will now also begin to ease.' Gazing into the distance as though for a last, backward glance, he then said in a voice consumed with sadness. 'We dug a grave and left him there in the cool of the reef where he could forever look upon the tall ships come sailing in.'

Though these words had tears flooding Janie thought there was more to come in this story and she hadn't yet finished her interrogation and she asked, 'You never said what happened to the pearls?'

'Took them on deck one moonlit night and threw them, one by one, back into the sea from whence they came. The night sky was full of stars and so very beautiful and I stayed on deck for hours in rapt contemplation.'

'The night you decided to enter the church?'

Looking at her in wry acknowledgement. She reached so easily into his most innermost reasoning with a capacity for understanding that never ceased to amaze, one that invited equal frankness of communication. 'Alone with my grief on the foredeck'' he said in explanation, 'with this calm and so wonderful night embracing me and somehow offering release from mortal anguish, and I knew, in that revealing hour, that my seafaring days were over and another more infinitely rewarding way of life was being offered. So I yielded to the night and made my promise to Almighty God to seek redemption in His service.'

All the tension had gone from Mathieson and his eyes shone clear and warm and she thought she had helped to exorcise the spectre that had haunted him and, with serene voice, she asked, 'What about the black pearl Adam gave you?'

'You really are a witch, Janie.' Reaching into the pouch on his belt he drew out a small bag of red velvet then, opening her hand, he loosened the drawstring and tipped it into her palm.

Her eyes opened wide at the beauty of the black pearl glowing, with lustre so deep it seemed to be burning into her soft skin, so dark and so devastatingly lovely. Eyes riveted to the glory of the black pearl she murmured in awe, 'Must be worth a fortune.'

'Just couldn't bring myself to throw it into the sea with the others . . . it seemed as if I would be breaking faith with his memory.' Replacing the pearl he said, 'I will make a present of it one day, to someone I love and who returns my love with trust and devotion.'

Her heart thumped! Not with the glory of the black pearl, but with longing and the wish that she alone could be the one he loved. Sharing! Helping in any way she could! At which encompassing thought she folded her arms akimbo and said in childishly defiant voice, 'I'm not the only one who knows.'

Startled! Almost resentful now, his eyebrows met together in frowning consternation. 'Because you couldn't keep it to yourself,' he said accusingly.

'Why should I? It's high time they learned the truth! How else are they to accept? To realise just what they are being offered? The dedication they are closing from their prudish minds. People need guidance,' she concluded haughtily. 'You wouldn't give it, so I told them!'

Her defiant posture brought a glimmer of smile and with a shake of his head he gave her a look of fond indulgence. 'I'm surely glad you are on my side.' The ship rolled underfoot, he suddenly had more urgent things to concern him. Storm clouds were gathering and the wind was getting up and filling the jib sails and heeling her more to larboard. Glancing at the fluttering masthead pennant, he said. 'Wind is fair for us.' Concentrating on the compass heading. The guiding star was lost from sight behind a thunderhead rain cloud and a roll of thunder announced its distant threat across the night. 'We have enough sail up to get us round the bay on time. Janie, love,' he instructed, 'go below for a foul weather oilskin, looks as if we are in for a wet ride.' A jagged streak split the sky to seaward and a roll of thunder followed immediately. The waves were beginning to heap up and foam white at the crests and came hissing up behind out of the dark. A fierce gust blasted the headsails taut as a drum skin and the *Rose* surged forward but, while pleased at their fast progress, this was the very situation he didn't want, and was relieved that they had only a scrap of sail hoisted, knowing only too well that he and Janie could never cope with a heavy press of canvas. From choice he would have liked another man aboard but Janie had insisted that only family should be at risk on this night, and her father was no sailor and his involvement would be too obvious: when reckoning, or blame, was certain to be accounted.

They had only a short distance to sail and soon their destination coastline came into vision. Sailing in close as he dare he then brought the ship head to wind. She stayed her forward drive and lay passive under the lee of the land. Leaving the sails to flap he scurried forward to drop the anchor and pay out the cable. As the anchor dug in he expertly lowered and secured the sails on the fore deck and, satisfied she was lying snug to her anchor, launched the ship's tender.

Running the longboat on to the sand and shingle. Jumping out, knee deep in water, he strained the boat up the beach away from the surging tide then helped Janie ashore. Above them the rain clouds split asunder. A flash of lightning danced an ominous path of crackling blue flame into the hillside, illuminating the bay and outlining the *Rose* in ghostly silhouette. Then the urgent rumble of the anchor chain snubbing in its hawsehole brought concern, shared by Janie as she scanned the cliff side. 'They ought to be here by now!' she exclaimed.

'If they miss the tide,' confirmed Mathieson, 'their chance could be lost for good.' His words heralded a rustle from the undergrowth and the appearance of the three fugitives. Descending in a hurry they scrambled the last few yards to the beach just as the first drops of rain began to fall.

'Thought you weren't coming,' said Simon as he embraced his sister, 'that perhaps you couldn't get the *Rose* out of Newlyn?' With a whoop of joy and excitement, he cried, 'Come on, Jonathan, let's get the hell away from here!' A streak of lightning greeted his cry and a might clap of thunder reverberated around the bay and rain splashed in horizontal sheets over them.

Facing each other for the last time. Their hands

met in firm clasp. 'You're going to be in deep trouble, Richard,' said Rudd with desperate longing in his voice. 'Give it best and come with us!'

The shake of Mathieson's head bore a finality that forbade any argument.

'Find those new horizons, Jonathan,' he said, 'the world is waiting for men such as you.' Smiling his tender smile as he added, 'I have found my new horizon and here will I work to make my place.'

'And where is my place?' asked Janie in sotto voice.

'Wherever your heart desires.'

'The decision has to be mine?'

'Yes.'

'You won't ask me to stay?' He made no reply, just averted his head, and she cried desperately, 'Ask me, Richard, I want to hear you ask me to stay with you!'

It was a cry from the very depths of her being but he just looked at her with a haunted expression in his eyes and on his face. 'Janie!' he gasped, 'why do you torment me so? Surely I have explained why I will not decide your life for you!'

Her eyes were staring and strange and she glanced from him to where Rudd stood by the longboat. A silent observer but with intent and worried expression on his face and all the while rain fell in torrents, streaming over their heads and trickling rivulets cold down their necks. Only

Janie wore protective clothing. Rudd's long hair lay plastered in sodden curls and water dripped from the beard that grew luxuriant after weeks of confinement. Holding out his hand. 'We have to go, Janie,' he said insistently.

'Then this is goodbye, Richard Mathieson.' Flinging her arms round his neck she pulled his head down and her soft lips fastened longingly on his and he thrust his arms round her waist, tight with the intensity of his embrace. Then, breaking free with a tormented gasp, he ran away along the hard-packed sand towards the rocky path that wound up the cliff side. Turning at the base of the cliff he could just make out the shape of the *Rose* and the tiny longboat as it rose on a crest close to the anchored ship.

Suddenly weary, but more in mind than body. Stumbling up the shingle path with the rain driving incessantly over him. His clothing was sodden and clinging like a second skin but he felt nothing but the pressure of two soft arms and the burning fire of her mouth. A jagged blue streak pierced the sky and a slow rumbling rolled across the night: matching his own shuddering torment. Stopping in his tracks with a wild look appearing on his face. 'You blind fool!' Racing back down the path. Leaping over rocks as if they were merely obstacles and in his way. Slithering out of control over loose stone and gravel and with panic in his hasty descent he regained the beach to stare seaward. The *Rose* was gone! Lightning split the sky. Searing! Crackling blue light: and in that brief flaring glow he caught a glimpse of the ship standing well out into the bay with her bow rearing and plunging into the white caps.

'Janie!' The shout roared from a gaping mouth, an almost hysterical cry instantly whipped away in a rush of wind and rain. 'Janie!' scything into the night sky. Eyes staring and piercing the rain curtain out to sea where the *Rose* was taking her away: and it was his own damn fault! She had been pleading, begging him to ask her to stay. And he had failed . . . again! Despairing sob wracking, and his head sagged and he sank exhausted on a slab of rock in a soaking wet and miserable huddle. Then, into the misery that enveloped him a muted, far off cry penetrated.

'Richard!'

Disbelief and desperate hope brought him from stupor. With head cocked for a hearing, he knew surging elation. On his feet! Fatigue forgotten and eyes searing the darkness, and a last flicker of lightning as the storm began to abate sent him speeding along the beach, for the heaven sent illumination nestled on and lit up the figure of Janie racing round the curve towards him. Her head was high and her hair streaming in the wind and again she called his name, 'Richard!' and he caught her flying body in sure hands and buried his face in the wet and wonderful fragrance of her.

'Janie! Janie! Thought I had lost you for

always! Hands on the back of her head he turned her face upwards and kissed her on the mouth with uncontrolled hunger. Gripping him tight: she wasn't letting go of him: ever! Tears and rain mingling down her cheeks and he could taste the wonderful salt of them as her lips moved in trembling joy against his own. Kissing her as if he would never stop and it was like she had never been kissed before, with the need that was in him, and in her. Releasing his hold with a breathless gasp. 'Had to lose you,' he said emotionally, 'before I could realise how much I love and need you.'

Happiness and reprieve in the words and he held her in crushing embrace and it hurt and she didn't care. 'When I saw you running so blindly away,' she cried in ecstatic voice, 'I knew I could never leave you.' Her eyes were huge and streaming with tears, but with happiness shining through the tears as she said, 'I have known all along that your ridiculous blend of pride and humility was the reason you wouldn't ask me to stay. Yet only tonight, here on the beach, did I at last realise that you needed me as much as I need you.'

'And Jonathan Rudd?'

'Jonathan needs only himself and his beloved *Rose* . . . think he was glad to get rid of me.' Smiling at the thought she said in secret voice, 'Do you know what his last words were?' Mathieson shook his head and looked curiously at her. She whispered in his ear, 'Make him happy, Janie. That is one hell of a man!' Then he was gone, rowing like fury to join his ship.' With these words she stood on tiptoe and kissed him and her arms were fierce round him. She was home and with him: and deliriously content. The rain ceased as suddenly as it had begun. The clouds disintegrated away over the cliff top and a brightening in the sky heralded the approach of a new day.

He stood at the helm, raising his face to the heavens. The rain clouds had scudded away. The crescent moon hung suspended and it was a shining incandescent curve of silver with just one bright star for company. He felt good. At sea: and free! Breathed a silent prayer. 'Thank you, Lord, for your Richard Mathieson and for allowing me to again know the feel of a rolling deck below my feet.' The wind backed and, as if in some mystic response to his prayer, a gust heeled the ship to starboard, giving her an exhilarating push down Channel. Her mainsail was deep reefed and she had just a small jib set flying. Even so, she lay pressed over with the wind strength. Simon and Jake alongside. They had all donned foul weather clothing and were buried in long black sea coats and sou'westers. Rudd whipped off his hat to free his hair to the wind. 'Thought we'd never see the *Rose* again.' Joyful words blended with relief, then he said to Simon, 'See if you can find that last bottle of brandy we had hidden in the bilge, and while below check on the food and water stores.'

As Simon went below Jake turned an enquiring eye. 'Where now, skipper?' he asked.

Rudd gave a fond glance back at the coast of Cornwall opening out behind them. 'We'll return to Newlyn one day,' he said. His eyes, gaunt sockets after weeks of confinement, became suddenly alive to an incredible bright blue as dreams re-awakened. 'But now,' he declared, 'we are off to seek our fortune in some far away ocean where the sea is blue and crystal clear under our keel.' Looking over his ship. 'I've been promising her this adventure.' His enthusiasm fired response in Jake but his next words brought an open-mouth, incredulous reaction 'We have been together a long time you and me, Jake,' said Rudd, 'and now, along with Simon, I'm making you equal partners with me in the *Rose*.' His eyes were on the far off haze where sky and sea came to meet each other as he boldly stated, 'Together we'll find islands not marked on any chart. Islands where mountains of green reach for the sky and where surf thunders on to beaches burnished gold by the tropic sun.' He looked so very young and boyish as dreams engulfed. 'We might never find our fortune,' he said with a grin, 'but I promise you one hell of a time searching for it.'

Jake was too flabbergasted to speak, then he managed to gasp. 'Partner!' Looking along the deck. 'Me! Jake Ward,' he said proudly. 'Partner in the *Rose*.' Speaking as if he couldn't believe it then, as acceptance took over, he exclaimed joyfully, 'Wait 'till I tell Simon!' Making as if to go below but Simon appeared in the hatchway bottle in hand and a smile on his face.

'Found it!' he said, adding, 'plenty enough water on board but little in the way of food.'

Taking a hearty swig, Rudd gasped as the fiery liquor went down then passed the bottle to Jake. 'Drink it down, lads, and don't worry about food, fishermen never go hungry when at sea.'

'Sail ho!' Jake's finger pointing with dramatic foreboding. 'Standing out from Mounts Bay.'

Training his telescope. Closing it with a determined snap.

'Gillard!'

'Have they seen us?' asked Simon.

'They're seamen are they not: be sure they've seen us!'

'Could intercept us on this course,' said Jake.

With the wind fresh from the southeast the *Rose* broad reached on a course that took them in a westerly direction down the English Channel. The Coastguard cutter was on an almost parallel but converging course.

'She's coming fast,' said Simon.

'We've five or six miles start,' said Rudd, 'on our fastest point of sailing and stand a fair chance of running into fog as we close the Scillies.' He then added bleakly, 'Could do with Mathieson at the helm, he'd relish the chance of getting all sail up!' Commands suddenly brisk. 'Shake the reefs out of the main, Simon. Set the outer foresail and stand by the mizzen staysail. If the wind eases we'll set it flying, and the topmast triangle also.' With as much sail as he dare set in these blustery conditions the *Rose* heeled rail down and plunged her bow into the first Atlantic swell.

Jake spat over the side. "Come on then, Mr Bloody Gillard! We'll give you a run for your money!'

Aboard the cutter, lowering his telescope. 'Almost wish we hadn't seen them,' said Gillard, 'keep her as she is coxswain.' Noting the additional canvas hoisted and heeling the *Rose* rail down he exclaimed, 'Rudd has too much sail up for this wind strength.' A quick calculation of his own sail area. 'Set the inner foresail, and stand by the topgallants.'

Intrepid had a crew of twelve, experienced men! Her hull had suffered no serious damage when grounding on the mud bank, and her mast had been skillfully renewed at Penzance shipyard. A sleek vessel she had been built for the Royal Navy and then transferred to the Coastguard. The ending of hostilities with France had left many such ships, and even more officers and men, surplus to requirements and all to the benefit of the emerging Coastguard, or Preventative Service. She had a fine turn of speed and Gillard focused on the towering press of sail and, satisfied for the moment, he commanded, 'Keep her full and bye, coxswain, promised Rudd I'd match him boat for boat one day.' Leveling his telescope again. 'Wonder what he's up to?' he mused, 'could come up a few degrees and run from us.'

Steadying the wheel, eyes calculating on his Captain, the coxswain announced, 'We're closing on her!' Then hesitantly. 'You know they'll hang if we take them back?'

'Speak when you are spoken to, Jackson, and keep your eyes on the binnacle! Not our concern. We have no obligation to Rudd and his men!'

Scowling at his Captain's sharp rebuke, Jackson murmured as if to himself, 'And none to that bastard Faraday either.'

His words echoed Gillard's own thoughts, and doubts. 'You're a good coxswain,' he snapped back, 'but stick to what you do best and allow me make the decisions!'

'Aye, aye, sir.'

The morning wore on and as the sun rose in a pale sky so did the wind force begin to ease and the two ships sailed on an endless, heaving carpet of dark grey water. *Intrepid* was proving the faster, perhaps a half-knot or more in the lighter breeze. Under the direction of Charles Gillard and the sure hands of her coxswain they slowly overhauled the pursued vessel. In the long Atlantic swell by now and as the two ships rose on a crest then dropped into the following deep trough they would lose sight for virtually minutes at a time but always *Intrepid* would come into view of the *Rose*, her closing insidious but menacing.

With every spare inch of canvas up, Rudd could do nothing more to increase speed. To add to his worries he could feel his ship unusually sluggish through the water. Which confirmed his impression that her underwater hull was thick with weed. A condition that weeks of lying idle in Newlyn dock had only made worse. Normally she would have been dried out on the scrubbing grid and her bottom scraped and scrubbed clean but now, in the light breeze, she was paying the penalty for his unavoidable neglect.

'How long do you think before they catch up with us?' asked Simon woefully.

'By late afternoon, maybe . . . our only hope is that we might run into fog as we get past the Scillies. We can usually rely on bad visibility near the Islands, trust today to be the exception.'

'May come down thick this afternoon?'

'If there is any fog about it will likely be clearing by then.' Striking his fist on the wheel Rudd swore out loud. 'There isn't a damn thing I can do about it! *Intrepid* is faster then we are and she'll close on us, as surely as darkness follows daylight!'

*   *   *

Bounding up the last few yards to gain the green sward of the hilltop. Pulling her up with him. Her skirt was dragging wet below the oilskin and she impatiently hoisted it above the knee. Modesty unimportant! Her only thought one of overwhelming content. Just to be with him! She had insisted on accompanying him on this venture to free the *Rose*. Justified in stating that only family should be at risk on the desperate, final night. One that had brought fulfillment to her fondest dreams and they stood looking out to sea with his arm round her and gripping her close to him. The storm was over. All the menacing rain clouds had fled and dawn was breathtaking and beautiful. The only remaining sign of the passing night being the crescent moon and the one, solitary star, lingering bright and clear as if reluctant to let go its early morning sight of the world below.

'Shine brightly, little star,' she whispered, 'and guide the *Rose* into safe waters.'

The words were said as a prayer, brought a glow of endearment and he unbuttoned her oilskin coat and brought her against him and traced the curve of her mouth with a gentle finger. 'Janie, darling,' he said, 'how can I make up for all the time I have wasted?'

She looked up and devoured him with her eyes. 'No matter how much time we have together it will never be enough,' then, invitingly, 'but you can make a start by kissing me again.' His mouth stifled the words. Her lips trembled in an incredible warmth and softness against his own then, with mounting intensity he held her tight and his mouth fastened on hers. She yielded to the strength of his embrace and they clung together and all the while the wind gusted wild, and unheeded. A slow, booming sound began to reverberate deep into her seething emotions. He felt it too and, as he pulled away, his eyes registered incredulous disbelief then crinkled, and there was wonder on his face:

'The church bell!' he said in awe, 'for a mad moment I thought the ringing was only from my ecstatic heart!'

'Me too.' Then she asked curiously. 'Who could be ringing the bell at this hour?'

'Who cares, I'm so delirious I could ring it myself!' Seizing her hand to pull her along in joyous abandon. As they drew near the church the ringing increased in volume, as if welcoming them back. Bursting in through the lych gate. The bell ceasing its crescendo: silent as they ran through the open door. Stopping short on the threshold. Great shout roaring as they came into view, and he stared in wonder at the scene inside the church at Perranwithick.

It seemed every adult man and woman from the village were there. Ladders and trestles up at the walls! Every man with a pot of paint and every woman a cloth: to catch and clean away the slightest drop that might fall. From the rafters and joists spanning the ceiling were slung stout planks of wood. Ceiling glowing: a delicate shade of magnolia. Solitary figure on the work platform painting the last touch of gilt to the ornamental plasterwork of the central, ceiling rose. The walls had been scraped clear of all flaking paint and already the upper sections were a new and pale cream. The chairs had been moved away and piled high in a corner and the little church stood proud in decorative splendour. Thomas White was there and guarding his organ lest a drop of paint dare fall. The atmosphere was rife with the smell of paint and polish but the one thing above all that made Mathieson want to sink down to his knees was the compelling sense of dedication filling his church that morning: reaching into the very depths of his being with overpowering humility and he gazed at them, speechless, as Janie's hand crept shyly into his. The spontaneous roar of greeting died away and Glyn Ralston took their hands in powerful grip and his eyes were moist.

'It does my heart good to see you! Oh. Janie!' he exclaimed, 'I thought I had lost not only Simon but you as well.' Unashamed tears in his eyes and he hugged them both with arms like solid branches of oak. 'Now, like a miracle you're back,' he said. 'You and Richard together as the Good Lord intended you to be.'

Mathieson's free hand gripped Glyn's shoulder and he smiled into the faces of the people as they thronged towards them. He barely knew the men folk crowding round but recognised a few. Will Perryman, for once without his cap. Coggeshall the blacksmith and Trewelyn the baker and the cadaverous figure of storekeeper Tremaine hiding in the background. Blanche Tremaine and the Ladies of the Committee standing before him somewhat shamefaced.

'We have been complete fools, Reverend,' she said in humble manner. 'Heard a story without any real foundation and in our small minds judged you unfairly, and even more because your brave actions of these last few weeks have brought pride back to our village and put us all to shame.' Gesturing at the scene of activity she then explained, 'This is in some small way the beginnings of our apology and regret and with it lies the hope that you will allow us back into your church.'

Leaving Janie's side he stepped forward but his cup was full and brimming over and he needed a little time before making reply. 'This is not my church, but yours,' he said at last. 'My task is to keep the doors open but the church belongs only to those who choose to worship here and if some action of mine has kept you from the sanctity that is rightfully your own, then, if there is a fault to be recognised, it must surely lie with me.' Looking at them, as if the speaking had restored familiarity, he smiled. 'Must admit, ladies,' he said, 'I have missed you at Sunday service, more than you can possibly imagine.' Looking around as he said this. Sunlight streaming through the windows: the ruby red glass shone like fire and reflected warmth and colour into the upturned faces and he raised his hand in exultation. 'Let the bells ring out,' he cried, 'so the world outside can share in our reunion!'

The bells tolled, the sound coming but faintly back as though rung from a distant steeple. Hurried bustle filling the interior: planks taken down from the scaffold. Ladders and trestles removed and carted outside and men down on their knees painting the last base section of the walls, and overall pervaded the happy satisfaction of the completion of the church's decoration.

The bells stayed their call! Outside in the roadway the clatter of horses reining to a halt! Lych gate crashing open and the uniformed figure of Wilder Faraday rushing up the steps with four men in close pursuit. The Captain wasn't his usual impeccable self. Disheveled: his breeches and boots were dirty and mud-stained and his face livid as he stormed to confront Mathieson. '*Rose of Endau* has been taken from Newlyn!' he shouted in a voice consumed with desperation. 'Where is she, Mathieson, and where is Rudd and his thieving crew?'

'I know not, except to hope they are out of your reach for all time.'

As he made reply Janie to his side to link arms in a significant gesture that had Faraday seething, they had conspired together, made a fool of him! Eyes flaming he thrust forward. 'Not so far removed as you may hope!' he snarled. 'Never trusted you, Mathieson! Always had you in my sights as a violent criminal: a murderer dressed in pious robe!' Voice afire with rage and frustration as he shouted at top voice, 'You can't hide behind your un-sacred and profane doors this time because I am taking you in custody on suspicion of unlawfully stealing an impounded vessel out of Newlyn harbour in the hours of darkness last night.'

A growl of outrage greeted this indictment. 'I don't think so,' said Glyn Ralston, 'we have been here all night painting the church and will swear that the Reverend has been here with us.'

Faraday showed only sneering contempt for this statement. 'You!' he scorned. 'Father of an escaped prisoner! Who do you think would find credibility in the word of someone so personally involved?'

'But they will believe the rest of us.' Blanche Tremaine and the Ladies of the Committee converging menacingly on the Excise officer with their men folk pressing in full support behind. Making no attempt to hide her antagonism she glared at him as though he was the Devil disguised in the uniform of authority and as though he had wormed out of a cesspit hole in the ground and she snapped with dislike rampant on her face, 'Can you hope to prevail against the whole village of Perranwithick?' The ladies moving forward in concert. The Excise men looking at them in alarm, for the sight of the Ladies in aggressive, charging mode was enough to strike dismay into any man and these men were no exception. The Ladies came on and Faraday retreated a pace. 'You're leaving, Captain' stated Blanche, 'or shall our men folk assist your departure?'

Beaten, for now, he cast a bale-eyed glance at Mathieson's sodden clothing. 'Don't think you are getting away with this,' he threatened, 'because I'll be back for you!'

'When the news of this latest failure reaches your superiors,' said Mathieson, 'I doubt you'll ever be back again. You'll be lucky to retain the rank of corporal!'

'Forward Ladies!' Blanche urging on her troops. Faraday took one look at the converging group and with a last, threatening snarl, turned on his heel and his men broke ranks and rushed in untidy haste out of the church and, watching them go, Blanche said with satisfaction and disdain, 'That's the end of you, Captain Faraday.' Abruptly regaining her mode of command. 'Time you got out of those wet clothes,' she instructed. 'Off with the both of you! You can leave us to clear away and put back the seating. When you return, all will be normal.'

Looking around his church with pride, and with humility. His eyes met those of Thomas White.

The organ throbbed into subtle life: a glorious, moving hymn to the dawn. To a new day, and a new beginning. He smiled, a gentle smile that warmed the hearts of the people of his parish. Reaching out his hand to Janie, he said:

'I think perhaps a little better than normal!'

24

Mid-afternoon. Wallowing on a sea almost flat calm. Breeze light, with the ship making barely two knots. Almost due east of the Scillies with the land just a vague blur on the near horizon. Visibility poor: Rudd estimating distance off at about five miles. Just behind in the broad slick of the wake, *Intrepid* eased up to windward. Carrying all her fair weather canvas she was a picture of grace in motion. But formidable! Her gun crew in suggestive formation around a long-barreled cannon poking its nose through the gun port in the starboard bow bulwarks.

'Pity we've no arms aboard,' suggested Jake, 'at least we could make them fight for it.'

'Could have blown us out of the water long since, but reckon Gillard is more intent on out-sailing, rather than sinking us.' In spite of the grave situation Rudd managed a grin as he added, 'Don't think he's forgiven us for running him on that mud shoal last time.' Jonathan had inherited the *Rose* from his father, a Master shipwright who had completed the building of the ship just before he died. She was Jonathan's love: and his life! And he was about to lose both! His thoughts were bleak in the extreme.

Intrepid creeping nearer all the time: only two hundred yards separating the two ships. 'Stand by, forward gun crew!' commanded Gillard.

Jackson cast a worried glance but looked away in response to a challenging glare.

'Fire one shot! High and well in front!'

'Wha-am! Bow cannon flaming fire and smoke: percussion slamming into unprepared eardrums. Rudd and his crew ducking in reflex action as the cannon ball whistled overhead. Water-spout disturbing the placid sea: but a long way in front.

'A request to heave-to if ever I heard one,' said Jake.

'Gillard had no intention of putting that shot into us,' said Rudd. 'Why should he? They'll be alongside soon enough.' Shrugging, he looked at his crew and said quietly, 'Either way, I'm not being taken back:! Rather would I end it cleanly with the *Rose* under my feet.' He had contemplated this decision for hours, churning the reluctant thought over in his secret mind and, now looking intently at Simon, he announced, 'I'm going to put you and Jake over the side in the longboat.'

Jake took a step forward to stand alongside as if he was aware and understood and accepted. 'I'm with you, skipper,' he said

Simon needed a minute to realise what they were on about then he joined them and stood proud with them. Looking fondly over the ship, up at the towering masts and the appealing curve of the white sails. 'Pity to scuttle her,' he said sadly, 'but the hangman's rope is no fitting end for sailing men such as we.' Then, in self-condemning voice. 'Why didn't you leave me in the sea that day? You would both be free and in some distant ocean by now.'

Rudd handed the wheel to Jake and placed his arm round Simon. 'Don't torment yourself, lad,' he said with great tenderness, 'just consider what you would have done were the position reversed.' Regarding Simon with affection, he then said, 'This is the way of things between comrades. We do what we have to do, each for the other and without thought of reward and certainly without cause for blame . . . or regret.'

Wha-am! The cannon of *Intrepid* booming again but the shot whistled high and wide. 'Reckon the Lieutenant has a tender heart,' said Rudd. Light-hearted words, then his face clouded over. 'Stand by the sea cocks, Simon.'

Aboard the cutter Jackson's keen eye was looking ahead. 'Mist coming up!' he announced.

'Too far off to be of service . . . yonder mist

is a few hours late!' Gillard stared in perplexed manner at the figures on the after deck of the *Rose* as his coxswain murmured:

'Rudd isn't going to make it easy for you, Captain, perhaps he doesn't recognise a heave-to signal across his bow?'

'He knows we have him,' replied Gillard irritably, 'he hasn't enough men to fight us off, so what the hell is he hoping for?'

'Perhaps something he has been hoping for all day,' said Jackson looking ahead at the approaching mist.

'That fog is too far off to give shelter, wondered why he persisted in running down the Channel this way but for once his luck has run out.' Unsure. Reviewing his position for a brief moment, he glanced sideways at Jackson. 'What would you do in his place?'

'Wouldn't fancy going back to that hellhole of a prison, not after breathing sea air again. And for what . . . to be stretched up by the neck?'

'No court in the land would hang men on such a minor charge?' speculated Gillard.

His freckled and finely drawn face held a look of concern, and Jackson noted this and thought his Captain didn't like the situation any more than he did. 'They certainly will if Faraday has his way,' he said with conviction. Thinking about this, he added, 'But there are all kinds of death! A man such as Rudd would die many times in prison confinement. First, the colour would go from his face, then his eyes would glaze over and dim, and finally all his dreams would shrivel and die inside him until his very soul faded away in hopelessness.' Deeply moved by his own eloquence, his voice almost broke as he raised his face to his Captain and said, 'I know what I would do in his place.'

Gillard studied his coxswain as if seeing him for the first time. Then, as the full implication began to register his brow deep-furrowed in consternation. 'You think he's going to scuttle?'

'Any minute now!'

'Pipe all hands aft,' commanded Gillard.

The shrill whistle of the bosun's pipe brought all hands on the double. They stood in line with their faces raised and wondering as he looked down on them from the quarterdeck. Jackson's hands were sure on the wheel, *Intrepid* came abeam and close enough to shield the wind and the sails of the *Rose* backed and fluttered and, as the bosun's whistle came clearly across the water, Rudd's call to Simon at the sea cocks was stifled. He exchanged puzzled glances with Jake as the ship lost way and came almost to a standstill under the lee of *Intrepid*.

Gillard: facing his men. Dressed in blue uniform jacket with two gold bars on the shoulder and looking every inch a Naval Lieutenant as he commanded, 'Crew of *Intrepid*, attention!' Looking at his smartly dressed sailors the Lieutenant couldn't resist a compliment. 'Men, you are a credit to me and to the ship!' Squaring his shoulders, he ordered, 'Right face!'

Ten unquestioning seamen turned as one and facing seaward and away from the *Rose*. Their Captain's voice ringing out loud and clear. 'Men! You all know the story of Nelson at Copenhagen.' Pausing for effect. 'I now ask . . . can anyone see the *Rose of Endau*?

'No! Sir!'

'Will you swear that you have not seen the *Rose of Endau*?'

'Aye, aye! Sir!' Resounding across the main deck, with feeling.

Gillard proudly ordered, 'Back to your posts and prepare to come about!'

The crew hesitated, as if pleased about this, and Jackson's voice came hoarsely from behind. 'Three cheers for our Captain!'

Never did men cheer so spontaneously and the exultant shouts soared over the water and, wondering what the hell was going on, Rudd saw *Intrepid* coming about and realisation brought renewed hope. 'Belay there, Simon,' he called, 'and come on deck fast! Think you ought to see this!'

Rushing out, his face a picture of incredulous delight Simon stared across to where the cutter was turning back. Away from them! With the gap between the two ships widening all the time. 'They're turning away!' he gasped.

Simon couldn't believe what he was seeing,

and Rudd said reflectively, 'Charles Gillard has made his point. That he could out sail us. I also think he is man of great compassion for there are few men large enough in stature to jeopardise their own future to save others to whom they have no obligation.' Head raising high to the heavens, he declared, 'More than this! He has presented us with the supreme gift of life and liberty and I solemnly swear, before you and Almighty God, never again to place these things at wanton risk. Jake,' he cried, 'dip our colours to *Intrepid*: and to her gallant Captain!'

Jake sprang to the base of the mizzenmast. The fluttering red ensign descended, significant and moving in salute. As the bow of *Intrepid* turned to windward so did her stern swing towards the *Rose*. The two captains faced each other across a few yards of placid water. Lieutenant Gillard raised his hand smartly to his tricorn hat in formal salute, and Rudd flung his own hand high in response and it was a salute of thanks and farewell: and a salute of respect. Looking on with surging emotion as Gillard turned back to his ship, and from *Intrepid* came the insistent trill of the bosun's whistle as she sailed away on a diverging path.

The wind came free. The sails filled. The helm once more responded. And the story finishes, as it started, aboard the *Rose of Endau*. Sailing free. Hull down: and disappearing into the grey chill of an Atlantic mist on her way ever southerly.

Epilogue

Sailing my Bermuda sloop one day along the south Cornish seaboard. Craggy cliffs. Mysterious coves . . . beaches of golden sand. A vintage gaff ketch standing close inshore: solitary, bearded figure at the helm. Imagination working overtime! Smugglers, and Excise men!

Rudd came easy. He was the first. All I had at the commencement. One of the last of the old-time smugglers! And so the writing began with Jonathan Rudd and his *Rose of Endau*.

I then sought to introduce a clash of personality between two men and envisaged this clash coming with the arrival of a ruthless and abrasive Excise Officer in the area. Mathieson was to be the vehicle for enmity between seamen and Excise but, strangely, he refused from the very beginning to incur any bad feeling for Rudd. They were two of a kind: blue-water men, and Mathieson would in no way tolerate a role as an

Excise man. Rather! And again, so very strange, he insisted . . . No! Demanded of me that I make him rector of the little church at Perranwithick. It seemed I had no choice but to go along with Mathieson and so the story progressed, at times with little in the way of contribution from me, almost as though dictated by other, more capable hands than mine.

Mathieson had much to say about his vocation in the church, and so much more he wanted to say and I had really had to shut him up before the reader tired of his rhetoric. So I channeled his enthusiasm into action rather than words. There has been much said by writers about characters wanting to take over a novel. When asked, "how do you deal with characters who try to monopolise?" one well-known author stated, "I kill them off, darling".

I had no such freedom with Richard Mathieson. My wife was in love with him!

THE END